Holliday Hotel Book 2

BY COURTNEY LYMAN

Kindle Digital Publishing books can be ordered through Amazon.

ISBN: 9781520897820

Cover art by Karin Mellin, Merge Left Marketing LLC

Other books by Courtney Lyman

KW Consulting Series:

Best Laid Plans
Smell the Roses
Dress for Success
Always a Bridesmaid

Holliday Hotel Series:

Resolution Room
Sweetheart Suite
Book 3 coming Spring 2018

Christmas novellas:

Christmas Angel
Snowfall
New Christmas book coming November 2017

For my in-laws,

Duane & Bobbye Lyman,

Who recently celebrated their 50th wedding anniversary!

"Love is patient and kind; love does not envy or boast; it is not arrogant or rude. It does not insist on its own way; it is not irritable or resentful; it does not rejoice at wrongdoing, but rejoices with the truth. Love bears all things, believes all things, hopes all things, endures all things. Love never ends."

1 Corinthians 13:4-8a

1

Carol wiped her eyes with her handkerchief. She had always been a sucker for weddings, but this one was particularly special to her. As the owner of Holliday Hotel, she was pleased to see her bed and breakfast used for its first wedding. Loving holidays like she did, a New Year's Day wedding gave her joy. But the best part of all was the couple standing under the willow tree by the lake.

Owen Coburn had been her handyman since she bought the old Victorian house and turned it into an inn. Carol had developed a close relationship with him as they worked together to restore the property. In fact, she was there when he had first met Willa Newman, one of her favorite guests.

Willa had come to the inn to celebrate New Year's Eve with her college roommates. It had become a tradition for them, but soon they were each getting married and starting their own families – except for Willa. Out of desperation, one year Willa had made a New Year's resolution that she wouldn't be alone by the next New Year's. Owen had seen his opportunity and had swept her off her feet.

Last New Year's he had proposed, and now they were getting married. Willa was beautiful in white against the glistening snow. Carol had thanked God that morning for the fresh snowfall from the night before so that their location would be pristine. Willa's long full skirt hit at her ankles and didn't have a train. She had long sleeves to protect against some of the chill, and over it all wore a white satin cape, trimmed in faux fur. The cape was elegant, and Carol was pleased that she had found a way to protect herself from the cold without sacrificing style.

Next to Willa were her three college roommates. Ebony, Crystal and Su stood proudly beside their friend in silver dresses and red capes. Ebony in particular had wanted Willa to see Owen in a new light, and had been almost as happy as Willa when she heard about their engagement.

Next to Owen were his two half brothers and his dog, Cody. Owen had only recently met his half brothers, but had developed a quick friendship with them. While many might wonder at the addition of his dog as a groomsman, Carol knew that the dog had played an interesting part in getting Willa and Owen together.

Carol's eyes roamed to the front of the small group where the family was gathered. Willa's parents sat on one side wiping their own tears of joy. On the other side was a sight that no one had expected to see. Owen's father sat side by side with his mother and step-father. Owen's half-sister also sat in the row with his family with a broad smile on her face.

Carol was certain that no one felt the cold because of the warmth of the love that was present. Still, she was thankful that the ceremony was short. As soon as she saw them exchange their first kiss as Mr. and Mrs. Owen Coburn, Carol slipped out of the last row and headed up to the bed and breakfast.

She stripped off her coat, hat, gloves, and scarf, and donned an apron in their place. Her daughters, Libbie and May, soon followed and silently the three of them put carefully arranged platters of appetizers on buffets in the dining room. A beautifully decorated cake already had a place of honor in front of the window. A fire was going in the living room fireplace, and May was setting up urns of hot coffee in there as well. Carol surveyed the space and was pleased. Owen and Willa's reception would be lovely.

The guests began to come in, carefully stomping the extra snow from their shoes before entering. Music played softly while the guests waited for the bride and groom to finish up some pictures. They chatted and warmed up as Carol and her daughters floated between groups making sure they were taken care of and comfortable.

Soon Willa and Owen entered with their families and the bridal party. The guests applauded and gathered around the couple, all wanting to offer them their congratulations. It seemed like no time had passed when Carol realized that the dances had been done, the cake cut and passed around, and the bouquet tossed. Guests began to drift away. Ebony, Crystal and Su were among the last to leave. They had stayed at Holliday Hotel in the Resolution Room with Willa the night before, but had packed to move into rooms with their own husbands for the rest of their stay. They each gave Carol an affectionate hug before leaving the newlywed couple behind.

Willa turned to Carol with tears glistening in her eyes. "How can I ever thank you?"

"It was my pleasure. I would have been disappointed if you had gotten married anywhere else." She pulled Willa close and hugged her tightly. "Are you sure you don't want the honeymoon suite?"

Willa laughed. "I know it's probably lovely, but I have a special place in my heart for Resolution Room."

Owen put his arm around his new wife. "If that's where she wants to be, then I'm happy there, too." He smiled up at Carol. "Besides it's only for one night, and then we're heading to the Caribbean."

Willa sighed. "I can't wait! I've never been there before."

"It will be wonderful. Head on up to your room now. I've got to clean up down here." She could already hear Libbie and May washing dishes in the kitchen.

Owen flashed Carol a bright smile as he grabbed Willa's hand and guided her to the stairs. "Thanks for everything," he said as they disappeared around the corner.

Carol started going around picking up dirty dishes and then went into the kitchen. Libbie was loading the dishwasher while May was washing the coffee urns. Fortunately, the pots and pans used to make the appetizers had already been cleaned. Carol couldn't stand a cluttered kitchen.

"You did a great job, Mom," Libbie said. The simple phrase from her serious daughter was a compliment indeed, and Carol glowed under the praise.

"It was absolutely lovely," May agreed. "Willa couldn't have asked for a better venue for her wedding or the reception."

"I heard several people talk about how they would like to come back and stay here some day," Libbie added. She looked up from her task. "Mom, I think it's time for you set up a website."

Carol sighed. "I know, but I don't know the first thing about it. I barely know how to use my computer to create reservations."

"That's why there are professionals to help you," Libbie pointed out.

"I have to agree with Libbie on this one," May added. "This wedding is going to bring in more visitors and a website will give them the information they need. You can even set it up to take care of the reservations for you."

Carol picked up a towel and started to dry the coffee urns. "You're right. I just don't know where to begin."

Libbie wiped her hands on her apron. "I found someone for you." At her mom's expression, she put up her hands. "If you don't like him, it's fine, we'll find someone else. His name is Tristan Romero. He lives right here in Willow Creek so you can meet in person instead of conducting all your business through emails." She handed her mom a business card.

Carol looked at the card and liked the simplicity of it. It simply said "Creation Designs, Tristan Romero" and then had his contact information. "I guess it wouldn't hurt to meet with him."

"Good! He's coming over for a meeting tomorrow." Libbie smiled as she removed her apron and placed it in the laundry.

"Libbie!"

"Mom, if I'd waited for you, it wouldn't get done. You would find some reason to put it off. Besides I'm only here for a few days, and I want to help with this." Carol knew that Libbie felt the need to protect her since her father had passed away. With that knowledge she softened a bit.

Still she looked at May for back up. May shook her head. "I don't agree with Libbie making the appointment for you, but I do think you need to get this started." She placed her arm around her mom's shoulders. "We'll help, and I'm sure Mr. Romero will do an excellent job."

Carol placed the business card on the refrigerator with a magnet. "All right, girls. I'll meet with him, but if I don't like him,

I'm not going through with it."

"Fair enough." Libbie smiled, and Carol realized that as far as her daughter was concerned, she had won the war.

2

Tristan Romero stood for a moment in front of the large Victorian house. He was tall and slender with a Latin complexion. His dark hair was cut short and his deep brown eyes were framed by trendy glasses. He looked at the inn with interest. The white siding was broken by forest green shutters, and window boxes, the latter of which were empty now that it was winter. The front door was a cheery bright red and the wraparound porch was inviting. Even with the chill in the air, Tristan thought it would be nice to sit on the porch with a good book. There was a forest on both sides and he just caught a glimpse of Harper Lake behind. Mrs. Holliday had a prime piece of real estate for her inn.

His eyes caught the wooden sign in the front yard. It was painted white with forest green letters. The crossbar of the H was made of holly leaves and berries giving a splash of red to the design. Tristan nodded in approval. It was noticeable enough to help guests find the location, but didn't detract from the beauty of the architecture.

Tristan walked up the steps of the porch with confidence. This website would bring in guests – not because of his work – but just because it was such a desirable place to stay. All he had to do was make sure that people could find it.

He entered the front door and surveyed the entryway as he removed his coat and gloves. Crown molding, hardwood floors, tasteful artwork all gave a welcoming, traditional feel to the bed and breakfast.

"May I help you?" The cheerful voice brought Tristan's eyes to the large wooden desk that sat near the stairway. A woman in her fifties sat behind it. She was short and curvy with twinkling eyes and pleasant smile. Dressed in slacks and sweater, and her hair was stylishly cut, she had achieved a balance of appearing professional and motherly at the same time.

"I'm looking for Mrs. Holliday." Tristan took a step forward. "My name is Tristan Romero. I believe she is expecting me."

Tristan didn't know if he was imagining things or not, but her smile seemed to falter for a brief moment. She quickly recovered and came out from behind the desk with her hand extended warmly. "I'm Carol Holliday. It's nice to meet you. Follow me." She led him down a short hallway beside the stairs. At the end of the hallway there were two doors. One appeared to be a guest room while the other was clearly marked "office". She opened the door and allowed him to enter first.

The room was small, dominated by a desk, with a few file cabinets against the wall, and a couple of chairs. Carol gestured to one of the chairs. "Make yourself comfortable. I'll be back in a moment."

Tristan sat in the chair that Carol had pointed to and let his eyes wander. The room had no windows, but she had managed to keep it bright and cheerful. There were a few lovely watercolor paintings on the wall by an artist he didn't recognize. The desk held piles of paper and an old computer as well as a printer. Tristan suspected that the office work was not Carol's favorite part of running a bed and breakfast.

The door opened and Tristan jumped to his feet to grab the large tray that Carol was carrying. She smiled her thanks and cleared a spot on the desk for him to put the tray on. When Tristan turned around he realized that another woman had entered behind Carol. The surprise must have been evident on his face because the woman's lips twitched in amusement.

"Mr. Romero, this is my daughter, Libbie Holliday. She's the one who contacted you about this meeting." There was a slight tension between the two women, and Tristan wondered if he would be getting this account after all. Libbie sat in the chair beside him while Carol took the chair behind the desk. Carol passed Tristan a plate of homemade cookies and then asked how he liked his coffee.

He answered black automatically and before he knew it he had a floral mug in his hand. He had never been at a meeting like this before. "I'm sorry about the cramped space," Carol apologized. "I'm fairly certain this was a closet before it was turned into an office."

As he juggled the napkin with the cookie and his mug of coffee trying to find where to place them for the meeting, Libbie chuckled. "My mom doesn't know how to do a meeting without food involved."

Tristan smiled. "I think I'll need lots of meetings to get this set up then," he teased. "That is, if you hire me."

Carol blushed. "I'm going to be honest, Mr. Romero. I know nothing about this sort of thing. I use my computer to enter data and email, but that's about it."

"Many of my clients know little about how to get started on something like this. That's why they hire me." He flashed his best smile. Something told him that he still needed to win Mrs. Holliday over.

"Mom's business is doing well, but I think it would do even better with the addition of a website," Libbie stated.

"More and more people primarily use the internet when booking travel arrangements," Tristan agreed. "Many people won't book with a hotel or inn that doesn't allow them to make reservations online. It's a valuable tool in the hospitality industry." As he said the word "hospitality" his eyes landed on the plate of cookies and he couldn't stop the smile from coming. Carol Holliday had hospitality down to a science.

Carol sighed. "I know that it's important. I'm just nervous about implementing it."

Tristan reached in the bag that he had brought with him and pulled out a brochure. He showed Carol the various options that he offered and pointed to the all inclusive package. "I know that probably every salesperson you meet will tell you that you need the biggest, most expensive package, but I want you to know that I don't normally do that. In your case, I would like you to consider it because I not only get it set up for you, but I'll maintain it for you as well. There's no contract so if at some point you feel confident that you can maintain it yourself, then you can just let me know. Also, if you feel like you don't need to update it every single month, I won't charge you for months where I didn't do any work on it."

"Mom plans lots of events around the different holidays throughout the year so I'm sure that she'll need to update the site frequently for those."

Tristan watched Carol's face as she scanned the brochure. She still seemed tentative. "If you'd like to see some of my work, I did the website for The Resort." He thought that perhaps seeing that he had done a website for another bed and breakfast might let her know that he was capable of handling her business. The Resort was a modern and trendy inn owned by Jack and Miranda Horne. He hoped that rivalry hadn't caused strained relationships between the two inns.

Carol's eyes lit up. "I know Jack and Miranda wouldn't hire just anybody. They would only get the best." Tristan didn't know what to do with her praise so he remained silent.

Libbie had pulled up The Resort's website on her mom's computer and showed it to Carol. Carol perused the site with interest. Her posture began to relax for the first time since he had entered. "I can see where this would be beneficial."

"I recognize that you and the Hornes have very different properties and tastes. I don't want you to think that your site would be identical to theirs. I want everyone to have a very personalized experience." He shifted his glasses nervously.

Carol turned her attention back to the brochure. She flipped over to the back then glanced up at him in surprise. "You're a Christian?" A broad smile lit her face.

"Yes, ma'am." Tristan was relieved. On the back he had placed a verse from Ephesians. *For we are his workmanship, created in Christ Jesus for good works, which God prepared beforehand, that we should walk in them.* Some of his clients were thrilled by it, some were clearly skeptical about hiring him. There were only a few who had opted not to hire him and sited the verse as a reason for going with someone else. He was glad Carol was pleased with it, because he had really wanted to do the website for this business since he stepped foot on the property. There was just something about this place.

Carol held out her hand. "I'm looking forward to seeing what you come up with. I think we will work together well."

Tristan smiled broadly as he shook her hand. "I think so, too." He gathered his things and was soon heading back to his car. He couldn't wait to start on this project.

3

Tristan was often seen around the inn after that. As he took pictures, gathered information, and got Carol's approval for his designs, Carol grew increasingly excited about the new website. She hadn't thought that she would since Libbie had practically forced her into it, but she could see the benefit of having one. She had been somewhat concerned that Tristan would make it too stark and masculine, or overcompensate and make it too frilly and girly, but he seemed to find a balance that pleased her.

Carol stood on the porch on the back of the inn wrapped in a coat and cupping a mug of coffee. She could see Tristan near the lake taking pictures near the willow tree where Willa and Owen had been married. Truth be told, Carol liked having Tristan around. She always made sure that he stopped by the kitchen and got some cookies and a cup of coffee before he left. He was warm and friendly, and she enjoyed their conversations together.

Tristan was heading back towards her now so she waved her hand. Even from a distance she could see his bright smile. He was a heartwarming person. She began to think of him as part of her family – much the way she had adopted Willa and Owen. Her daughters teased her that instead of picking up stray dogs and cats, she picked up stray people. She couldn't help it. When she liked someone, she showed it.

"That's a beautiful spot," Tristan said as he mounted the porch steps. "Of course, this place is full of beautiful spots."

"I certainly think so." Carol beamed with pride. The inn was the realization of a lifelong dream. It had been somewhat risky, but she was pleased with the results. "Seeing you by that tree reminded me that some friends of mine were recently married in that location. It was a lovely wedding. Maybe they would let me put one of their wedding photos on the website so people can see that the inn makes a good wedding location."

"As long as both they and their photographer give permission, that would be a wonderful idea. I'll make sure to give the photographer credit, of course, which may help his business as well."

"Come inside, and I'll get you their contact information." Carol went to open the door, but Tristan beat her to it and held it open while she entered. Carol liked a young man with old-fashioned manners.

They went into the kitchen, and Carol got Tristan a warm brownie and a cup of coffee before taking a business card off the fridge. She handed him the card as she sat opposite him at the small table in the nook of a bay window.

"I'm surprised I haven't gained weight since starting this project," Tristan teased after he swallowed his first bite of brownie.

"Oh you burn off the extra calories tromping around the property," Carol assured him. She loved feeding people. It wasn't a chore to make breakfast every morning for her guests – unless she had one of those picky people. No gluten, no meat, no dairy, no eggs, no this, no that: the lists seemed to get longer and longer.

"Coburn and Son," Tristan read from the business card. "I've seen their truck out and about town."

"Owen did all the renovations when I bought this old house. It was in rough condition." She affectionately glanced over her kitchen. This room was one of her favorite places with the industrial appliances, granite and stainless steel work spaces, and warm wood cabinets.

"He did an amazing job." Tristan pocketed the card. "I'll give them a call later." He put the last bite of brownie in his mouth and shook his head when Carol offered more coffee. He stood and placed his mug in the sink. "I need to get back home, but thank you so much for your hospitality."

"It's what I do," Carol said modestly with a shrug.

Tristan was nearly out the front door when he abruptly turned back. "I forgot to tell you that I was thinking of hiring a graphic designer to create a logo for Holliday Hotel. Would that be okay?"

"A logo?"

"I like your 'H' on your sign out front with the holly leaves, but I feel like there's more to Holliday Hotel than just that. Graphic design isn't my strong suit so occasionally I hire someone to create a logo for a customer if they don't have one yet."

Carol nodded slowly. "I'm sure that will be fine. I trust your judgment."

"Great! I recently got this ad from a graphic artist in the Bay Area. I haven't used her before, but having seen some of her work, I think she'd be the perfect fit."

4

Amy Juliette walked into her office with a spring in her step. Her office space was small, but artistically decorated. While most of her colleagues in art school were on the trendy side, Amy thought of herself as more traditionally elegant and classic. Her office reflected that with white walls like an art gallery dotted with her own work. There were two desks in the room, both of them antiques. One was situated at the front near the door for her assistant, Katie Miller, while the other in the back was her own. An antique loveseat was near the front door for anyone who might need to wait for her and two antique wingback chairs were in front of her desk.

Amy loved her office space, loved being her own boss. Smiling with satisfaction, she hung up her coat and headed for her desk. She always arrived thirty minutes before Katie. Starting the day off in silence so she could plan for what lay ahead suited her very well.

Pausing before a framed mirror behind her desk, she checked her reflection. Her black hair was cut in a bob that reached her chin, her blue eyes were in stunning contrast to her dark hair, and her ivory skin tone complimented both. She was aware that she often looked cool, arrogant, or aloof, but she found that it kept people distant which was just fine with her.

She smoothed her hands over her black pencil skirt and pale blue blouse before taking her seat. Her carefully manicured fingers flew over her keyboard as she responded to messages. Most of her work was done through email and her website. She rarely had face to face meetings, and when she did she found them to be difficult and a waste of her time. People could be so irritating.

Her first email was from a man named Tristan Romero. He was building a website for a bed and breakfast and wanted to know if she would design a logo for it. She looked through the email several times. Her success since getting out of school had given her the luxury of being able to refuse clients if she didn't see it working for any reason. She liked many things about Tristan's email. He was not local so he wouldn't want to meet in person – that was always a bonus. He seemed to be willing to give her free reign. She hated people who wanted to micro-manage her work. On top of that, he was thorough, including photos of the inn for her to look at so she could get a feel for the place. She liked what she saw, too – an old Victorian house with a wrap-around porch, shutters, and window boxes. The few pictures he had taken of the inside showed elegant furnishings and decorations. It was lovely.

One thing bothered her – the inn's theme. Holidays. She nearly spat the word out under her breath. If it were a normal bed and breakfast, she would be on board, but a themed inn? She shook her head. He hadn't included any pictures of the guest rooms, but she could just picture them covered from floor to ceiling in cheap holiday décor, garish and ugly. How could anyone take such a charming old place and ruin it with a cheesy theme?

Leaning back in her chair, she closed her eyes to picture the owner of the inn – an old lady with unkempt hair, definitely a cheek pincher, someone who bored you to tears with pictures of her grandkids. She sighed. Such a person would want something cutesy, cartoonish. She was fully capable of creating that, but it wasn't what she enjoyed doing.

Katie came in just as she had her hands poised over the keyboard to answer Mr. Romero's email telling him that she was unable to take the account. Amy paused and watched her assistant. In a lot of ways, Katie was her polar opposite. Her hair was brownish-blonde and always seemed in need of a trim. Not that it mattered because Katie always had it thrown up in a messy bun. Her eyes were hazel and hidden behind wire framed glasses. She had a few freckles across the bridge of her nose. She was short and her clothes always managed to look rumpled and bland. Today she wore brown slacks with a tan sweater, both of which were too big.

Amy smiled affectionately. People were always surprised when they saw the two of them – one polished and refined, the other carelessly put together and warm – but maybe it was their differences that made them such a great team.

Katie gave her a warm smile and headed over to her desk. "What's on the agenda for today?"

"I've got to put the final adjustments on the ad for that new fusion restaurant. Then I really need to start the brochure for the dentist office. I've been putting it off too long." She rattled off a few more items while Katie listened intently. She knew that she didn't have to tell Katie what she should do. Katie had a great knack for hearing Amy's schedule and knowing exactly what she needed to do to help Amy get her work done. "Pretty typical day," Amy finished up.

"Busy, but not stressful – just the way I like it," Katie said cheerily. She started back to her desk. Amy stared at the email for a moment and then called Katie back over.

"Maybe you can help me with this. I got an email from a web designer who wants me to do a logo for a bed and breakfast."

"Ooh, that's right up your alley. What's the problem?" Amy loved that Katie instinctively knew that she was hesitating.

Amy pulled up the picture of the inn and showed it to Katie. "The name of the place is Holliday Hotel. It's owned by a lady named Carol Holliday and all the rooms are holiday themed." Her contempt was clearly evident as she said the word 'holiday'. Oh how she hated that word!

"Oh," Katie said simply. She stared at the photo for a while. "I know holidays aren't your favorite thing, Ms. Scrooge." She smiled to take any sting out of the comment. "But I still think that this could be perfect for you."

Amy snorted. "You know that this place is probably filled with plastic decorations and cheap art."

"I don't think so. Just look at that house, Amy. It's gorgeous and elegant. It's well taken care of and beautifully situated. I think you'll regret turning this down." Amy started to speak, but Katie stopped her. "You know you will! You'll pull up that photo over and over and you'll sketch ideas for the inn as they come to you. You might as well get paid for doing it."

Amy looked at the inn one more time. There was a classic timelessness about the house. Surely she could find something that would work. "You're right. Thank you." She immediately set to writing a response back to Tristan.

Katie patted her shoulder. "Good girl. I can't wait to see what you come up with."

5

Carol heard the front door open. She frowned as she looked up from the bills she was paying in her office. She wasn't expecting any new guests to arrive today. January was a slow time for her since holiday vacations were over and everyone was settling back into the daily routine.

She pushed out of her chair and went to the front of the house. What she saw caused her to squeal with delight. "Willa! Owen! You're home!" She embraced each of them warmly and led them into the kitchen. Willa and Owen were all smiles as they held hands and sat beside each other at the counter top stools. Carol poured them both coffee – she seemed to have a constant supply, and it never tasted bitter or stale – and cut them a piece of coffee cake. Once she had them settled, she leaned on the counter across from them, cradling her own mug in her hands. "So how was your trip?" Her eyes sparkled as she asked the question, and she burst out laughing at the blush that flooded Willa's face. "That good, huh?"

"It was a wonderful trip. Beautiful location. Wonderful company. Couldn't have asked for more," Owen answered as he gazed lovingly at his new wife.

"I'm so glad, but I'm even happier that you're home. Has school begun yet, Willa?"

Willa was a kindergarten teacher. She had been hired on with the elementary school in the summer and moved to Willow Creek in the fall. Owen had moved back in with his father while Willa took possession of his apartment. From what Carol had heard, it was now a completely different place full of feminine touches.

"It has started, but I'll go back on Monday. I've had a sub

while I've been gone." She smiled up at Owen. "It'll be weird when the kids call me Mrs. Coburn instead of Miss Newman."

"Weird in a good way, I hope."

"Weird in the best way." Willa rested her head on her husband's shoulder, and tears flooded Carol's eyes for a moment. She quickly blinked them away. Her own husband, Gabe, had been gone for eight years, but there were still moments when the memories nearly took her breath away. Watching Willa and Owen had reminded her of how she had leaned on her own husband and seen him gazing at her with the same adoration.

Carol cleared her throat. "How is Cody doing?"

Cody was Owen's dog. He was old, but a faithful, loving member of the family. Owen's face clouded for a moment. "He's having more and more trouble getting around. I'm not sure we'll have him much longer." He squeezed Willa's shoulders. "But he adores having Willa with us. I can tell because he chewed up her favorite pair of shoes. I think he did it just so she couldn't walk away from us." His eyes had a teasing glint as Willa sighed.

"Dogs and men do not understand the importance of shoes in a woman's life."

Carol threw her head back and laughed. "No, they don't. That's why we girls have to stick together."

"Anything new happen while we were away?" Owen asked as he dug into his coffee cake.

Carol drummed her fingers on the countertop. "Let's see. The city council approved construction for a new medical clinic. It's supposed to help people get treatment more quickly, kind of serve as a mini-hospital of sorts. Of course, serious cases will still need to be transported to the big hospital, but I think it'll be a good addition to our town."

"Good for the town and good for business," Owen responded with a smile. "I wonder if Dad put a bid in yet."

"I don't think it's gotten that far yet." Carol was pleased that though Owen and his father had been through a rough patch recently, they had worked it out. Their relationship – both personal and business – seemed to be stronger than ever now that they had been able to talk things through.

Carol took a sip of her coffee. "Oh, and I'm getting a website!"

"That'll be fantastic!" Willa exclaimed. "It should really be helpful for getting new guests."

"I'm hoping so. I hope it will also help me with booking, collecting payments, and cancellations. Tristan Romero is building it for me."

Willa didn't show any recognition to the name, but Owen's face lit up. "I did some work on his grandma's house. She needed some things put in to help her after her stroke. He seems like a good guy."

"He is. He's been very helpful and communicative. I've loved that he includes me in the process." Carol refilled Owen's coffee mug. "He's over nearly as often as you used to be."

"Trying to steal my place, is he?" Owen said laughingly. He looked thoughtfully at Willa. "I suppose I won't be over as often I was."

"Probably not, but that's as it should be." Carol felt her heart glow with warmth for these two. She wanted them to feel free to visit whenever they wanted, but she knew they needed to be alone as well. "Just know that you are both welcome in my home anytime."

Willa smiled. "You may regret that."

"I doubt that." She laid her hand on top of Willa's.

The slamming of the front door made all three of them jump. They turned in unison to the entryway of the kitchen as the sound of boots stomping across the hardwood floors filled their ears. "That woman is going to drive me crazy!"

A young man with black hair and dark eyes framed by trendy glasses stood in the doorway with his hands clenched at his sides. His eyes widened as he saw Willa and Owen at the counter and the anger left his face. "I'm so sorry. I didn't realize that you had company."

"That's okay, Tristan. I'd like you to meet Owen and Willa Coburn – although I guess you've already met Owen before. This is the couple who got married by the willow tree earlier this month."

Tristan approached them with his arm extended to shake their hands. "Oh yes! I thought you looked familiar. Thanks for letting me use your wedding photos on the website. I think more people are going to want to have their weddings here because of them."

"We're glad to help with anything for Carol. She's done so much for us." Willa glanced over at Carol with affection. But Carol waved off her comment as she would a pesky gnat.

"What woman were you raging at when you came in?" The change of subject worked. Tristan's brow furrowed once more.

"It's that graphic designer that I wanted to prepare your logo. I thought she would be a perfect fit for us, but she's not working out at all."

"What's wrong with her work?"

Tristan put a stack of papers on the counter and let the three of them sort through them. As they finished all three wore a look of confusion that was nearly comical.

"This is what she thinks I would like?" Carol wasn't sure if she should be hurt or amused. One of the drawings showed a frumpy old lady wearing a witch's hat, a heart covered apron, and carrying an Easter basket and a Christmas tree. Another had her lovely Victorian home drawn in a cartoonish fashion covered in holiday paraphernalia. Yet another simply had a stark HH encircled by generic twining lines. Carol sighed. "Is this all she's come up with?"

Tristan shook his head. "These are only the best ones. There are several more that I've rejected. It's like she can't get the right feel for this place. It's either too cutesy, or too whimsical, or too formal. The balance is all wrong." He sighed. "I'm sorry. I should have gone with someone I had worked with before, someone I trusted. Instead I got us into this." He gestured weakly at the images littering the countertop.

"Maybe Holliday Hotel is someplace you have to visit to really understand," Willa said thoughtfully, almost as if she was talking to herself.

"That's it! She needs to experience it for herself!" Carol

grabbed the papers and pushed them into Tristan's hands. "Tell her that she needs to come stay here – and not for some overnight trip. I want her to at least be here a week, longer if she needs to, but she needs to experience Holliday Hotel."

Tristan's lip twitched. "I have a feeling that she's going to hate me for this."

6

"I hate him for this!" Amy threw her purse and jacket down on one of the wingback chairs in front of her desk. Katie jumped and whirled around.

"I thought you were going to lunch."

"I was, but I stopped to check my email first. Obviously that was a mistake." She sat down hard in her chair and began typing aggressively.

Katie walked over and glanced at the email that Amy was composing. She gasped. "You can't say that to a client!"

Amy sighed and pressed the backspace button, knowing that Katie was right. Though her blood was boiling she couldn't afford to make enemies. She took a deep breath as Katie took the chair opposite her.

"What's going on?"

"He wants me to go there. He says I'm not 'capturing the essence' of the inn. Nothing I've done has pleased him. Now he wants me to go to some podunk town in the middle of winter." She knew she was rambling, but she also knew that Katie would be able to follow her. Katie had always been able to read her well.

Katie leaned forward and grabbed a stack of papers off Amy's desk. She flipped through them one by one, frowning in dismay at each. "This is what you've shown him for the Holliday Hotel logo?" Amy nodded. Katie put the pages back on her desk and shook her head. "I don't wonder that he wants you to visit. These are not your best work."

"Don't you turn on me, too." Amy's heart sank. Katie was her biggest support. If she felt like the artwork wasn't up to the challenge, she knew it was bad.

She could tell Katie was searching carefully for the right words to say by the way her eyes darted around the room as if looking for inspiration. "Look! In most cases you have no reason to meet a client face to face. You get a good feel for them and you deliver amazing artwork. But this one is different. They're further away, unknown to you, and obviously looking for something other than what you've provided. So go meet them in person. You can take your laptop, work from there as well as you can here, and maybe inspiration will strike."

"I can't just up and leave."

"Yes, you can, and I think this is something you need to do." Katie stood up. "I can take care of the office. I'll go make your travel arrangements now."

Amy was stunned. She felt as if her best friend had just slapped her. Leaping to her feet, she cried, "Wait a second! I didn't say I was going."

Katie was already plugging away at her computer. "You didn't," she agreed. "I did." She looked up at Amy. "You haven't had a vacation since we opened. Use this as a working vacation. Go. Get some rest. And while you're at it, come up with something brilliant for Holliday Hotel." She smiled. "I know it's in there somewhere."

Amy sighed. "I'm going to lunch." She went back and gathered her things knowing that by the time she returned Katie would have made all the arrangements needed for her to travel to Willow Creek. She felt defeated.

As she walked to her favorite deli down the street, defeat turned into anger. How dare that man tell her what to do? She was talented! Everyone knew it. Her style was distinctive, but she was adaptable. She could do this logo.

"He wants me to quit!" She wasn't aware that she had spoken out loud until the man behind the counter looked at her strangely. She apologized and paid for her soup before finding an empty table.

It was becoming clear. Tristan Romero wanted her to quit, then he would claim that she hadn't filled her end of the contract and use that to refuse to pay her. Since she'd already sent him some drafts, he'd use those to create a logo for the website. She huffed so hard that some of her soup spattered on the table. Wiping it up, she glanced around to make sure no one had noticed.

She finished eating quickly and marched back to her office. Mr. Romero was going to get the surprise of his life when he found out that she was actually coming. She smiled in anticipation. The look on his face would make the trouble worth it.

A picture of Tristan was already forming in her mind. He'd be heavy. Sitting at a desk all day was pretty sedentary. He'd have balding gray hair, thick glasses, and thick lips to match. His clothes would be wrinkled and stained. Probably divorced and a woman hater because of it. That would explain his inability to accept her work. Although it didn't explain why he'd hired her in the first place.

She frowned as she pushed the elevator button to get to her floor. As the chime sounded, a light bulb went off in her head. Of course, he'd hire a woman! His plot would have counted on her being too weak to fight back and too stupid to figure out his plan. Wouldn't he be surprised when his plan backfired on him?

She flung open her office door causing Katie to jump. "I'm going to Willow Creek!"

7

Tristan smiled at the email. It was stiffly formal. He was sure she had rewritten it several times before sending it. The idea of what her first few drafts may have sounded like brought forth a chuckle.

His phone rang, and he wasn't surprised to see Carol's number on the caller ID.

"She's actually coming!" Carol sounded surprised and nervous, as if she had heard that her favorite movie star was coming to stay at the inn.

"I figured she would. She seems like a competitive person. She would have seen my invitation as a challenge."

"How did you figure that?"

Tristan shrugged even though Carol couldn't see him. "I don't know. There's something in her emails that strikes me that way."

"Well, in any case I'm glad she's coming. Although, I haven't been this nervous since we first opened. I put her in the honeymoon suite." Her words came out in a rush.

"I'm surprised it was available." He double checked the dates that Amy had sent him. She had said that she was going to be using this time as a working vacation so she was going to be in town for an extended stay. She was coming in the first of February and leaving the day after Valentine's Day. "I thought the honeymoon suite would be booked for the holiday."

"It usually is, but I just got a cancellation and figured I'd want her in the best room I have." Carol sighed. "Am I trying too hard? Maybe I should put her in a different room."

"I'm sure it'll be fine. She probably won't want to leave." Tristan paced his office which was in his grandmother's basement.

He actually figured that Ms. Amy Juliette would be packing her designer bags and heading home before she'd completed a week, but he knew that would only add to Carol's anxiety. She'd feel like she should go above and beyond to make sure that her guest stayed the full two weeks.

"I get the feeling that Ms. Juliette doesn't have a very high opinion of me or the inn," Carol said quietly. "I feel like I have to win her over."

Tristan's lips compressed. He had gotten the same feeling, but he had hoped that Carol hadn't felt that way, too. There was something about Carol that made him want to protect her. "You simply have to be you, and let the inn speak for itself. If that doesn't win her over, then she's not worth our time. I'll just pay her, and we'll move on."

"Okay." Carol's voice wobbled a bit as if she were holding in tears, and Tristan was glad that he had a few days before the graphic artist showed up, because right now, he was angry at her for causing doubt and pain to such a wonderful woman.

"Leave it in God's hands. He'll take care of us."

"Of course. Thanks, Tristan. I always feel better after I talk to you."

Tristan put the phone on his desk, balancing it on a stack of papers. Organization was not a skill he had mastered over the years. He knew the mess always bugged his grandma. She would ask him to let her clean it up for him, but he insisted that he'd never be able to find anything. Recently though it was getting more difficult for her to manage the basement stairs which made it easier for him to insist that she leave his office alone, although it saddened him considerably.

Thoughts of his grandma always brought a smile to his face. He looked at the clock and decided it was time for a lunch break. He left his office, carefully closing the door behind him, and walked into his grandma's living room.

When a stroke had left Carmen Romero partially paralyzed, Tristan had moved from Los Angeles to Willow Creek in order to take care of her. Of his siblings, his job was the only one that had the flexibility to work from home. They had agreed that Carmen shouldn't be moved out of the house she had moved into as a bride, so Tristan had moved to her.

"How are you doing, Grandma?" Tristan came over to sit on the couch next her favorite recliner. She was chewing on the end of a pen as she studied a crossword puzzle.

"I'd be better if I could figure out this word."

"You'll figure it out. You always do. I'm going to make some lunch."

"I'm not hungry."

Tristan paused and looked back at Carmen sadly. Trying to get her to eat was a challenge every day. It was like she had given up after the stroke. "I'll make you some anyway. You may want it later." He went into the kitchen that hadn't been updated in decades. There was no dishwasher, the appliances were an avocado green, and the floor was linoleum. But it was clean. Tristan made sure that even though his office was a disaster, the rest of the house met his grandma's strict expectations. He fixed a can of soup and filled two bowls. Bringing them to a small dining room table, he tried to convince Carmen one more time to join him. "I'm going to be so lonely eating here by myself." He made his eyes large and gave her an exaggerated pout that never failed to make her laugh.

"Oh all right," she said still chuckling. She reached for her walker and pulled herself up. "You're a pesky as your grandfather was."

"He taught me everything I know." Tristan held Carmen's chair, another trait that his grandfather had taught him. They said grace and began to eat. As he watched his grandma lift the spoon to her mouth he gave thanks again that the paralysis had not affected her dominant side. She was able to eat and write with her right hand as she had before, but he hadn't realized how often both hands were used until he came to help his grandma. He knew that many everyday tasks were difficult for her now, but she quietly allowed him to help her when she needed it.

"The artist that's developing the logo for Holliday Hotel is coming to town for a visit. Carol and I thought it would be helpful to actually see the inn."

"He's coming at a cold time." Carmen concentrated on blowing on her soup.

"She."

"What?"

"*She's* coming at a cold time."

"Oh, the artist is a *she*!" Carmen set down her spoon and a twinkle lit her eyes. "Is she pretty?"

Tristan laughed. "I don't know. I've never met her."

"Do you like her?"

"I don't know. I've never met her."

Carmen huffed. "What do you know?"

"I know that her style is usually elegant, almost old-fashioned, but that she's been struggling with getting me a decent logo for the website I'm designing. I thought she'd be the perfect fit, but I guess I was wrong."

"Hm. She's trying too hard."

Tristan looked at his grandma in surprise. She always seemed to be able to read a situation intuitively. He had commented on it before and she just said that with age came wisdom. "That's a possibility." He put the last bite of soup in his mouth. "I think she has the idea that the inn is a cheesy tourist trap."

Carmen nodded. "City girl?"

"San Francisco."

Carmen grunted. Tristan was pleased to see that she had nearly finished off her own bowl of soup. Sometimes if he distracted her with conversation she seemed to eat better. "What's her name?"

"Amy Juliette."

"Sounds like a stage name," Carmen laughed. "Your grandpa and I used to play this game whenever we were going to meet someone where we would each guess what that person would look like." She slid her gaze to him mischievously. "Bet I could get closer than you."

Tristan smiled. "You're on." He closed his eyes. "With her temper, I'd say she's a redhead with wild curls, green eyes and freckles. She has sharp features. She's short – Napoleon complex –

and skinny." He opened his eyes. "Your turn."

Carmen's eyes sparkled. "You said that her designs were elegant and a name like Amy Juliette – oh, this is interesting. I'm guessing she's tall and slender and graceful. Her hair is – oh she's definitely a brunette, gray eyes with dark lashes and full lips – not too full though. I bet she's lovely."

Tristan grunted as he gathered their dishes. "You always taught me that lovely is as lovely does. I've yet to see anything lovely out of her."

8

"Tell me again why you booked this trip for two full weeks." Amy had her phone on speaker as she navigated the twisted mountain roads.

"We've been over this before." Katie's voice was full of exasperation. "You need a break. You've been working hard for too long. Relax. Enjoy the time away."

"Right. I can't relax. I have too much to do."

"You have your computer and your art supplies. Use them."

Amy sighed. "I'm going to hate this place."

"Have you seen the pictures? The place is gorgeous. It'll be the perfect place to give you new inspiration – especially for the Holliday Hotel logo."

"Outside is gorgeous, but inside it will look like Cupid threw up all over." Amy slowed as she entered a town. A quaint wooden sign proclaimed it to be Willow Creek. "Looks like I'm here. I guess I better figure out where this place is."

"Ok. Look, Amy, I think this is going to be good for you. Try to enjoy yourself."

"I make no promises." She disconnected the call and focused on the GPS directions. She knew Katie was trying to be helpful, but for the first time in their time together Amy felt frustrated with her. Who was she to tell her to take a vacation? Arrange it even? What was she supposed to do if she couldn't stand this place? No hotel gave refunds. She'd be out the money if she moved to another inn. Two weeks in a corny holiday hole did not sound appealing.

She saw the sign for Holliday Hotel and pulled into the small parking lot. Thick trees on either side gave the large Victorian home an isolated feel. The house really was lovely with its white siding, dark green shutters and bright red door. The wraparound porch was perfect. She had half expected the house to be decked out in heart shaped lights, cheap cupid cutouts and red paper hearts in the windows. After taking a deep breath, she got out of her car.

As she placed her hand on the knob to enter, a feeling of trepidation filled her. The outside might be normal, but what would the inside look like? She stepped in and again was surprised. The front area was beautiful, decorated with antiques that fit the age of the house. A large wooden front desk sat directly in front of her. A short hallway was beside the desk and a staircase on the other side of the hallway. The stairs had been restored to what seemed like their original stateliness.

A lady behind the desk greeted her cheerfully. She was probably mid-fifties, short and curvy. Her hair and her clothes were stylish, and her bright smile was welcoming. Amy approached the desk. "I'm checking in. My name is Amy Juliette."

The smile faded briefly, but was recovered. "Oh yes. I'm Carol Holliday." The lady held her hand out. "It's so nice to finally meet you in person."

Amy couldn't believe her eyes. This was Carol Holliday? No frumpy old lady here. "It's a pleasure," she murmured.

"Would you like to go straight to your room or would you like a tour first? Maybe we should hold off on the tour until tomorrow when you've had time to rest." The words poured out of Mrs. Holliday like a fountain.

"Um, room first, I guess." Amy had never felt so steamrolled in her life. Nothing was what she had expected, and was it her imagination or was Mrs. Holliday nervous, almost frightened by her?

"Of course." Carol grabbed a key and headed up the stairs. "I put you in one of our two suites. It's actually our honeymoon suite." She smiled almost apologetically. "I felt like you would be most comfortable there."

The suite was on the third floor. Carol explained that the two suites occupied the whole third floor. One of them faced the street, and the other faced the lake on the back of the property. The honeymoon suite faced the back. "It has a beautiful view," Carol promised. "It's, of course, our valentine room. The Sweetheart Suite." She stopped in front of a door with a small wooden plaque on it. The sign was painted white with the words in pale pink and one simple heart in a corner. Amy took a breath as Carol opened the door expecting to be flooded with red and pink, cupids and hearts.

Carol stepped to the side to allow Amy to enter. She stepped inside hesitantly, then stopped in wonder. She was standing in a living area. A fireplace took the primary focus along one wall, the wood around it restored to the original Victorian elegance. The walls were a soft gray and the floors were hardwood. An antique loveseat sat in front of the fireplace covered in a white fabric with delicate pink rosebuds on it. French doors led out to a balcony overlooking the lake. Along one side of the room, two antique wingback chairs sat with a small table between them. The mantle simply had a bud vase with two pink roses in it. A watercolor painting hung over the fireplace of a couple holding hands and walking beside the lake.

Amy was shocked at how elegant the room was. It was restful, not overly crowded and free of cheap valentine gimmicks. "This is lovely," she breathed.

Carol beamed. "Thank you! I'm rather proud of this room. I wanted it to be a refuge for a newly married couple."

Amy glanced back at Carol. "Well, I think you've achieved your goal then. I think that most couples would love to stay here."

Carol blushed. "I'll show you the rest." She walked through an archway. Amy followed and discovered a small kitchenette. A few cupboards, a sink, a small refrigerator, stove top, microwave, toaster and coffee pot took up most of the small space. Along one wall was a small wooden table with two chairs. Carol opened the fridge and revealed that it was stocked with fruit, milk, and juice. A cupboard was opened to reveal bread, muffins, and coffee. "I've found that most newlyweds don't really want to socialize with other guests," Carol explained with a smile. "Anticipating that, I added the kitchenette so that they can have breakfast alone whenever they want. You are more than welcome to come down for breakfast, but if you would rather eat alone you can help yourself."

"That was some ingenious forethought on your part." The idea of dining alone was actually very appealing to Amy. She was used to being on her own. "How do you know when to restock the supplies?"

"When we clean the room each day, we also check the kitchen. It works well." Carol led her through another archway and into a large bedroom. The bed was the focal point. It was a wooden canopy bed, draped with gauzy white fabric. The bedding was pure white which stood out against the darker gray of the walls. There was a bay window looking out towards to lake and a window seat piled with white, pink, and gray pillows of different patterns. A small, antique desk was on one wall beside a dresser. Black and white photos of couples in various stages of life occupied the walls. The windows had shades to draw and were framed by more gauzy white drapes. On the dresser sat an ice bucket with apple cider in it and two goblets.

Amy placed her suitcase on the bed and looked around in amazement. The room was romantic, yet elegant. Somehow she had pictured something gaudy, more along the lines of Las Vegas with a heart-shaped bed, but she had been very wrong. She was beginning to understand why her logos had been unappealing to Mrs. Holliday and Mr. Romero. She hadn't understood what Holliday Hotel was about at all.

She wandered to where there were two doors in a wall. One revealed a closet, while the other led into the bathroom. The toilet was in a separate little room which Amy was sure was appreciated by the couples who stayed there. A large sink and countertop with a mirror above it was in the center. On the opposite side from the toilet was a large glass shower, but what drew Amy's attention was a deep claw-footed bathtub. A shelf above the tub had bath salts, and bubble bath, as well as the basic toiletries. Large, white towels hung on the towel rack and two thick, white bathrobes hung on pegs beside them.

"I don't know what to say," she said as she returned to the bedroom where Carol was waiting. "This room is amazing."

Carol smiled brightly. "I'm glad you like it. I had so much fun designing these rooms." She moved towards the doorway. "I'll let you get settled in. If you feel like a tour later, just come get me. If I'm not at the front desk, I'm most likely in the kitchen."

Amy heard the door to the suite close and took another look through the rooms. She was in awe of the taste and comfort and elegance that was revealed at every turn. She sighed. It looked like she was going to have to start the process all over with a brand new perspective.

9

Tristan walked into the dining room at Holliday Hotel and frowned as he glanced at the occupants. Amy Juliette didn't appear to be there. There was a family of four, a young couple, and middle aged man by himself. Tristan had expected to find her at breakfast to be able to talk to her about the logo. He kicked himself for not scheduling the time with her. He shouldn't have assumed anything.

Carol came in with a fresh pitcher of juice. There was a heart covered apron wrapped around her waist. She set the juice on the buffet and then joined Tristan by the door. "I think she's eating breakfast alone in the suite." Tristan marveled at Carol's intuition.

"Why would she eat alone?" He eyed the chafing dishes of eggs, bacon, sausage and the fresh cinnamon rolls on the buffet. "No, the real question is why would she turn down this spread for a breakfast alone?"

Carol chuckled. "Go grab a plate and sit down."

"But I'm not a guest."

"There's plenty, and it makes me happy to feed hungry young men. Now, do as you're told."

Tristan didn't need any further urging. With a plate heaped full, he took a seat at a table, and soon Carol joined him, cradling a mug of coffee in her hands. "To get back to your question, I get the feeling that Amy is used to being alone. She's comfortable on her own."

Tristan swallowed his mouthful of food. "What was your first impression of her? You're a good judge of character."

"I have to admit, she intimidated me at first. She's so polished and professional. She came in with a look that told me that she was ready to hate everything." Carol smiled slightly. "She couldn't hide how surprised she was about her room, though. I think she was surprised about me and the inn as well."

"I don't know what she expected." Tristan kept his attention on his food.

"I think she expected a little, old lady with a house full of clutter, knick knacks, and cheap, over the top holiday décor." Carol sipped her coffee. "It was such a relief when she was obviously impressed. She especially liked the suite."

"Well, of course, she did! This place is amazing!" Tristan pushed his empty plate away. "I'm glad she can see it. I was starting to wonder about her."

"No, she's someone who can certainly see beauty. I think she'll turn out to be a good choice. She simply needed a firsthand experience." Carol stood up and picked up Tristan's plate. "If you want to meet with her, she's on the third floor in Sweetheart Suite."

"Is it weird to go up to her room?" Tristan looked uncomfortable. "What if she's still sleeping or not – ready?"

"You could call or text her first if you're concerned. I'll meet up with you later. I need to clean up the dining room right now."

Tristan wandered into the entryway indecisively. He looked towards the stairs, then pulled out his phone. He put one foot on the bottom step and then removed it. He paced the area, raking his hair in frustration. He owned his own business and made decisions all the time. Why was this hard for him? Hearing footsteps, he turned around. The woman descending the stairs was absolutely beautiful. He was sure his jaw dropped. She was slim and elegant. She had bobbed dark hair and bright blue eyes. She looked like a movie star.

As she reached the bottom, she noticed him standing there staring at her. "What?" she snapped.

Tristan shook his head. "I'm so sorry. It's nothing."

The lady rolled her eyes and headed towards the kitchen. It suddenly hit Tristan that this woman fit Carol's description of Amy Juliette as 'polished and professional'. He took a step after her. "You wouldn't happen to be Amy Juliette, would you?"

The woman stopped and turned around slowly, suspicion

etched on her features. "I am. Who are you?"

Tristan smiled and extended his hand. "I'm Tristan Romero. I was trying to decide if I should call you or just head up to your room." As she shook his hand, Tristan noticed that her fingers were frigid, like her expression. He had the distinct impression that she was the original ice princess.

"Calling is always the more favorable option. Text or email would work just as well." Tristan put his hands in his pockets awkwardly feeling as if he'd been slapped.

"Okay, good to know. So, do you have time to sit down and meet with me now?"

Amy's eyes shifted towards the kitchen. "I was just going to see Mrs. Holliday and get a tour. Could we schedule it for later?"

"Sure, absolutely. Maybe we could meet over dinner?"

A corner of her mouth tipped up cynically. "I don't really do dinner meetings."

Tristan suddenly understood the iciness. With him gawking at her as she was coming down the stairs, she must think that he was hitting on her. "Oh! Sorry. Of course. Well, you tell me the time and place. I think it'd be good to have Mrs. Holliday there as well so she can give her vision and input. Why don't you discuss it with her and then text me a time? I'm pretty flexible today." He waved weakly, and left before Amy could answer. He had only had time to notice that her brows had contracted in confusion when he had mentioned Mrs. Holliday joining them. Good. Maybe he had started to dispel the idea that he was interested in her.

He was still feeling awkward and embarrassed when he stepped into his home. His grandma was watching a game show in the living room. As it was his custom, he stopped by to give her a kiss on the cheek and let her know he was home.

"You're home earlier than I expected," Carmen said, as she muted the television.

"Well, I didn't actually get to the meeting." He slumped on the couch near his grandma and closed his eyes.

Carmen frowned in confusion. "What do you mean? You didn't meet the elegant Amy Juliette?" He opened his eyes to see her mouth twitch.

"I saw her and met her briefly. She quickly dismissed me and let me know that she would contact me later."

"What do you mean she dismissed you? Who does she think she is?"

"The ice princess," Tristan answered without thinking.

Carmen laughed heartily. "Sounds like she made quite an impression on you."

Tristan's mouth quirked in amusement. "She was cold in expression and manners – even her fingers were cold. She immediately set up a barrier between us."

"A barrier? You're working together."

Tristan sighed. "I think she's used to fending off males."

Carmen's eyes shone with laughter. "And did she have reason to think she needed to fend you off?"

Tristan chuckled. "Remember the game we played where we tried to guess what she looked like? Well, you were definitely closer than I was. Dark hair, pale skin, icy blue eyes, slender – I'll admit that at first I was attracted." He blushed. "I may have been staring."

Carmen couldn't keep the laughter in any more. "My poor Tristan! Bowled over by the ice princess!"

Tristan smiled in sympathy. "Yeah, well, it didn't last for long. As soon as she opened her mouth she was rude and condescending. Any attraction I may have felt was quickly replaced by embarrassment and frustration."

Carmen patted his arm. "I'm so proud that you aren't taken in by a pretty face, but you care about the heart. A pretty face may fade, but a good heart will last a lifetime."

Tristan was beginning to feel better with his grandmother's encouragement. "I don't even know her. If she isn't a Christian, then there isn't a future there anyway. All I know about her is that she is a talented artist. I just want is to get this logo done and send her back so I can finish the Holliday Hotel website. And speaking of work," he got up and stretched. "I'll leave you to your game shows while I get back to work."

As he left the room he could hear Carmen muttering. Experience told him that she was probably praying. He wondered what he had said that made her feel the need to go before the Lord.

10

Amy watched Tristan leave. She had a feeling that she had embarrassed him somehow or that he was flustered. When she had seen him at the bottom of the stairs she had been annoyed. She wasn't unaware that men found her attractive, but instead of being flattered by it, it simply irritated her. Then he had introduced himself, and she had wondered if maybe she had misinterpreted the reason he had been staring. Her defense mode had started back up when he had suggested a dinner meeting. In her experience, she had found that male clients tended to hope that giving her a little wine would make her willing to give them something in return. His hasty agreement to meet on her terms and even to have Mrs. Holliday with them had again left her questioning if she had jumped to conclusions.

She shook her head and went to the kitchen. She would have to figure out Tristan Romero later. Or if she was lucky, she could get out of this town before she needed to figure anyone out.

Carol was putting dishes in the dishwasher when she came in. Her apron covered in hearts was more along the lines of what she had been expecting throughout the inn. The sight simply made her smile. Carol looked up and gave her a welcoming smile.

"Did you eat in your room? If not, I have more that I can get for you."

"I already ate. Thank you. I was hoping to get a tour now, but it looks like you're busy. Maybe I'll come back later."

"Why don't you grab a cup of coffee and sit down at the counter? I wouldn't be opposed to having some company as I clean up." Carol nodded to where the coffee mugs were placed and encouraged her to help herself. Amy followed her directions and took her place at the counter. "How did you sleep last night?"

"Like a log. My room is very comfortable. I'm surprised it was available."

"I had a cancellation. Usually it is booked this time of year." Carol began to wash the pans. "I was glad I was able to put you in it. I'm fond of all the rooms, but I felt like Sweetheart Suite was the best place for you. It's the most elegant of the rooms. At least, that's my opinion."

"How did you get started doing this?"

"I'm a Christmas baby so I always had a love for Christmas, but I also developed a love for all holidays. Even as a little girl, I would celebrate each one. I'd make decorations or cards or find some way to celebrate. Later when I was married, Gabe and I talked about what we'd like to do someday, and he brought up the idea of owning a bed and breakfast. I got all excited and said that each room could have a holiday theme." Carol took a breath. "Gabe didn't get to see our dream come true, but he helped me be able to afford to do it. Between what he had saved and the life insurance policy he had, I had plenty to buy this house, fix it up, and get it going."

"It seems like you're doing well."

Carol smiled proudly. "It's exceeded my expectations."

"I have to admit that this is not what I had expected." Amy looked around the modern kitchen and almost wished she could have the opportunity to cook something in it – almost.

Carol looked at her for a long moment while drying her hands on a towel. "I know." She didn't say more, but Amy knew that her preconceived notions had somehow hurt Carol. She thought about the logos she had designed and realized that they had been condescending. She felt the heat rush to her face, but before she could say anything more, Carol suggested that they take the tour.

Carol led her through the living room, dining room, briefly showed her the small office, and then took her upstairs. Although most of the rooms were full, Amy was able to see that each room had a simple wooden plaque bearing the room's name and something that symbolized the holiday it represented. Carol was able to show her Resolution Room and Amy had to admit that she was impressed. The room was more modern, but still comfortable and tastefully done.

"Some of my first guests were a group of college roommates who came to celebrate New Year's together their senior year. They've come every year since, and I always save this room for them. They're now some dear friends of mine. I think that's part of what I love about this place. Certainly, I have guests who come and go and never leave a mark, but the ones that do are worth it."

Amy smiled, but said nothing. She did what she could to keep people at arm's length. The idea of welcoming strangers in and hoping that they would become friends was completely foreign.

Carol led her outside where they walked around the wraparound porch. Amy noted all the comfortable corners that had been created to sit and relax in. Porch swings, rocking chairs, small tables with a couple of seats on either side, and lounge chairs had places on the porch, but it didn't feel crowded. Instead it felt like you could bring out a book, find an isolated spot, and enjoy the solitude.

They walked down to the lake which was still frozen, although Carol warned her that it wasn't solid enough for ice skating. She explained that when it was, there were ice skates available to her guests. "I make very sure that the lake is safe for skating before I allow the skates to be used. And of course, for insurance purposes, I have to have my guests sign waivers." Carol smiled slightly. "My very practical daughter, Libbie, made sure of that."

"You have a daughter?"

"I have two. Libbie is an accountant. She's very smart, very sensible, and very serious. She takes care of me, especially now that her dad has passed away. May is an interior decorator and an artist. She's very sensitive, very compassionate, and very friendly. She loves on me – if that makes sense." Carol chuckled. "They're night and day, but I love them each so much."

"Sounds like you have a nice family."

"I do. I've been blessed. How about you?"

Amy stuck her hands in her pockets and gazed unseeingly at the lake "My family – is not as nice as yours." She was silent for several moments, inwardly waging a war about how much to tell. Finally, she decided that she was only here temporarily, so it wasn't worth getting into. "Is there anything else you'd like to show me?"

"Why don't we go to my apartment and I'll make us some tea?" Carol led the way to an outside door that went to her basement apartment.

The space was open, bright and clean. The smaller kitchen was still very up to the minute and Amy found herself seated at a small table while her hostess made a pot of tea. She brought over cups and saucers, sugar, and milk with the tea. Amy fixed her tea the way she liked it.

"I don't drink tea often so it feels like a special occasion when I have it," Amy admitted as she enjoyed the aroma coming from her cup.

"I've always found that there's something relaxing about having a chat over a cup of tea."

Amy's back stiffened. "What do you mean chat?"

Carol's eyebrows raised. "I only mean we have a lot of business to discuss."

"Oh, of course." Amy relaxed again. She could tell that Carol longed to ask more, but that she refrained. For that she was grateful. "I feel like I have a better grasp on your business now. I think I should be able to come up with something."

"I feel certain that you will."

Amy began to feel uncomfortable with Carol. She felt like Carol could see deeper inside her than she was comfortable letting anyone get. "So, I ran into Mr. Romero before I came to get you. He said to let him know when the three of us could get together."

Carol shrugged. "Why don't I make dinner for all of us tonight? That would probably be easiest."

"Isn't there a restaurant or something where we could meet? I don't want to put you out."

"I was already planning on having soup and a salad. It's

already simmering in the crock pot. There's plenty to share."

Amy recognized the scent of chicken tortilla soup now. She felt like Carol might have been a born hostess. "Well, as long as you're sure."

"Absolutely. Why don't you tell Tristan and you can just come to the inside door when you're ready? Let's say around six?"

Amy stood up, suddenly eager to leave. "Yeah, six sounds great. Thank you."

Carol looked at her quizzically, but stood up with her and walked her to where the stairs led to the rest of the inn. "Thanks for coming down to see the hotel for yourself," Carol said earnestly. "It means so much to me."

Amy smiled weakly, remembering how she practically came kicking and screaming. "No problem." She rushed up the stairs as if she were being chased by a bear. But she knew better. It wasn't a bear that she was escaping. She was running from her overwhelming urge to sob out her life story to Carol.

She leaned against Carol's door breathing heavily and pushing tears down. It had been a long time since someone had shown that much genuine interest and concern for her. It was nearly her undoing.

11

Tristan was glad that Carol had invited them to her apartment for dinner. With Amy's reproving look still fresh in his mind when he had suggested a dinner meeting, he wanted the dinner to seem as much the opposite of a date as it could. Even if he had been interested in her, he was in no position to date anyway. His grandma needed him, and he needed to be able to devote his full attention to her right now. He smiled in amusement as he gave his imagination freedom. He could just picture dating the extremely citified Amy Juliette – going hiking through the woods that surrounded Willow Creek in her expensive business clothes, going out on the lake to fish, seeing a movie at the theater with only one screen, eating at greasy diners. Then once they were deeply in love, he would propose and offer her the opportunity to live in a small town in the same house as his grandmother. What bride wouldn't jump at the chance to share her groom with an elderly lady who needed lots of medical care? He chuckled. No. Amy Juliette might be beautiful, but she was not for him.

He knocked on the door of Carol's apartment. He didn't have to wait long before Carol admitted him. She was wearing a simple white apron over her jeans and sweater, and looking the exact opposite of how Amy had drawn her in the caricature logo.

"It smells wonderful in here." Tristan had all the cooking duties at home. Although he wasn't a gourmet, he was able to put together some tasty meals. Looking after his grandma had forced him to improve his skills in that area. "What do you put in your soup?"

"It's easy. I'll get you the recipe before you leave." They stepped into the kitchen and Tristan saw that he was the first to arrive.

"Is there some way I can help?"

"Why don't you cut the avocados?" She reached into a closet and pulled an apron off a hook. "Here. I don't want you to mess up your clothes." She put it on him and stepped back with a smile. "That was Gabe's. He always wore it whenever he grilled for me."

Tristan glanced down and saw that the black apron was embroidered with the words "Kiss the Cook" on it along with a pair of bright red lips. He chuckled. "Did it work?" He pointed at the scripted words.

"Oh, yes!" Carol's eyes twinkled. "But he didn't need that to get a kiss from me." She placed a cutting board, knife, and the avocados on the counter and busied herself with more preparations.

After Tristan had sliced one of the avocados there was a light rap on the door. Carol quickly went to answer and soon came back with Amy. "Go ahead and put these on the table," Carol instructed, placing dishes in Amy's hands. She stood there for a moment staring at the dishes, but finally did as she had been told. Tristan wondered why she was acting so strangely. Then he remembered that she was a city girl and her meetings were probably mostly over fancy dinners at restaurants, not home cooked, family style meals.

They finished getting the table set and putting the food out. Amy took her seat and Carol sat across from her. Tristan was about to sit down next to Carol when he caught Amy looking at him.

"What is it?" He wondered if he had somehow gotten avocado on his face.

"I was just admiring your apron," Amy answered with a small smile.

Tristan had completely forgotten about the garment. He smiled in embarrassment and took it off. Sitting down, he said, "It's more of a suggestion than a command."

Carol laughed heartily. She kissed his cheek in a motherly fashion. "There! Now it's all taken care of." When she got her laughter under control, she asked Tristan to pray for the meal.

Tristan noticed that Amy quickly set down the silverware she had picked up. He figured that they probably both had red cheeks now, and was thankful for the opportunity for both of them to close their eyes and compose themselves before needing to interact with each other. "Lord, we thank You so much for Carol and her willingness to have us over for dinner. Thank You for the food we're about to enjoy. I pray that as we discuss Carol's website and logo that You will give us all wisdom so that we can help her succeed in this venture. We thank You for the success she's already had. Thank You for Amy's willingness to come to us and get a good feel for Holliday Hotel. We pray that you'll guide her as she designs the logo, that it would be an inspiration from you, perfect for this inn. In Jesus' name we pray, amen."

Amy opened her eyes slowly and began to eat her food in silence. Soon Tristan and Carol were chatting, but Amy remained awkwardly quiet.

"Are you okay, Amy?" Carol couldn't keep herself from expressing her concern.

Amy smiled wanly. "I'm fine."

Tristan didn't know if Amy was embarrassed about the prayer or upset by it. Maybe she was still uncomfortable with this situation. "I read recently that it's difficult for graphic designers to get hired out of college, but you seem like you're doing well." He tried to make her feel more at ease by drawing her into the conversation.

"I also have business and marketing degrees so that helps."

"Did you start your own business right out of college?" Carol asked.

"No, I was with another firm. The owner of that became a mentor to me. She decided that it was time for her to retire a couple of years after I joined her, and she suggested that I go into business for myself. She told me that she would recommend her clients to me to help get me started, and she kept her word."

"That's great. Tristan showed me your portfolio, and it's very impressive." For some reason, Carol's comment made Amy blush.

"Thank you. I'm glad you still have confidence in me." She put her silverware down again and pushed her plate away from her as if she couldn't stand to take another bite.

"Are you sure you're all right?" Carol persisted.

Amy closed her eyes and sighed. "I've just been thinking all day about how I misjudged you and your business. My logo ideas must have been so hurtful. I felt so arrogantly superior when I did them." She put her head in her hands. "I'm so sorry."

Carol came around the table to embrace her. "It's fine. I'm just glad you don't have the same opinion about me now that you've met me."

Amy looked at her with moist eyes. "Are you sure you still want me to design your logo?"

"Like I said, your portfolio is very impressive. I'm eager to see what you come up with now."

The subject moved on to lighter things, and they continued to chit chat through the meal. They all pitched in to help clean up, though Amy seemed to do so hesitantly. When finished, they sat back down at the kitchen table and drank coffee with their dessert.

"I'm so glad that you were able to see Holliday Hotel for yourself," Tristan stated again. "I think you have the talent to do something amazing. You were only lacking vision since you hadn't seen anything like this before."

"Do you think that you'll be able to come up with something now that you've been here?" Carol asked.

"I think so. I'll be honest though, and let you know that I'm not brimming over with ideas right this second."

"You have some time here. Maybe once you've been able to relax for a while inspiration will hit," Carol suggested.

Amy shrugged. "I've never been good at relaxing."

Tristan smiled. "I think you'll figure it out while you're here." He glanced at the clock. "I really should get home."

"Hold on. I packed some of the dinner up for you to take to your grandma." Carol rushed into the kitchen and came back with containers for him to carry. He thanked her and headed home.

As he drove, his mind went back over the meeting with Amy. She somehow seemed less confident than she had earlier that day – or through any other communication he'd had with her. What had happened?

12

Amy sat at Carol's table and wondered what had happened to her. She came to this town full of confidence, and now she felt incompetent. She had never felt this way – not even as a recent graduate on her first account. She always assumed she could do anything, and had proved it, too. There was something different about this account.

Carol came and refilled her coffee with a smile. No, it wasn't the account that was different. It was the people. Carol sat across from her.

"Do you have plans for tomorrow?"

"Not really." Amy couldn't believe it was her that was saying that. She always had plans. What was she supposed to do all day?

"You've had a tour of the hotel. Maybe you should tour the town tomorrow."

The thought of looking over the little town of Willow Creek left her uninspired. "Why don't you just tell me about the town instead?"

Carol leaned back in her chair and studied Amy's face. "I think you'd like it more than you think you would." Amy's face flushed again. How could this woman read her so well? "I suppose in a lot of ways it's like any small town. There's a town square and a small park. There are shops and restaurants. My place is one of four bed-and-breakfasts."

"There are four?" Amy was surprised that there would be enough tourists to allow for that many inns.

"We get our share of people who want to escape city life. Between the hiking, the bike trails, and the lake we have quite a few outdoorsy people who visit. Then we have art festivals that bring in the artsy folks. It's not a bustling place, but we have our own charm."

"I guess so." Amy sipped her coffee. "Are the other inns like yours?"

"No, each one is very different. One is sort of like a cottage, another is very trendy and modern, and the third is a series of cabins right on the lake. They each appeal to different groups."

Amy finished her coffee and went to put her mug in the sink. "I feel so strange here." Even as she said it, she wondered what was making her confide in this woman who was little more than a stranger.

"In what way?"

Amy folded her arms across her stomach. "Like I'm out of sync. My confidence is at an all time low, I have no plans, no destination, no drive. I just don't feel like me."

Carol's eyes were sympathetic. "I think you were caught off guard. All your presuppositions were wrong, and now you're questioning yourself. You'll get back on your feet sooner than you think."

Back in her room, Amy thought about Carol's words. She had been shaken when she had discovered how completely wrong she had been about everything. Wandering the room, she remembered how surprised she had been when she had first seen it. No, shock described it better.

She stood in front of a framed piece of needlework. She had noticed it before, but hadn't taken the time to really look at it. It was a beautiful piece, and must have taken some time to complete. It looked like a poem.

" Love is patient and kind;" she read aloud, "love does not envy or boast; it is not arrogant or rude. It does not insist on its own way; it is not irritable or resentful; it does not rejoice at wrongdoing, but rejoices with the truth. Love bears all things, believes all things, hopes all things, endures all things. Love never ends." She snorted. What an idealistic view of love! It sounds pretty, but that wasn't the way the world worked. At least, she'd never seen or experienced a love like that. The world would certainly be a different place if that was what love looked like.

After turning on the gas fireplace, Amy grabbed her sketch pad and sat on the couch. Although most of her work had her on the computer, she found that sketching with paper and pencil relaxed her. She began drawing without even really knowing what she was doing. Her fingers moved across the page mindlessly, leaving her brain to puzzle over how she was going to get back to her normal self. Maybe she should go home. Waking up in her own room would probably snap her out whatever this was. Or being in her office, working hard on a difficult account.

She frowned. This was a difficult account. Why couldn't she come up with a design? That's all she had to do – come up with a logo, go home, and life would back to normal. No more holidays, no more hotels, no more Tristan, and no more love poems.

Her fingers stopped moving and her mind came back from where it had wandered to look at what she had created. She gasped and stared at the picture. A man with dark hair and glasses smiled back at her, his apron reading "kiss the cook". Why had she drawn Tristan? Could he be the reason why she felt so odd?

13

Amy found herself walking the streets of Willow Creek around lunchtime the next day. Sheer boredom had forced her to go exploring. She hadn't expected it to be worth her while, but sitting in her room was no longer an option. Besides, it gave some time for housekeeping to freshen up her room and restock her kitchenette.

At first glance Willow Creek was like any other small town in America. There was a town square, a park, police/fire station, bank, and a few other shops and restaurants. When she took a closer look at the shops though, they weren't the typical touristy small town stores. Instead there was a gallery of fine art, jewelry and clothing boutiques, mixed with outdoor sporting stores. She saw a day spa, salon, and coffee shop, and found herself wanting to explore the shops, but not today. For now she just wanted to get a feel for this place.

As she passed a small café, her stomach reminded her that she hadn't eaten lunch yet. She stepped inside and enjoyed the aromas of fresh baked bread and simmering soup. Glancing around for a place to sit, she noticed someone waving at her.

Tristan sat with an elderly woman. His cheerful smile spoke of nothing beyond kindness. *Love is patient and kind.* Shaking her head, she cleared the first line of the poem from her mind. She felt her cheeks warming as she remembered the sketch that she had drawn the night before. Quickly deciding that eating alone was not enticing, she headed in his direction.

"Amy, this is my grandmother, Carmen Romero. Grandma, this is Amy Juliette," Tristan introduced the two women. He sat in a chair next to his grandma and Amy took the seat across from him.

She shook the old woman's hand and murmured a greeting.

"So this is Amy." Carmen studied her intently. "She's not exactly how I pictured her."

Amy looked at Tristan, unsure of what she meant or how she should interpret the statement. Tristan smiled. "My grandparents played a game before they were to meet a new person where each would guess what the person would look like. Grandma and I played it with you. She won."

"Okay," Amy drawled out slowly. After a beat she added, "I don't know what to do with that information."

Carmen gave a shout of laughter. "I wouldn't either. Tristan thought you'd be a redhead. But I was sure you'd be a brunette. Maybe because it rhymes with Juliette."

Amy was relieved when the waitress came over to spare her from having to reply. This conversation made no sense. When the waitress left, Tristan mercifully changed the subject. "What have you been doing today?"

"I decided to get a flavor for the town so I've been on a tour of Willow Creek."

"If you need a tour guide, Tristan could show you around."

"Oh, Grandma. Maybe Ms. Juliette would rather be on her own." Tristan nervously rearranged his silverware.

"Nonsense! Why would she want to be on her own when she could have her own private tour?" Carmen insisted.

Tristan opened his mouth, but Amy jumped in before he could speak. "If you have time, I would be happy to have you join me. I'm sure I would learn more with a guide than I would alone." She didn't know what made her give the offer. Maybe it was just to avoid the awkwardness of seeing the two of them argue. Or maybe it was because Tristan Romero was intriguing. Whatever the reason, the offer was out there now, and she couldn't retract it.

Tristan looked at her for a moment with uncertainty. "Um, sure. After lunch I'll take Grandma back home, and then I'll take you around town."

As the waitress placed their meals in front of them, Amy remembered her embarrassment at Carol's when she hadn't waited for the prayer. She kept her hands folded in her lap and her eyes lowered, hoping that no one would ask her to give the blessing. To her relief, Carmen volunteered.

"Lord, thank you for this food, for my grandson, and for his friend. I pray that you will guide and direct Amy and Tristan as they work together. I know that what they do will glorify You. In Jesus name, amen."

Amy glanced at the older woman before digging into her apple walnut salad. She was pretty sure that God had nothing to do with her work, and the only one getting any glory for it would be her. Not wanting to get into a theological debate, however, she opted to focus on her lunch instead of saying what was on her mind.

Soon her attention was brought back to Carmen. She had ordered the chicken fried steak, but she was having difficulty cutting it. Tristan's eyes were riveted on his grandma, but he allowed her the opportunity to try. Only when he saw that she was tiring, did he speak up. "Why don't you let me cut your steak for you?" Carmen gratefully pushed her plate towards him.

Tristan pushed his own plate aside. He carefully cut the meat into tiny bites and then pushed the plate back over to his grandma. She got a piece, but her hand shook as she raised it to her mouth and it fell back on her plate. As she struggled to get another bite, Tristan offered to help her once again. She sighed, but allowed him to feed her.

"It's a terrible thing to get old," she told Amy. "It's hard to lose your independence." She accepted another bite from Tristan. After a moment, she smiled up at him. "Listen to me complaining! How can I be discouraged when I have you to help me?"

Tristan smiled lovingly at her. "It's normal to be discouraged. No matter what you may think, you're not perfect."

Carmen laughed heartily. "You know that better than anyone." She put her wrinkled hand on top of his. "Thank you for always allowing me the opportunity to try it for myself first."

"I know that you have good days and bad days. I'm so thankful for those days when you don't need my help – not because I don't want to help, but because I know those days mean so much to you.

I always want to give you the chance to have a good day."

Amy watched the interaction between the two with interest. She had never seen a tighter bond between a grandma and her grandson. She wondered if they had always been close, or if it was something that had developed recently.

As Carmen finished her last bite, Tristan pulled his own plate closer. His beef stew in a bread bowl had to be cold by that point, but he cheerfully dug in without complaint. *Love is patient and kind.* Amy felt warmth spread through her as she realized that she was witnessing such a love firsthand. Tristan's patience and kindness to Carmen came from a deep love for her. Amy wondered what it must feel like to experience a love like that.

They finished and settled the bill, then Tristan told Amy where he would meet her and promised to return in just a few minutes. Amy wandered around the square, looking at the memorials that were placed around the area. There was a statue of the man who the lake was named after, and a plaque dedicated to those who had served in the military. One caught her eye in particular though. It was a bronze piece of a little girl taking her first toddling steps between her mother and father. The plaque near it called the piece "Love is Patient" and declared that it had been sculpted by a local artist. Amy hadn't thought about how a parent helping their child learn to walk was an example of patient love. It would be faster to just pick the child up and go, but love knew that it was best for her to learn to walk on her own. There would be times that she fell, she would move slowly to start, but it was worth it so that one day they could see her run.

"I've always liked this piece myself." Amy turned at the sound of Tristan's voice. "There's such joy on each of their faces."

Amy looked back at the art and noticed the facial expressions for the first time. The snow that dusted the top of the images couldn't dampen the warm glow that their faces showed. "It's lovely. You can see the love in their eyes."

"Love between the parents and love for the child," Tristan agreed. "Shall we explore?" She half-expected him to offer his arm in an old-fashioned gesture of chivalry, but he simply motioned for her to proceed him and fell into step beside her. "I know you weren't thrilled with Willow Creek when I asked you to come, but has your tour helped you see the town in a different light?"

"It has. I didn't expect so many stylish places, or art galleries, or salons. I guess I figured it would be kind of – kitschy."

"I was surprised when I first got here, too."

Amy looked at him in astonishment. "I thought you had always lived here."

Tristan shook his head. "Nope. We grew up in southern California. My grandparents lived here since they were married. By the time I was in college and then starting my career, I never seemed to find time to get up here to visit. Even when Grandpa died, I only found time for a short trip. At the time I was living in Los Angeles, and starting a new job, so I didn't feel like I could get away."

"When did you move here?"

"When my grandma had a stroke. The doctors told us that she needed care. We got together as a family and discussed the best way to approach it. We talked about a care home, but none of us really wanted her to have to leave her home if she didn't need to. My sister, Kylee, couldn't come stay with her because her husband, Jordan, is in the Coast Guard. They really can't just pick up and move wherever they want to." He chuckled. "My brother, Brendan, is a missionary so he wasn't able to stay with her. My dad would have been happy to look after his mother, but not long before my grandma's stroke, my mom found out she had breast cancer. So my dad needed to take care of my mom, and I was the only one left. I was in the process of starting my own business, and could do it from home. With email and the internet, I would still have plenty of clients. It seemed like the best solution."

"I'm so sorry to hear that. Is your mom okay now?"

"Yeah, Mom responded well to the treatments, but by that time I was already moved in, and Grandma and I had comfortable relationship."

"Do you ever miss Los Angeles?" Amy couldn't imagine leaving San Francisco for such a small town.

"I suppose there are times, but I've never regretted my choice – especially when I see my grandma and remember how much help she needs." Tristan put his hands in his pockets as they walked. "I'm reminded almost daily that she isn't going to be here forever, and I treasure this time with her."

"Is your grandma able to live alone or do you live with her?"

"I moved right in with her. It's a small house, but with only the two of us there, we're comfortable." They walked in silence for a while.

"I don't think I could do what you did."

"I would have said the same thing. We never know what we can accomplish until we actually are faced with a situation that forces us to make a decision." Tristan looked around at the street they were walking down. "When I first came here, it seemed so slow, empty, and boring. I was sure that as soon as I was able to I would leave this place and head back to the city. But Willow Creek grew on me, and the more time I spent with Grandma, the more I couldn't imagine leaving her."

"Were you close to your grandma before you moved here?"

Tristan sighed. "Not particularly. Once I grew up I kind of got busy and lost touch." He stopped in front of a coffee shop. "Want to go get warmed up?"

Amy hadn't realized how cold she was until she stepped into the coffee shop. The warm air stung her frozen cheeks. Tristan's story had absorbed her to the point that she could've walked for hours. They ordered their drinks and sat at a table.

"There's a poem hanging in my room at Holliday Hotel. The first line of it kept going through my mind as I watched you with your grandma today. It says 'Love is patient and kind'."

Tristan smiled in amusement. "I guess it's a sort of poem. It's actually a passage from the Bible. It's found in 1 Corinthians 13, and it tells us all about what love should look like." He looked in her eyes intently. "I'm pleased that my actions made you think of it."

Amy felt her face warm. She hadn't been prone to blushing, but there was something about these people that made her feel things like she'd never felt them before. "Well, you were so patient and kind with her, and I could tell that you did it because you truly love her, not because you were obligated."

Tristan studied his coffee. "Unfortunately, it probably started as an obligation. I think the love came later."

"Still it's impressive. I've never experienced a love like that before."

Tristan blinked. "Your family wasn't patient or kind to you?"

Amy snorted. "Yeah, patience is not a family trait. And my dad always said that the only point in being kind was if you got something in return. He didn't teach us to be intentionally mean or anything. He just didn't think we should go out of our way to be kind either."

"I think we had two very different childhoods."

Amy cupped her hands around her coffee. "I'm sure of it."

14

Curled up on the window seat in her room with a book in her hand, Amy couldn't remember the last time she had time to just sit and read. Although the book had been a New York Times best seller, she couldn't seem to keep her focus on the story. Her mind kept wandering back to Tristan and Carmen.

She knew that there were people who took care of their family members, but that had never been her experience. When her grandma had developed Alzheimer's, her mom had put her in the cheapest care center she could find. Grudgingly her mom would visit on Mother's Day and her grandma's birthday. Amy had been embarrassed by her mom's attitude towards her own mother, but knew that her mom wouldn't listen to her if she had said anything. When her grandmother had finally passed away, the only sentiment her mom had expressed was relief that she wouldn't be paying for her care anymore. Amy recalled how often her mother had complained that the old woman was just clinging to life to spite her.

And her mom was the more compassionate parent. Her dad hadn't had anything to do with his parents for as long as she could remember. She had never met her paternal grandparents, didn't even know much about them.

Amy swung her feet to the floor and went over to the needlework. It seemed to take on a new significance now that she knew that it was from the Bible, and not just a poem. "Love is patient and kind, love does not envy or boast." She paused. "Love does not envy or boast." Again her experience was completely different from such a love. Was it possible that it existed? She hadn't thought that love could be patient or kind either, but Tristan had proven her wrong.

Pulling herself away from the words on the wall, she put on a jacket, hat and fingerless gloves and went onto the balcony with her sketchpad in hand. She sat on the glider and gently rocked it with her toe while she drew the lake, the willow, the snow drifts. Such a stark scene. Yet it was beautiful in its own way. She was certain that it was a view that would be enchanting no matter what time of year it was.

Flipping the page, her fingers deftly started creating the letter H over and over again. Some were large, others small, some scripted, others in print – nothing seemed just right. In frustration she turned to the next page where she wrote "Holliday Hotel" over and over again.

Sighing she turned her attention back to the scenery in front of her. A dad and a little girl were out building a snowman. The little girl was struggling to lift the middle part onto the bottom section. Quickly, the father joined her and helped her lift it up. The girl's face lit up as she looked up at her father. Impulsively, she hugged her daddy's leg. He scooped her up, tossed her into the air before catching her in a big bear hug. The sound of the girl's giggles reached Amy and she couldn't help the smile that stretched across her own face. *Love is patient and kind.*

Why had she never experienced that kind of love?

******

When Amy was four years old, she went on her first sleepover, and that was when she discovered that not all families were like hers. Her friend's parents hadn't yelled at each other, or at her. They had come in to say good-night and had whispered terms of endearment to their daughter and were kind to Amy as well.

Knowing that there were other families out there, loving ones, had made her return home difficult. Even at such a young age, she had learned to sit through the fights silently to avoid becoming part of it. Now, she would close her eyes and imagine she had parents like her friend. But the yelling wouldn't be drowned out, and she would reopen her eyes to reality.

By six, Amy had become adept at keeping out of her parents'

ways. She had become self-sufficient, and if there was something she couldn't do herself, she did without. At this point, she fed herself, dressed herself, got ready for school and bed all alone – and it was better this way. Somehow no matter how hard she tried, her mother always found fault and her father always swore at her. Being independent made her nearly invisible to her parents, and that was just fine with her.

Without their attention, Amy could pretend she had a family like the other kids. Her pretend mom made homemade cookies for her after school, and her pretend dad had affectionate nicknames for her like Lovebug. Then the yelling would begin, and she could no longer pretend that her family was loving and kind.

She never really knew how her mom and dad had ended up married. They seemed to be miserable together. But Rhonda and Larry Juliette somehow must have at one point loved each other. Occasionally, she would see her parents kiss or hug, but experience told her that it was a temporary truce and things would go back to normal too soon.

One night, Amy woke suddenly by the sound of crashing glass. She slid out of bed and tiptoed to the top of the stairs. From there she could see into the living room and hear everything. She knew better than to let her parents know she was there, but something told her that this fight was different.

"I'll ask you again, Larry," her mother seethed. "Where were you tonight?"

"I'm not accountable to you. You can't control me." He sat on the couch and tried to turn on the television with the clicker. Rhonda grabbed it out of his hands and hurled it against the wall. The plastic shell broke open and tiny buttons scattered around the room. Larry jumped off the couch. He swore as he grabbed her by the shoulders and gave her a shake that made Amy cringe. "What I do isn't any of your business!" He released her and attempted to gather up the tiny pieces of the clicker.

Rhonda steadied herself on an arm chair. "You were with Helen again, weren't you?" Her voice was low. She pulled herself up to her full height. In Amy's mind, her mom had never looked stronger than in that moment. Her dark blonde hair was mussed, and her face was pale, but her ice blue eyes flashed with something from deep within – something that a six year old couldn't quite grasp.

Larry stood slowly and looked at his wife. He looked weary, yet defiant. "What if I was?"

Rhonda swore. "Larry, I've put up with Tina, Melissa, Brandy, and who knows how many others, but my best friend?"

A wicked smile curved Larry's full lips. Amy had heard some call her dad handsome, but she had never thought so. He had thick, dark, wavy hair with a Tom Selleck mustache. His green eyes often seemed cruel to Amy as they did now as he mocked her mother. "I can't help it if they come flocking to me."

Rhonda shook her head. "I don't even care anymore how many woman you can or can't get. I'm more concerned that you took away my best friend from me. You could be with every woman in the whole state of California for all I care, but you could have left the one person I cared most about."

Larry folded his arms over his chest. "Seems like you care more for her than she did for you. Or maybe she just cares more for me."

Rhonda let out a low scream and came at him with her nails like claws. She left a scratch on his cheek before he slapped her hard enough that she fell against the couch. As she lay there unmoving for a moment, Amy felt scared, but soon she heard the sound of her mother's sobbing. Slowly she stood up. "I'm done."

"Good. Let's go to bed." Larry began to head for their bedroom.

"No. I'm done. Done with us. Done with you. I want you to leave." Rhonda's voice was low, but intense.

Amy felt her stomach clench. She'd known kids who came from divorced homes. She understood what was happening to her family. What would happen to he? Who would she live with?

"Why should I leave? It's my house." Larry stood tensely.

Rhonda walked calmly over to the closet and pulled out a suitcase. She thrust it into his hands roughly. "That's where you're wrong. Your credit was too bad to have on the lease. The house is only in my name. You have no right here."

Larry swore and slammed his way into the bedroom. Amy could hear him throwing things, stomping around, breaking things. Finally he stormed out and headed to the front door. With his hand on the knob, he turned back one last time. "This is your last chance, Rhonda. Once I leave, I'm not coming back."

"I'm sure Helen would be ecstatic to have you stay with her and her husband. Good-bye, Larry." Rhonda walked stiffly to the bedroom and closed the door gently. The click seemed to echo through the house decisively. Larry took a step toward the closed door, then turned on his heel and slammed the front door behind him.

After a few moments, Amy slipped down the stairs. She stood at her mom's bedroom door and could hear her crying inside. She knew better than to intrude though. Quietly, she turned off all the lights, made sure the doors were locked, and went back up to her bedroom. As she lay in bed, she stared up at the ceiling. She couldn't place her feelings. She wasn't really sad. Life had been too miserable before for that emotion. There would have been a sense of relief if she had felt that her mom would take care of her, but her mom was as selfish as her dad, and often viewed Amy as a nuisance that prevented her from having fun. Instead, the strongest emotion she felt was worry. Would she be carted back and forth between her parents? Who would get her the most? Did either of them even want her?

Eventually, she turned on her side. Tears slipped down her cheeks. Emotionally exhausted, she slipped into a deep sleep, hoping that things would get better now, but without feeling any confidence that they would.

******

The coldness in her fingers eventually snapped Amy out of her memories. She flexed her fingers carefully as she stood up to go inside. Removing her jacket she thought of making a pot of coffee, but decided against it. Carol always kept hot coffee ready in the kitchen. She wouldn't have to wait this way. On her way out the door, she passed the needlework.

Love does not envy or boast.

She laughed shortly. Her mom's envy and her dad's boasting had certainly not exemplified love. Yet they had claimed to love each other. She thought back to the very few relationships she'd had. Rico Booth had been envious of any male client she had. Ivor Herschel had done nothing, but talk about his own accomplishments. The final one, Wright Shepard, had seemed to want her to be envious of any pretty girl that crossed his path. All three had declared that they loved her. And yet, these verses declared that wasn't love at all.

She headed down the stairs, deep in thought. What was love? Amy was certain that she had never experienced love – not a true love. She wasn't even sure she had demonstrated such a love. Patience and kindness were never strong virtues of hers. Having learned to be independent at a young age, she was frustrated with people who seemed needy or clingy. She could easily walk past someone who needed help if stopping to be kind was even remotely inconvenient.

In the kitchen, Carol was rolling out sugar cookie dough. A heart shaped cookie cutter sat nearby. She looked up with smile. "What have you been up to today?" she asked brightly.

"I was sitting on the balcony and got lost in my thoughts. I need a cup of coffee to warm up." She went and got her coffee on her own, knowing that Carol always kept an open kitchen. Reaching in the cookie jar that was on the counter, she pulled out a chocolate chip cookie then took her treats to the counter near Carol. "Are the cookies for anything special?"

"I'm having a kindergarten class over for a field trip on Valentine's Day. I figured I should get them ready now since they freeze well. I get busy near the holidays."

"I would imagine so." Amy chewed her bite of cookie thoughtfully. "You do quite a bit more than just run an inn, don't you?"

Carol looked confused. "No, my life is pretty much all about this house."

"Yeah, but I've already been hearing about your Valentine's dinner. Then you're having children over earlier in the day. Those aren't things that a normal innkeeper does."

"Well, I guess I can't help myself. I love the holidays, and I want to help others celebrate." She began cutting the shaped cookies and placing them on a cookie sheet.

"Who helps you celebrate?"

Carol glanced up. "Everyone who comes to my gatherings helps me celebrate."

"That can't be right. That's work. When do you celebrate?"

Carol put the cookie cutter down and leaned on the counter. "I truly do celebrate with those who come here. New Year's Eve is a big celebration in this house, full of friends who help me welcome in the New Year. Valentine's Day has seen several engagements take place in my dining room, and I celebrate with each one. I could go on down the list, but the truth is, it doesn't have to be about me to celebrate." She picked the cookie cutter back up. "But to ease your mind, my daughters both come into town on Valentine's for me. After we clean up from the dinner we go to my apartment and watch chick flicks. My oldest daughter always makes sure I have roses just like her father used to give me every year when he was still with us."

Amy warmed her hands by wrapping them around the mug of hot coffee. "I'm glad you have family to be with."

"Do you have family? I've not been able to get to know you personally. We've been so focused on the logo." Carol smiled at her so genuinely that Amy was sure that it was an honest desire to know her better that had prompted the question, not just curiosity.

"I have family, but we're not close."

"I'm sorry to hear that. I don't know what I would do without my girls."

"I've felt like I was kind of on my own my whole life. Even when I was little and living with my parents, I never felt like I was part of that family." Amy was surprised at the words she spoke. She had never really talked with anyone about it before. She wasn't even sure that she had realized how she felt before.

"Were you – harmed in any way as a child?" Carol asked gently.

"No, I wasn't abused at all. It was more that I was – neglected. I didn't seem to matter to anyone."

Carol stopped working. "There was no one for you? Not a grandparent or aunt or sibling?"

Amy shook her head. "I never knew my dad's parents. My mom only visited her parents when she absolutely had to, and when they would watch me they would complain so much about how my mom took advantage of them by using them as a babysitter that I never really felt wanted there either. I was an only child – well, I have half-siblings, but I was never close to any of them - and my parent's siblings were too involved with their own families to pay much attention to me. I don't think they had any clue that I was lonely."

"What a tough little girl you must have been!" Carol looked at her with wonder.

"Well, that tough little girl has become a tough woman. It's helped me succeed beyond what most people predicted. So I guess in some ways I'm grateful for it." Amy sipped her coffee. "There's a needlework framed in my room. Who did it?"

"I did. It was so fitting for the Sweetheart Suite."

"I've been drawn to it. At first I thought it was poetry, but Tristan told me it was from the Bible. I've never seen or experienced or felt a love like it describes. Love was always selfish. Maybe the only love my family is capable of experiencing is love for themselves."

Carol reached out and took hold of Amy's hands. "Anybody is capable of a love like that, but not on their own. A love like that comes from God."

Amy stiffened. "God doesn't exist. Or if He does, He doesn't care about someone like me." She pulled her hands away and headed back to her room, ignoring the pained expression on Carol's face.

15

Amy felt restless after her conversation with Carol. She paced her room for a while then decided to get some fresh air. After wandering around the town for half an hour, she followed an impulse that led her straight to the Romero home. She had a business card on her for Creation Designs and used her phone's GPS to find the address.

Standing in front of the small white house, she wondered what she was doing there. Why had she sought this family out? Yet something beyond her compelled her to continue. Before she knew it, she had climbed the steps of the porch and rang the doorbell. After waiting briefly, she turned on her heel, anxious to leave. The door opened with a squeak, and a masculine voice called her name questioningly.

She put a smile on her face and turned back around. "Hi. I came because . . ." she faltered. Sighing, she continued, "To be honest, I don't know why I'm here. I simply felt like I needed to come."

Tristan opened the door wider and motioned for her to come inside. He took her coat and things, and it struck her that no man had ever shown her such courtesy before. Leading her into the living room he called out, "Grandma, we have a visitor."

Carmen stirred on the couch where she had been napping. She blinked a few times and then smiled. "Well, hello, Miss Juliette. Come sit next to me." She patted the couch seat next to her. Amy gladly joined her.

"I'll go get us all something warm to drink. Would you prefer coffee or tea?" Tristan asked.

"Tea sounds good. Thank you." Amy twisted the edge of her

sweater in her hands.

"You've got something on your mind." Carmen was studying her closely.

Amy tried to laugh. "It's nothing."

"People drink tea when they're working out life problems." The old lady nodded wisely. "Coffee is to keep you going. Tea slows you down. Gives you time to really think things through."

A chuckle escaped from Amy. "I'll have to remember that."

"It's true." Carmen laid a hand on Amy's hand. "So what's on your mind?"

"I'd rather not talk about it, if you don't mind." Amy wasn't even sure she knew what she was wrestling with herself. And she certainly didn't want to open up before people who were practically strangers.

"That's fine. Help me figure out the answers to *Family Feud* instead." Using the remote, she un-muted the television so they could hear Steve Harvey give out the clues.

Tristan came back in with a tray. "I didn't know how you took your tea so I brought everything." When he set it down on the coffee table, Amy realized that he meant what he said. The tray held sugar cubes, artificial sweetener, milk, cream, honey, and lemon. He handed a cup that was already prepared to his grandma while Amy fixed her own with a little sugar and milk. "I think I'll get back to work and let you ladies of leisure enjoy your game show."

Amy was glad when he left. There was something about Tristan that made her want to sob out her life story on his shoulder. And she knew that would be a mistake. It was best to keep things professional between them.

After a while though, Amy noticed that Carmen was fading again. She stood up to leave, trying not to disturb her, but she awoke anyway.

"Are you leaving already?"

"I'm afraid I've worn you out."

"Nonsense!" Carmen waved her hands dismissively. "It's been nice to have someone to talk with besides Tristan. I love that boy, but sometimes having fresh company is a nice change."

"I suppose it would be."

"Why don't you go down to his office? It's in the basement. You can see where he works and what he's working on, and I'll rest up so that you can join us for dinner." As Amy opened her mouth, Carmen seemed to sense that she was going to politely refuse. "I won't take no for an answer so you may as well save your breath."

Amy laughed softly. "Well, all right then. I'll see you in a little bit." After a moment's hesitation, she added, "Can I do anything for you before I leave?"

"Could you hand me that afghan over there?" She pointed to a much-used, faded, and fraying blanket draped over a chair. Amy happily helped her get settled under it and lifted the foot of the couch's recliner so she would be more comfortable. As she headed for the basement door, she shook her head in surprise. She'd been looking out for herself for so long, that she often didn't think about the needs of others. It wasn't that she was intentionally selfish – it was a by-product of taking care of herself from such a young age.

She descended into the basement. Tristan was sitting at a computer, his fingers flying over the keyboard. The final step creaked as she stepped on it, and Tristan turned around. He smiled as he removed his glasses and rubbed his eyes.

"I'm glad you came down. I could use a break."

"What are you working on?" She looked over his shoulder.

"Carol's website. Here's where your logo will go." He pointed to the top of the page.

"It looks great. I should have come to see this before. I think it will help me decide what kind of style I need to go with." The website was elegant. Photos of the inn, a wedding, and different holiday celebrations were displayed. A tab led to a description of each of the guest rooms and a button allowed the user to check each room for availability and book it. A calendar link showed upcoming events at the inn and in Willow Creek as well as the surrounding community. "You've been thorough. I'm impressed."

Out of the corner of her eye, something else caught her

attention. A wall was covered with framed certificates, awards, and degrees. She wandered over and studied them. The shear amount of them was staggering in itself, but as she read them over, she recognized several prestigious awards.

"Wow. This is extraordinary! Why haven't you ever mentioned this?"

Tristan shrugged. "It never seemed worth mentioning. Would it have changed anything?"

Amy thought back to her initial ideas about both Tristan and Carol. Had she known about his credentials, it certainly would have altered her opinion. She would have been more considerate, more eager to please. Sighing, she admitted, "Sadly, yes. I think it would have."

"I've never seen any point in bragging about my accomplishments. I figure my work will speak for itself. I learned that from my grandpa. Follow me." He led her to another room in the basement. Cardboard boxes were stacked neatly against the walls. They were carefully marked in Sharpie. Tristan walked over to one labeled 'Grandpa's things'. He opened it up and pulled out a box filled with military medals. "I didn't even know these existed until my Grandpa had died. We were going through his things and found them."

Amy fingered the medals reverently. "A Purple Heart. Did you know he had been wounded?"

Tristan shook his head. "Later my grandma told me that the bullet missed his heart by mere inches. After we found the medals, I also found these." He pulled out a stack of papers. Leafing through them, Amy found that they were awards and certificates from school and then later from his job. "When I asked Grandma why Grandpa had never mentioned these things, she said that he felt that his actions could speak louder than any piece of paper or any bit of metal."

"This is amazing. I can't believe you never knew about it."

"He was amazing. And he was right. I admired him and loved him for who he was not for the accomplishments he had done." With a smile he added, "He was a braver, stronger man than I'll ever be." There was no trace of envy in his voice, just a simple pride that showed his deep love for his grandfather.

Love does not envy or boast.

Tristan wasn't envious of his grandpa's accomplishments, even though he didn't believe he would equal them. And he didn't brag about his own awards.

"Why do you have your certificates on the wall? If you don't want them noticed, having them framed seems to defeat the purpose."

Tristan blushed. "That's my grandma's doing. She insisted that they be hung up and I agreed only if they were put in the basement. No one usually comes down here."

They headed back into the main room of the basement. "How are you coming on the logo?" Tristan seemed anxious to change the subject.

"I'm struggling," she admitted honestly. "I just can't seem to find the right feel."

"You'll get there." He sounded so confident, and she wished that she shared his feelings.

"Maybe. You might want to look at hiring someone else. At least have a back-up plan."

Tristan's brow furrowed. "When I first contacted you, I found an artist who was confident. You were chosen because I had seen your talent at work, and knew that I couldn't find anyone better. What's happened to you?"

Amy wandered back over to Tristan's desk and stared at the website. "I don't know. When I came here I knew who I was, but now I feel – lost."

A small smile tugged at Tristan's lips. "Sometimes it's when we feel most lost that we become found."

"There's something about this town, about you and Carol, that is challenging everything I've ever believed."

Amy felt Tristan close the distance between them. "Such as?" There seemed to be an eagerness underscoring his question.

"I don't know. Life. Love." She shrugged helplessly.

Tristan's lips compressed as he thought for a moment. "That's a start."

Amy whirled to look at him. "A start to what?"

"To finding what you need to become found." He gestured toward the stairs. "Let's go get some dinner. Things always make more sense on a full stomach."

16

Letting herself back into Holliday Hotel after dinner that night, Amy found Carol at the front desk. She instinctively walked over to her and leaned on the desk.

Carol looked up at her with sympathy. "Long night?"

Amy looked up at the clock and was surprised to see that it was only a little after eight. "Exhausting, somehow." She straightened up. "By the way, your website is looking fantastic."

Carol smiled. "I never doubted it." She studied Amy for a few moments. "How's the logo coming?"

Amy sighed heavily. "I can't seem to come up with anything. I've never had this problem in my career before."

Carol patted her shoulder in a motherly way. "I'm sure it will come eventually." She looked at her for a long moment. "Would you like to talk about what's going on?"

To Amy's great surprise, she burst into tears. Judging by Carol's expression, it was a shock to her as well. She hurried around the front desk and wrapped her arm around Amy's shoulder, gently guiding her into the living room. They sat on the couch and for several minutes Amy just sobbed against Carol's shoulder.

"I'm so sorry," Amy sniffled as she used the tissue that Carol offered her. "I don't know when I last cried."

"Maybe that's part of the problem. You've had to be strong for too long. We all need to cry at times."

Amy leaned back against the couch. "I feel like something is chasing me. It's the strangest thing. I keep being drawn to that needlework in my room – almost against my will. 'Love is patient and kind; love does not envy or boast;' – and I know that I've never seen or experienced a love like that."

"Maybe the Person chasing you wants to offer you love like that." Carol's eyes twinkled with a secret understanding.

"You think someone loves me, and I'm running away from him?"

"I know Someone loves you, and you are running away from Him."

Amy tried to think for a moment, but the only person who came to mind was Tristan, and that would make sense since he would be the only man both she and Carol knew. Perhaps Tristan had confided in Carol, and she was trying to get the two of them together. Yet Tristan hadn't seemed to see her as anything other than a business associate. Sure he'd been kind and patient with her. And he'd never seemed to be envious or boastful. Wait! That was the definition of love in the verse. Maybe he was trying to tell her something.

"Oh," she said weakly. She wasn't sure how she felt about this. He was nice, and he was attractive in a way. But he had Carmen to take care of, and she needed to get back to her life soon. Long distance relationships weren't ideal. She was going to have to politely let him know that she wasn't interested.

Carol frowned as she watched Amy. "I'm not sure you understood what I was saying."

Amy got up from the couch. "No, I did. But I think running is the best solution for all of us. I know you would like it to be different, but it can't be. I'm sorry." She was aware of Carol shaking her head slowly, and hated it that she had to disappoint her. She had grown fond of the innkeeper. But she was doing what was best for all of them.

As she entered her room, she drew near the needlework again. "Love is patient and kind; love does not envy or boast; it is not arrogant or rude." She sighed. Arrogant and rude seemed to go hand in hand – and unfortunately had been prevalent in her life.

******

"Hurry up!" Rhonda's stride was too long for Amy's little eight year old legs to keep up with. She struggled to follow her mom knowing that Rhonda had a temper, and that whenever they were meeting up with her dad it was always simmering, ready to explode at the least excuse.

Their divorce hadn't made her parents any happier. Her dad had moved quickly from one woman to the next, but had recently gotten married again. Now Amy had a half-sibling on the way. Her mom said that the baby was the only reason her dad had gotten married again, but Amy liked to think that he would be happier now. She hadn't seen him since his marriage, but she would be seeing him now that it was time for her annual Thanksgiving trip to Larry's house.

The divorce agreement had left Amy with Rhonda for most of the year. She spent Easter, Father's Day, and Thanksgiving with her dad, but the rest of the time she was with her mom. Rhonda said that it was because that's all Larry wanted to see of his daughter. Amy would have liked to think her mom was just angry, but in her visits to her dad she had felt like she was more of a nuisance than a welcomed guest.

Staying with her mom wasn't much better. In fact, she often found herself at neighbor's homes, her grandmother's house, or with a babysitter. Her grandma would mutter that she was too old to be raising another kid, and the neighbors would whisper and stop talking when she came in. Her favorite babysitter called her "pobrecita" which she had recently learned meant "poor little girl". She wondered what was wrong with her that no one seemed to want her.

Her mom arrived at the park bench where they were to meet Larry and sat down, swinging her foot impatiently. Amy tossed her backpack to the ground and sat next to her mom. Rhonda glanced at her watch and sighed. "Your father is never on time. As if I don't have anything better to do."

Amy pulled out a sketchpad and began drawing a picture of the fountain that they were sitting in front of. Her teacher had told her that she had talent, and she had found that it was a great way to escape from life when it started getting too tough for her to handle. Her mom was happy that she was quiet so she rarely complained about buying her more art supplies.

"Finally!" her mom huffed as she rose to her feet. "You're always late. I have a date to get to, you know."

"Good for you," Larry said drily. "He hasn't gotten to know you very well, has he?"

Rhonda turned red. "He knows me better than you ever did."

"Poor guy." He turned to Amy. "Ready to go, kid?"

Silently, Amy put her sketchpad back in her bag and stood up. There was no hug, no excitement. This was just how life was for her.

Meeting his new wife, Ruthie, was awkward. She tried too hard to make friends with Amy only to have Larry mock her for her efforts. Amy soon found that her dad was no happier, no nicer with Ruthie than he was with Rhonda.

When they thought she was asleep, she'd hear them arguing. Her step-mom had a shrill voice that carried, and she would stare at the ceiling trying to decipher what they were saying. It soon became clear to her that Larry was up to the same things he had been when he was married to Rhonda, and Ruthie didn't appreciate his attentions to other women any more than her mom had. He kept claiming that he couldn't help that women were drawn to him and would ridicule her for being insecure.

Amy decided two things on that trip. The first was that she was going to get out on her own as soon as she possibly could. Neither of her parents seemed to want her, and she didn't need them – at least that's what she told herself. The second was that she would never put herself in a situation where she needed anyone. She could be strong on her own. She didn't need a husband – didn't ever want one. She was intelligent and talented. There was no way she would depend on anyone. Others only let you down.

******

Amy held fast to her decisions made as an eight year old. She had received a full scholarship to the college of her choice, and had worked in order to stay at a nearby apartment. It hadn't been easy, but she had graduated at the top of her class and had immediately gotten a fantastic job. Now here she was, with a business of her own, reliant on no one, confident in who she was – and lonely.

She shook her head. No not lonely. She was solitary, and she liked it that way.

Her phone rang, and she looked down to find it was her mom. She sighed and rolled her eyes, but answered the call anyway. Her mom hadn't needed her as a child, but found her indispensable to relay gossip to as an adult.

"Hi, Mom. What's up?" She turned on the fireplace and sat on the couch.

"That secretary of yours told me you're in some small town, and that I wouldn't be able to get in touch with you." Indignation filled her voice.

"I'm sure she didn't expect a small mountain town to have great cell service."

"Next time, you two should get your stories straight."

Amy sighed. "Mom, I'm in a town called Willow Creek on a working vacation. We didn't know if I'd be able to get phone calls or not."

"Um-hm. Anyway, I have something important to tell you."

"Really?" Amy couldn't keep the sarcasm from her voice. Her mom always thought she had earth-shattering news which turned out to be simply gossip.

Rhonda either ignored her tone, or didn't listen enough to hear it. Amy guessed it was the latter. "Your father is getting divorced from wife number four. And here's the best part," she paused to create a dramatic moment. "She's the one who found someone new this time." She squealed and laughed hysterically. "He's finally getting what he deserves. Now he knows what it feels like."

Amy grimaced. Her mother's joy was disturbing, yet she couldn't deny that it was exactly what Larry deserved. "Well, I hope he learns from it."

"Oh honey! That man is convinced he is God's gift to women everywhere. He won't learn. He'll blame her somehow – say that he was too much man for her or something." Amy had to admit that it sounded a lot like something Larry would say. His most recent wife, Parker, was young enough to be his daughter, but he wouldn't see that being an issue. Parker was bleached blonde, tanning bed bronze, and had more silicone in her than sense. A former cocktail waitress in Las Vegas, she was convinced she was an up and coming star. "I'm sending her a congratulations card." Her mom giggled.

"Oh, Mom. Is that necessary?"

"Oh come on! It's tradition. I've sent all his other wives cards after their divorces. I still send Christmas cards to each of them. It's a sisterhood full of the women who were dumb enough to fall for that man and survived it."

Amy sighed. "Ok. At least there were no children involved this time."

"Children are resilient. They all survive and turn out just fine." Amy knew that her mom often felt defensive when she brought up the toll divorce takes on the children. She didn't want to admit that it had any effect on Amy's mental wellbeing. But Amy knew that some of her half-siblings had deeper wounds than she had, and not all of them had coped as well as she had - although she was starting to wonder if submerging herself in isolation was coping with things well.

Not wanting to argue, she simply said, "True."

"So what are you doing in some rural village? City life getting to you?"

Amy rose to go make coffee. Obviously her mom wanted a long chat. She explained why she was there, and that she was having trouble with her design. But her mom only seemed to pick up on one point of her story.

"So there's a man? It's been a while since you've had a boyfriend. I was starting to think you were getting ready to become a nun."

"I don't need a man, Mom."

"None of us needs a man. But they can have their uses." Rhonda giggled, and Amy rolled her eyes. "So tell me about this Tristan."

"There's nothing to tell. He and I are working together, and that is all."

Rhonda made a disappointed noise, then brightened. "I'm going to hope that working together will change things. You never know what proximity can do."

"Well, it better happen quickly because I'm only going to be here for a little while longer."

"Love can happen in the space of a heartbeat."

Amy's eyes found the verses posted on the wall once again. "I'm learning that love looks different than what I always thought. I'm not sure I've ever seen or felt true love before." Although her mom took great delight in her words, thinking that she was indeed falling for Tristan, Amy knew that this was an individual journey in a strange way. It was something she needed to figure out alone before she shared it with others.

17

Amy sat on the porch of Holliday Hotel. With a blanket over her lap and a warm mug of coffee on the small table next to her she was plenty warm. There was something about the view of the lake that drew her. She had her sketch pad with her and was determined to make a dent on designing a logo.

After several failed attempts, she finally had something she liked. The "Hs" were scripted with the rest of the words in an elegant print. The second upright bar of the "H" in Holliday was aligned with the first upright bar in the word Hotel below it. The letters were done in a silvery gray. She looked at her work critically. It didn't seem like enough, but she didn't want to make it too elaobrate either.

Hearing a footstep on the wooden porch, she glanced up. Carol was coming towards her with a smile. She sat in the chair next to her and began twisting her fingers nervously. "How's it going?"

"I think I finally have something started for your logo." Amy showed her the design and was pleased to see Carol's face light up.

"That's wonderful. Simple and elegant." Carol looked out across the lake for a moment. Suddenly, she took a deep breath. "I have a favor to ask you."

Amy set her sketch pad down and picked up her coffee. "Okay. What do you need?"

"A friend of mine, Willa Coburn, is a kindergarten teacher here in town and is going to bring her class to the inn on Valentine's Day as a field trip." Carol glanced over at Amy nervously. "I think I told you that already. She knows that I would love to host a children's Valentine's party." Carol smiled warmly at the thought of having a room full of young children.

"Sounds like something you would enjoy." Amy waited to hear what this had to do with her. Her heart raced as she thought about a bunch of wild, undisciplined children running with abandon through Carol's lovely rooms. She had never really liked kids much – even when she was a kid herself. Kids were messy and needy.

"It really is. The thing is that I need help. With my annual Valentine's dinner that night, it makes my day a little bit more busy than normal. My daughters are coming to help with the dinner, but I just found out they won't be here until that afternoon. Is there any way you could help me?"

"How could I help?"

"You could load the cookies onto trays, help me decorate, keep the punch bowl filled – things like that."

"So I wouldn't have to do anything with the kids then?" Amy had been nervous about refusing her hostess. Carol had been so kind to her, she would hate to disappoint her, but children? No. That was too much. Filling trays and punch bowls – that she could do.

"Oh, no. Willa and I can take care of the kids. Plus there will be parents here as well." Carol looked at her hopefully. "So do you think you could help? I know it'll be your last day of vacation. I hate to make you work, but you were the first person I thought of."

What was the next line of the verses about love? Oh yes. *It does not insist on its own way.* This wouldn't be her ideal way to spend her final day of vacation, but Carol needed her. How could she be selfish enough to deny Carol a little bit of her time? She'd have the rest of the day. "I can do that. In fact, I would be happy to help."

Relief washed over Carol's face. "I'm so glad. I didn't know who to ask next." She looked at Amy for a moment. "You know, the first guests that I had who became special to me were Willa and her friends. It hasn't really happened again until you came along."

Amy smiled warmly. She briefly had a feeling that her life, her views on love, would have been radically different if this woman had been her mother. "You've become special to me, too. I feel like

I'm undergoing some sort of transformation just being here, but I'm still not sure what I'm being changed into."

Carol's facial expression was cryptic as she replied, "I think I do." She rose from her seat. "The logo you created is great. I'm so glad Tristan contacted you about doing it."

"Me, too. It's been a good challenge for me." She smiled in chagrin before adding, "It was a good lesson in not jumping to conclusions, too."

Carol smiled, and this time Amy didn't see lingering hurt in her face. *It is not irritable or resentful.* If anyone had the right to feel resentful about how Amy had first depicted her, first thought about her, it was Carol. Yet she had shown nothing, but compassion for her. She had even come to think of Amy as someone special in her life.

What was it that made Tristan and Carol so different from her own parents, or from most of the people in her life for that matter? They lived out those verses on love so completely. It was apparent that they deeply believed in what the Bible said and wanted to live it out.

"Do you attend church?" Amy surprised herself with her question.

"Every week," Carol answered with a smile. "Would you like to join me?"

Amy hesitated. She felt as if there was an invisible hand pushing her in a direction that she had never had any desire to go before. "Yes, I think I would."

Carol absolutely beamed. "That's wonderful! I'll meet you in the entryway at eight-thirty on Sunday." When she finished, she headed back into the house as if afraid that Amy would change her mind.

Amy wasn't so sure she wouldn't change her mind either, but deep down she knew that she couldn't disappoint Carol. She would be there, whether she wanted to or not.

18

Tristan was making lunch for his grandma when his phone let him know he had a notification. A quick glance showed him that Amy had sent a text message. He put his phone aside for a moment so that he could get his grandma taken care of first. For a moment he thought back to when his own needs and wants had come first. Since he'd come to live with Carmen, his life focused around her, because she needed him. It wasn't always easy. The innate selfishness that lives inside people sometimes reared its ugly head. But he had never regretted his decision.

"Here you go, Grandma." He set a plate in front of her, and she grinned her appreciation. He sat down with her. When he had moved in, he had determined to have as many of his meals with her as possible. Taking care of her made him aware that there were a limited number of meals left for them to have together. He didn't want to miss a single one.

After praying for their meal, Carmen eyed the phone sitting next to his plate. "You have a message."

"I do. It's from Amy."

"Aren't you going to check it?"

Tristan chuckled. "You know I never look at my phone during our meals. Your curiosity is going to have to wait."

Carmen huffed in pretended offense. "My curiosity indeed!" She took a bite. "It might be important."

"It's not." Tristan could barely keep his countenance. It cracked him up to watch her. She was horrible at waiting.

"How do you know?"

"Because if it were important she would call." He looked at her. "Besides, I can't imagine that there would be anything urgent for Amy to tell me."

Carmen sighed and gave up. She dug into her food as quickly as she could though, and Tristan knew that she was anxious to finish her meal so that he would check his messages. It amused him, but also relieved him to see that she was showing signs of having an appetite. When she finished, she confirmed his supposition by reminding him that he still had a message.

He laughed. "I'll get it in a moment." Picking up both their plates, he carefully washed them and put them away. When he got back, Carmen had his phone in her hands and was trying to figure out how to unlock the screen. He held his hand out for the phone, and she sheepishly placed it in his hand. "You're as bad as my nephews."

Carmen smiled unrepentantly. "It was worth a shot."

Opening the message, he said, "She wants me to come over to look at a draft of the logo." He looked at his grandma in concern. "Will you be okay by yourself for a little while?"

"Of course I will." She waved off his concern and used her walker to move back to her favorite chair. She grabbed a book off the end table. "I wanted to finish this book anyway." He made sure that she had everything she could possibly need nearby – water, the TV remote, the phone.

"If you need any help, remember to call Mrs. Yates next door." The neighbor was a retired nurse who had often come to help with Carmen when Tristan needed to be gone for longer periods of time.

"I know, Father." Carmen looked up at him in exasperation. "We go through this every time you leave."

"Sorry." He kissed her forehead. "I just want to make sure you're well taken care of."

"You do take good care of me. But you shouldn't have me hindering you from doing what you need to do. Go. I'll be fine."

Tristan sighed. It was so easy to worry about her. Each winter, he was certain that she got a little frailer, a little slower. As he walked out of the house, he quickly sent up a prayer for God to protect his grandma while he was gone, and to keep his mind focused on what needed to be done instead of torn between his work and Carmen. Feeling a little better, he climbed into his car and drove to Holliday Hotel.

Carol stepped out of the kitchen wiping her hands on a heart covered apron when she heard the door open. With a bright smile she said, "I was hoping you would stop by today."

"You were? Got a new cookie recipe you want me to taste," he teased.

Carol laughed. "Not this time. Why don't we go sit down so we can talk?"

Tristan paused. "I actually came because Amy wanted to meet with me. I hate to keep her waiting."

"Oh. Of course. She's on the back porch last I knew. After you're done, why don't you come find me?"

"Absolutely. Thanks for understanding." Tristan was relieved that Carol didn't press him to talk with her first. It shouldn't have surprised him though. Carol was always willing for others to precede her. As he stepped out on the back porch, he pulled his coat tighter around him. The wind was picking up. He found Amy curled up on a chair, wrapped in a blanket, and fast asleep. He contemplated his options, not knowing if he should wake her, wait for her to wake up, or leave and come back later. All of a sudden, she cried out and sat upright. Tristan could tell by her glazed expression that she was still dreaming as the tears fell down her face. He knelt on the cold wooden boards next to her and gathered her into his arms. "It's okay. It's just a dream." He soothed her as best he could. Eventually, he felt her arms tighten around him, and she buried her face in his shoulder, crying as if her heart was breaking. Rubbing her back, he wondered what she had been dreaming about that had terrified her so badly.

Finally, she pushed back from him and wiped her eyes with the sleeve of her coat. "I'm so sorry. It was an awful dream. I've never had any like it before."

"Do you want to talk about it?" He got to his feet stiffly and sat in the chair next to her. Her nose was red, he didn't know if it was from the cold or the crying, and her eyes were still damp and pink. Mascara left trails down her cheeks and her hair was tousled. Yet he thought that she was even more attractive than ever. Maybe it was because she had always had a barrier around her, she had felt distant, but now she seemed vulnerable, like she needed someone – like she needed him.

Amy shook her head. "No, I would rather forget about it. It's not important." She tried to compose herself. She wiped the make-up off her cheeks, ran a hand through her short hair, and sat up straighter. "Let's get to business." She pulled out her sketchpad. "Here's what I've come up with so far. I don't think it's done, but it's the best start I've had so far."

Tristan took the pad and looked over the design on it. "This is perfect. It fits this place and Carol very well."

Amy smiled slightly. "I've never had a logo take me so long. I hope I'll be able to finish it before I have to leave."

"Now that you have a start, I'm sure the rest will be easy." He handed back the paper to her and started to get up.

"Before you go," Amy stopped. She fidgeted with the edge of the blanket. Tristan sat back down and turned his attention to her. He didn't press her, simply waited for her to continue in her time. "I wanted to make sure that you understood that nothing could ever happen between us. I mean, you're a great guy, and I really respect you, but we're from two different worlds."

Tristan was stunned. Had he said or done something that had made her believe that he was starting to fall for her? Maybe she was just embarrassed from crying in his arms. How did someone tactfully agree to a statement like that? He rubbed his hands together and stared at his feet for a moment. "When I made the decision to come here and take care of Grandma, I also came to the conclusion that it would also put on hold any ideas of dating or marriage. Grandma needs my undivided attention, and that's not fair to any woman." He looked up at her and took a deep breath. "When you said that we're from two different worlds, you were right. I think you were talking about big city compared to country life, but it's more than that. I dedicated my life to God years ago and part of that commitment to Him was that any woman in my life would also be committed to Him. Anything else is just setting up for failure because we'd be too different in our beliefs to make it work." Amy's cheeks had flushed. "I'm sorry if I unintentionally led you to believe that I felt more for you than I do."

"No," she waved him off awkwardly. "No, I just wanted to make sure we were on the same page and we are! So it's great."

"Okay," he drawled. "Well, Carol wanted to talk with me about something so unless you have something else . . ." He left the sentence open.

"No, we're good. Go see Carol." She smiled awkwardly, and Tristan felt like he had handled the situation badly.

Not wanting to make it worse though, he decided a hasty retreat was in order. He slipped into the kitchen and shed his coat immediately at the sudden warmth. "It's toasty in here." He sat at the counter where Carol was using the mixer.

"It gets a little warm when the oven is on. I don't feel like it's too warm though."

Tristan realized that he may be feeling some extra heat from embarrassment and decided to change the subject. "So what did you want to talk to me about?"

"Amy," she said simply. He was glad that she was focused on pouring the batter into a muffin tin to notice the flush that crept up his neck.

"What about Amy?"

"A couple things. First, I think that God is really pursuing her. He's been using the verses about love that I posted in the Sweetheart Suite to show her what love really is. She told me today that she feels like she's going through a transformation." Carol sighed as she placed the muffins in the oven. "I love seeing God draw people to Him."

"That's really exciting." Tristan hoped with all of his heart that he hadn't hurt things just now. He had been honest, but he wasn't sure that it had been handled in the best way.

"Also, I know you and Carmen always come to my Valentine dinner. Would you mind inviting Amy to join you guys?" She leaned on the counter across from Tristan so he was sure that she noticed the blood draining from his face.

"I'm not sure that would be so good."

"Why not?"

"Well, it's awkward. Amy just let me know that she wasn't interested in me, and I told her that I wasn't interested either."

Carol frowned. "How does something like that come up?"

"I don't know if I said or did something that made her think that I was falling for her, or what, but she wanted to let me know that it wouldn't work out between us, and I agreed."

Carol's eyes widened. "Oh no. I think I know what happened. That night she had dinner at your house she came home and was upset. We got to talking about the verses, and she said that she felt like someone was chasing her. I told her that Someone – meaning God – was chasing her and offering her love. I bet she thought I meant you. I'm so sorry. I was sure that she didn't quite understand me at the time, but I didn't correct her."

"It's all right. I wish we could have left things the way they were though." Tristan stood up. "I don't know if she would accept an invitation from me now."

"If you find a way to ask her, would you?" Carol's eyes pleaded with him. "I know it's asking a lot, but I hate the thought of her being all alone of Valentine's Day."

"I'll see what I can do." Tristan hugged Carol and knew that somehow he would find a way to invite Amy. He just hoped it didn't add to the confusion.

19

As soon as Tristan left, Amy buried her head in her hands. She wished she had never opened her big mouth. Of course Tristan was being kind because that's who he was not because he was in love with her. Why had she ever thought otherwise? It was those dumb verses in her room. They had her all confused.

Suddenly realizing how cold she was, she hurried up to her room, thankful that Tristan and Carol were nowhere around. She started the fireplace and went to the kitchenette to make coffee. On her way back in, the verse seemed to mock her. She pointed her finger at it and yelled, "You've got me all confused! I used to know how to tell the difference between a guy who wanted to be a friend and someone who wanted more, but now I don't know what to think. What do you want from me anyway?"

Love is patient and kind; love does not envy or boast; it is not arrogant or rude. It does not insist on its own way; it is not irritable or resentful;

Irritable. That was how she felt right now. She was irritated that Tristan had so flatly refused her. Sure, she had refused him first, but still. A girl didn't want to hear that he hadn't wanted her anyway. And because she wasn't a Christian like him? That was just intolerant. He was bigoted and narrow minded and, and . . . patient, kind, humble, polite.

She thought about how he had patiently waited for her to say her piece without prodding her or interrupting. In retrospect, his reply had been kind as well. She could tell that he had hated to have to say what he did and that he tried to phrase it as kindly as possible.

Even in his answer, he had shown how much he had given up

when he decided to come to Willow Creek. He had determined to remain alone in order to take care of his grandma. She was sure that it had been a sacrifice in many ways to give up the life that he had to come here, but he hadn't demanded his own way.

He could have felt irritated with her for forcing him to say he wasn't interested in her either. Yet he had spoken gently and honestly. She felt her own irritation slipping away.

She sighed. She had never felt so confused before. *It does not rejoice in wrongdoing, but rejoices with the truth.* She went and sat on the couch, tucking her feet under herself. Remembering her mom's phone call about her dad's most recent marriage failure she decided that her mom didn't know what love was. Her mom gleefully rejoiced in Parker's affair. Amy had always hated her father's infidelity, but she hated it also that he had to experience it as well. Maybe he would understand why faithfulness was an important component to a happy marriage now.

Rejoices with the truth. What was truth? Her college professors had indicated that truth was relative. That what was true to one, may not be true to another. There were many ways to see things, to experience things. Truth didn't have to be absolute. In fact, it couldn't be. All you had to do was listen to two people tell you an eye witness account of an event. Both would be telling you their truth, but it would be possible for their stories to be different because of their angle, their preconceived notions, their background, or any number of other reasons.

She had gladly accepted their teaching, but now she wished that there was something – anything – that was absolutely true. She was positive that both Tristan and Carol would tell her that God was absolute, that the Bible was truth, but she didn't know if she could believe that. She'd never seen God or felt Him. If He existed, He didn't seem to care about her.

Who has been pursuing you then?

The thought came as clearly to her mind as if someone had sat down next to her and spoken the words aloud. Her heart beat faster. Who was pursuing her? She had no doubt that she was being chased. She felt it. She didn't know Who it was or why, but she knew that something or Someone was after her.

Her nightmare on the porch had focused in on this idea. She had been running - she didn't know from what. She simply knew that she had to get away. But she ended up stopping suddenly on the brink of a cliff. Teetering on the edge, she looked down and saw that below her was fire as far as her eyes could see. She could hear people screaming and sobbing, crying for help, but she couldn't help them, and she wasn't sure she could save herself from joining them. She began to pitch forward –

And then she had woken up, being held in Tristan's arms and being comforted by him.

Perhaps it was this moment that had made her confess that she wasn't interested in him. It had felt too natural to cry on his shoulder. Or maybe it was the fear that she would get too comfortable relying on someone else to help bear her burdens. She had spent her whole life caring for herself. She didn't need anyone now.

She covered her face with her hands as she groaned in embarrassment. Why hadn't she waited for him to make an obvious move that seemed like he was interested – like asking her out on a date – before she refused him? Knowing that she could beat herself up about her error forever, she decided to do something more productive.

Taking out her laptop she searched other B-and-Bs to see what kind of logos they had. There were so many varieties. Quaint cottages next to elegant homes followed by mountain cabins and each one had its own personality. Some were classy, while others were homey, and still others rustic.

Amy sighed and put her laptop away. She knew the logo wasn't finished, yet couldn't decide what was missing. She went to the window seat in the bedroom and pulled out her sketchpad again. Drawing for fun was something she didn't often take the time to do anymore, but what were vacations for if not to rediscover the things you loved to do?

She sketched the lake and the stark, bare trees. She was falling in love with this view. For a few moments she leaned her head back and just sat there enjoying the silence and peacefulness that surrounded her.

A piercing ring startled her out of her reverie. She jumped to grab her phone and answered without bothering to look at who was calling.

"Have you talked to Dad?" The soft voice of Angela, her half sister, came over the line. Angela was Ruthie's oldest daughter. While Amy had three siblings from her dad's other marriages, Angela was the only one who contacted her regularly. She was also the only one who seemed to have a soft spot for their father.

"No, but my mom called to tell me the news." Amy put her feet on the floor. Angela wasn't a gossip so she knew that she hadn't just called to talk about the divorce. She also wouldn't revel in any pain that her dad might be experiencing.

Angela sighed. "I know you'll probably find this hard to believe given your past with our dad, but I think he's taking this divorce really hard."

Amy stood up and began pacing the bedroom. "It wouldn't be too surprising. This is the first marriage that he was faithful and his wife wasn't."

"Dad looks older all of a sudden. I'm worried about him." She could hear Angela gnawing on her nails as she spoke, a habit she developed as a child and had never outgrown. Come to think of it, all of her dad's children had a bad habit that had begun as children and had become part of them.

"What are you worried about?" Amy couldn't imagine Larry taking long to rebound from this. Within a month he'd have another girlfriend, and he'd be his normal self again.

"He seems depressed, vulnerable. I don't know how to describe it. I just feel like something's not right."

Amy heaved a sigh. She knew that Angela had a plan to help their dad. "What are you going to do to help him?"

"Not me. You."

Amy laughed shortly. The bitter sound startled her. "No way. There is nothing I can say or do to help him. You know that."

"I think all of us should get together and help cheer him up, but we need you to take charge. You're the oldest, and even though we're not all close, I know the others would listen to you better than they would listen to me."

Amy knew that she was right. Everyone knew that Angela was the soft-hearted one. She was always trying to get them all together for holidays, birthdays, always making excuses for Larry, always trying to be the big, happy family that they were not. If she called everyone, they would blow her off thinking it was just another try at salvaging her family. But if Amy called everyone, they would take notice. They all understood that Amy had issues with their father. She never got together with the rest 'just because'. If she arranged for all of them to gather, it would be for something serious.

"I need more information. I'm still not convinced Dad's fourth divorce is worth stirring everyone up about."

"I called to talk to Dad and he was crying - *crying*! Have you ever seen Dad cry?"

"No, but Angela it's also the first time he's been the one being left. I'm sure he'll be fine."

"He was distracted, kept forgetting things. He kept talking about what a terrible father he had been to all of us. He asked about each of us, but he kept calling me by your name. He seemed to think that you were still in college and the rest of us were still kids."

Amy sat back down on the window seat. "Honestly, Angela, he probably has lost track of where we all are. It's not like we're all close."

"No, this was different. I think he's heading for a mental collapse."

Amy rubbed the bridge of her nose, feeling a headache coming on. "Fine. I'll call him and see what I think, but I'm not promising anything. I'm already on vacation, and I can't up and leave my work again."

"All right. Thanks Amy! I'll be praying for you." With that the call was disconnected. Amy always forgot that Angela was a Christian. Not because she didn't live like one. Mostly because

Amy tried to keep her half-siblings at a distance. The less interested and involved she was with them, the less they could potentially hurt her.

Amy thought about her dysfunctional family. Angela had been the first half-sibling. Born when Amy was eight, she had looked up to her big sister and for a few years, Angela had made going to visit her dad tolerable. It was obvious that the little girl was smitten by her big sister. When Amy was there, Angela would toddle after her wherever she went.

Two years later, April had arrived, but her dad's second marriage was ending, and Amy rarely got to see the two girls. At that point, Amy had decided to keep her distance from all of her siblings. It hurt too much to have Angela pulled away from her. She could only blame herself for getting attached. Not long after she had made that decision, Ruthie had contacted Rhonda and told her that the counselor they had been seeing had suggested that they keep in contact with Amy for Angela's sake, to give her a little consistency. Rhonda had been happy to let Amy go to their home, but Amy remained aloof, afraid of giving her heart to people who would most likely abandon her eventually. So April never developed the same attachment to Amy although Angela had remained devoted to her.

A year later, her dad's new wife, Coral, gave birth to his only son, Craig. Even though Amy still went to see her dad on certain holidays, she made sure to keep her space from the chubby baby. Her new step-mom had complained that Amy was jealous of the baby and tried to stop her visits. Surprisingly, Larry wouldn't give in on it, and Amy's visits continued. His marriage to Coral hadn't lasted much longer so it hadn't mattered too much anyway.

After that, Larry had seemed content to remain single. He had flirted, dated, and moved in with women for the next ten years. When Amy was twenty-one, he married Parker, a woman only a couple years older than Amy. Since she was now an adult, she didn't spend time with Larry or his women anymore. She had actually been surprised that her dad's current marriage had last seven years. It was the longest marriage he'd had since he had been married to Rhonda.

Amy closed her eyes and leaned her head on the cold glass of the window. Angela was now twenty and in college. April was eighteen and a senior in high school, and Craig just a year younger. Amy felt decades older than her siblings. She knew that Angela wasn't prone to exaggeration so if she was worried about Larry, then she should definitely check on him.

She picked up the phone and stared at it for a moment. She should call her dad – but, not tonight.

20

Sunday morning found Amy waiting by the front door for Carol. She paced the small space, rechecked her appearance in the mirror for the hundredth time, and considered escaping back up the stairs. She brushed her hands over the top of her black slacks and smoothed the oversized white sweater. Hearing a footstep she turned to see Carol approaching with a bright smile.

"I was hoping you would come." Carol wore a black dress with a red scarf tied artistically around her neck.

"Don't you need to be here for breakfast?" Amy knew it was a stupid question born out of fright.

Carol laughed. "On Sundays, I have a more continental-style breakfast. Everything is set out, and I'll clean up when I get back." She wrapped her arm around Amy. "Don't worry. I promise this will be painless."

Amy tried to smile, but found that it was forced. Somehow she felt drawn to go although she was digging in her heels as hard as she could. The Person who was chasing her was now pulling her to attend church. She climbed into Carol's car and clenched her hands so tightly around her purse that her knuckles turned white.

Before she put the car in drive, Carol turned to look at her young guest. "Are you sure you want to go? I won't be upset if you choose not to."

Here was her opportunity. She could back out gracefully, say that she didn't know what had come over her, and head back to her room without any guilt. Instead what came out of her mouth was, "I really feel like I need to go to church today." What? Who said that? Certainly she hadn't. She didn't need anything or anyone – especially not religion.

But Carol heard her words and smiled as she began to drive to the chapel at the edge of town. Amy didn't know what was coming over her. This thing had to stop. But how do you tell an invisible force to leave you alone? She was beginning to feel like she was possessed or something.

The chapel was picturesque with its stonework and bell tower. It looked like something that had been built years ago and had withstood the test of time. Amy went inside hesitantly, but was instantly in awe. In the front of the church the entire wall had been replaced with glass to view the mountains and forests beyond the church. The wood pews and the dark green carpet of the floor reflected the colors found in the creation outside.

Carol smiled and greeted people as she made her way down the aisle until she reached a pew about halfway down. She slipped in leaving ample space for Amy to slide in next to her. Pulling out the bulletin Amy became absorbed in reading every word to avoid eye contact with others. She was sure they could see that she didn't belong. There had to be some secret handshake or spoken code that would reveal that she was an outsider. Maybe Christians had a sixth sense and could just tell by looking at you that you weren't one of them.

Amy breathed a sigh of relief when the service started. She tapped her hand on the pew in front of her, keeping time to the beat of the music. The words to the music were all about love, but not a romantic love. It was a love that reflected the verses posted in her room. *Love is patient and kind; love does not envy or boast; it is not arrogant or rude. It does not insist on its own way; it is not irritable or resentful; it does not rejoice at wrongdoing, but rejoices with the truth.* What were the next words? She couldn't recall. As the music played the verses repeated through her mind over and over and over again.

Okay I get it! She mentally shouted at the voice in her head.

Do you? Keep listening. I think you still have a lot to learn about what love is and what it isn't. Amy stood perfectly still. She slowly glanced at Carol, but she was still happily singing along. Apparently the voice was for her alone. She tried to calm her beating heart as they sat down and prayed. The One who had been chasing her was in her thoughts now. How could she escape Him if He was inside of her?

The pastor got up to the pulpit and Amy leaned back in the pew. The bulletin had told her that his name was Aaron Westley. However, she had no real intention of listening to the sermon, and found herself looking at the snow covered forest floor through the window behind the pastor.

"The world has twisted what love is to the point where people couldn't identify real love if it came up and introduced itself to them." Pastor Westley's words got Amy's attention, and she swung her gaze quickly to him.

Keep listening.

"According to the world love makes you feel good – if it feels good, do it. Love is changeable. It's here today and gone tomorrow. Love is passion and lust – both of which can and do fade. You know why the world has altered what true love looks like? Because real love reflects God, and the world doesn't want to have to deal with His existence. They say if God is love then why is there suffering? Or why would a loving God send anyone to hell?" Aaron looked around the congregation. Amy felt like his eyes were boring into her own. She had said those things before. "I want to show you what God's love really looks like."

Amy nearly pointed at herself in question. He seemed to be speaking directly to her.

Keep listening.

"Turn in your Bibles to John 3:16. This is the best known and quoted verse in the Bible. Many of us have heard it since we were children. In a lot of ways, it makes it so that it almost loses all meaning – like a children's song or nursery rhyme. But the reason why we teach this verse to our children is because it so clearly shows what God's love is." The rustling of pages had stopped by now. "Let's read together. 'For God so loved the world, that he gave his only Son, that whoever believes in him should not perish but have eternal life.' God *loved* the world. He loved it so much that He gave us a gift, a gift that none of us deserved, a gift that was more valuable than we could ever repay. He gave us His Son – His *only* Son. He didn't send us a back up, or one of many. He gave us something that could never be replaced." The pastor took a step to the side of the pulpit and leaned on it. "Remember that terrible earthquake that happened in China back in 2008 and school buildings had collapsed? Do you remember the anguish on the parents' faces? It's always difficult to lose a child. It's the worst possible grief, but this was more. Because in most cases, that child was their only child. It left a hole that nothing could fill."

Amy noticed women wiping tears from their eyes. A few pulled their children tighter against them. One woman leaned hard against her husband and silently let the tears fall down her face. These were people who either knew how unspeakable it would be to lose a beloved child or had experienced that agony.

"Now who among us would voluntarily give our child to a people that we knew would reject him, ridicule him, spit on him, and eventually kill him. Not a single one of us. I know I wouldn't. My children's lives are precious to me. Do you think that Jesus' life was any less precious to God?" The pastor looked around the congregation.

"So why would God do that? It was because of love. Not a Hallmark card kind of love, but a deep, abiding love. The Greek word for that kind of love is agape which means unconditional love. God didn't say if you're good enough, I'll send my Son for you. Or if you give enough, I'll send Him. He didn't even ask us to love Him first. In fact, the Bible tells us that it was the opposite. 1 John 4:19 says 'We love because he first loved us.' The only reason we can experience or show an unconditional love is because God loved us first." Pastor Westley went back to his text.

"So God's sacrificial gift to us was because of love, and it was for a specific purpose. It was so that we would not perish – we would not die – but have eternal life with Him.

I talked earlier about how the world asks how a loving God could send people to hell, but there's a couple things to remember. First, God is holy and Heaven is perfect. In our natural state we would defile Heaven. God's holiness cannot permit us to do that.

The second thing to remember is that God doesn't send us to hell. We're already on our way there. God is longing for us to take the detour that He has provided so that we don't end up in hell." The pastor paused. "I want you to see this next verse, so let's turn to 2 Peter 3:9."

Again the sound of pages rustling filled the chapel. Amy sat quietly, her head spinning with this new information. She had never heard God explained so clearly before.

"2 Peter 3:9 says, 'The Lord is not slow to fulfill his promise as some count slowness, but is patient toward you, not wishing that any should perish, but that all should reach repentance.'

God is patiently waiting for us to follow Him. He doesn't want anyone to die apart from Him, but He allows us to choose." Aaron smiled. "It seems so easy, and yet it's so difficult – especially for those of us who feel like we're independent, and need nothing." Amy held her breath as once again the pastor's eyes seemed to be drawn to her.

"Our original verse says it's as easy as believing. 'Whoever believes in him should not perish.' This belief is more than a head knowledge belief, but a deep heart belief. It has the meaning of entrusting yourself to Him. It's a deep conviction that can't be swayed. It means to absolutely trust in Jesus." The pastor smiled. "It seems too easy, and yet it can be the most difficult decision. To entrust yourself to God means that you have to relinquish your control and let Him take charge. Many of us struggle with that daily – even after salvation. We say, 'Lord, we believe in You' and then we tell Him, 'I've got this under control'."

The pastor stepped away from the pulpit. "I remind myself of my own small son. Jacob is three and when he's in trouble, he reaches out for his daddy. The other day we heard him call out for his daddy, and I ran in to find him on top of his dresser unable to get himself down. He was quick to call me when he needed help, but at his age, what we hear most often is 'I do it myself'. We try to help him and guide him only to have him scream 'I do it myself!'" Aaron laughed. "I think too often I sound a lot like my three old to God. He's there longing to guide me and yet I stand there and scream, 'I can do it myself.'"

Amy squirmed in her seat. All this talk of being too independent, unable to ask for help, was a little too close to home for her.

"But this belief is more than trusting God for everyday tasks," the pastor continued. "This is the belief of salvation. Acts 16:31 is another verse we learn as a child. 'Believe in the Lord Jesus, and you will be saved.' We are all sinners. That sin automatically separates us from God, but He loved us so much that He provided a way to get back to Him by sending His Son to take the punishment for our sin, the death penalty for our sin, so that we could have life with Him for eternity." Pastor Westley looked across the congregation again.

"Have you taken that step and believed in Jesus to save you from your sin? It's the biggest decision you'll ever make, and the best. You'll never know real love until you know the love of God. That unconditional love is like nothing the world could ever give you. It's only when you know His love that you can love others with that same love. I would love to talk to you more about His love and belief in Him if you have questions. Let's pray."

Amy had no idea what the pastor prayed about. She only knew that something was happening to her. That real love that she had been searching for was close, she could feel it. But she knew she didn't quite have it yet.

Quiet noise around her alerted her to the fact that service was over, and she had missed the ending. She raised her head and found Carol watching her questioningly. "Are you okay?"

Amy summoned up a smile. "Of course. Thanks for inviting me." She gathered up her things and began to head towards the door. As she made her way down the aisle, a hand reached out for her. Startled, she looked into the kind eyes of Carmen Romero.

"I thought that was you," she said with a smile on her face. Amy glanced around, trying not to be obvious. She had hoped that Tristan wouldn't be here to see her. It was going to be awkward to say the least at their next encounter. She didn't want him to think she was at church because of what he had said. She must not have done a good job at being discreet, because Carmen's smile widened as she said, "He doesn't attend this church."

"What?"

"Tristan doesn't attend church here. I prefer it here, but he felt like he needed a church with a young adult group."

"Oh." Amy didn't really know how to respond to that information. She was glad he wasn't there, but didn't want to admit she had been looking for him.

"I'm actually glad I ran into you though. I wanted to invite you to Valentine's dinner with Tristan and me. Every year he takes me to Holliday Hotel's dinner. Since you'll already be there and you're here by yourself I thought it would be nice for you to join us. No one should be alone on Valentine's Day."

Amy's smile felt weak. "It wouldn't be the first one I spent alone."

"You can't miss Carol's Valentine's dinner! It's one of my favorite events of the year."

"I'll think about it." Amy squeezed the older woman's hand. "Thanks for thinking of me." Feeling incredibly rude, she extricated herself and slipped out of the stone chapel. She took a deep breath enjoying the cold air filling her lungs. She had begun to feel warm in the church. Too many people, too much heat – too much guilt.

"There you are," Carol said coming up behind her. "I got stopped by a friend of mine, but I'm ready to go now if you are."

"I'm very ready to go." Amy hurried to the car anxious to leave this place behind. As the car pulled away, she glanced back to the stone chapel. *God so loved . . . you.*

21

"You invited her to Valentine's dinner?" Tristan stared at his grandmother in disbelief. In fact, since he had picked her up from her church the story she had to tell seemed unbelievable. That Amy Juliette had been in church was amazing enough, but that his grandma had invited her to join them for Valentine's was even more astounding. He hadn't told Carmen about Carol's request that they invite Amy. With their last conversation still plaguing him, he hadn't been sure it would be welcome. "What did she say?"

"She promised to think about it and thanked me like a perfect lady." Carmen set her fork down next to her plate. Tristan tried not to worry as he noticed how little she had eaten. "I think she's lonely."

"She doesn't know anyone here. I'm sure she has people – friends or family- back home."

Carmen shook her head. "No. She's a solitary person. I don't think she has anyone."

Tristan folded his arms and leaned on the dining room table. "What makes you think that?"

"Just a hunch I guess. She purposefully keeps herself distant from everyone. She's protecting herself from being hurt by keeping everyone at arm's length. Has she told you anything about herself?"

Tristan tried to think back. "I know she had a very different upbringing from me. I get the feeling that she didn't have a very happy childhood."

Carmen nodded. "That would make sense. Poor kid."

Tristan had to smile. "I think she's doing well for herself for being a 'poor kid'." He started gathering the dishes.

"Still, she's lonely. I know it's by her choice, but I think she's getting to an age where she's realized that she's missing something."

"She's missing God." Tristan paused. He wasn't sure where the thought had come from, but he had started praying for her spiritual wellbeing since their awkward conversation. Somehow he just knew that what she really needed was Jesus. That could be the sole reason why God had led him to pull her in to help on the logo. So that she could meet Him.

"Yes, she is. I pray she finds Him."

"I've been praying for that, too."

"Then I pray she finds you." Tristan nearly dropped the stack of dishes he was carrying to the kitchen.

"What did you say?"

"I said, after she finds God, I pray she finds you." Carmen looked at him with such intensity that he blinked. "I'm not going to be around forever. I don't want you to be alone."

"I won't be alone. I've got mom and dad. I've got my family. I've got friends here in Willow Creek." Tristan went into the kitchen, but Carmen followed him.

"You would make someone a wonderful husband, and you were made to be a father. I love seeing you with your nephews. You weren't meant to be alone." Carmen was insistent.

Tristan placed his hands gently on his grandmother's shoulders and looked her in the eyes. "If God has someone for me, I will gladly make her my wife. But I'm not going to get married just so that I won't be alone."

"Obviously. That would be a terrible mistake."

"I'm glad we agree on that." He turned back to the dishes.

"The truth is that I've been praying for a long time that God would bring you a wife, and when I met Amy I felt like she was the answer to my prayers."

Tristan looked back at his grandma. "How could she be? She's not a Christian."

"Yet."

"What?"

"She's not a Christian yet." Carmen pulled out a chair in the breakfast nook and took a seat. "I feel like it won't be long until she is a Christian though. She has the look of someone that God is working on."

Tristan placed the last dish in the cupboard and dried his hands on a dish towel. "What kind of look is that?"

"A look that someone is fighting something or Someone who they don't know. I remember seeing that look in the mirror when God was working on me." Carmen looked at Tristan as he took a seat opposite her. "I don't claim to be a prophet. Maybe I'm just an old woman who wants to know that her family is taken care of before I go. I only ask that you keep your heart open to God's leading."

Tristan held his grandma's hands. "You know I will. You taught me well."

"That's all I want." She stood up slowly and made her way to her normal spot in the living room.

Tristan sat at the kitchen table and thought over what Carmen had said. He pulled out his phone and dialed Amy's number.

22

Amy hesitated to answer Tristan's call. Since getting home from church she had craved solitude. She had a lot to think about. So much was going on inside her mind and heart that she just wanted time to sort it all out. Slowly, she answered the phone.

"I wanted to reiterate my grandma's invitation to join us for Valentine's Day dinner. I know that our last talk together was sort of awkward, and I didn't want you to refuse because of that. I think that the conversation we had was actually a good one because it let us both know that we're on the same page so there's no stress or discomfort." He trailed off as if sensing that he was rambling.

"Absolutely. We know that we are simply together on business and there's no need to agonize about feelings or emotions."

"Right." He paused. "So will you come?"

Amy took a deep breath. "I'm not sure. I'm not a big fan of Valentine's Day."

"To be honest, I'm not either. I've always felt like we should be telling the people we love how we feel all year and that Valentine's Day is just an excuse for restaurants, card companies, candy makers and florists to make an extra dollar."

"Exactly. There's no need to invite me so I won't be lonely."

"We invited you because we enjoy your company." Amy heard Tristan's sigh over the phone. "I started bringing my grandma to Holliday Hotel because Valentine's Day always made her miss my grandpa. It's always been the two of us, but she wants you there because she genuinely likes you. We both do."

Amy was glad she was already sitting on the couch in the living room of her suite. She knew that Tristan was being honest. Unlike most of the men she came in contact with, Tristan wasn't just being nice so that he could make a move. He was genuine, and he was becoming a friend. She hadn't realized how badly she needed a friend until she came to Willow Creek and met Carol, Tristan and Carmen. She felt closer to these three than people she had known for years. "If I feel up to it, I'll come. I'm helping Carol with a kindergarten field trip earlier in the day so I may just want some peace and quiet by evening," she chuckled.

"That sounds like a good idea. We'll wait to see how you're feeling then." Tristan paused for a moment. "Thanks for not holding our last conversation against me."

"I think we both probably regretted some of the things that were said. I shouldn't have assumed that you were interested in me. I'm sorry I put you on the spot like that."

"That's okay. I'm sorry I wasn't gentler in my response."

Amy smiled. "I'm sure it was the last thing you were expecting."

"It did take me by surprise," he admitted. "I'll let you go. Thanks again for being so gracious."

Amy hung up the phone and glanced out the window. A light snow was falling turning the world into a glistening, white fresh slate. She had come to Willow Creek against her will, but now she dreaded that the time to leave was coming soon. Katie had been right to send her away for a work vacation. She needed the time to rest so that she could refocus.

She pulled on her coat, gloves, and hat to go out on the balcony and enjoy the snowfall. She knew she wouldn't be out there long, but was determined to enjoy it while she could. Leaning against the railing of the balcony, she thought about the church service she had attended. So much of it had seemed aimed directly at her. If she had known the pastor, she would have thought that he had written his sermon just to guilt her. As it was, she half suspected that Carol had tipped him off. Except she knew better than that.

"God, You're the One who is pursuing me, aren't you?" She spoke quietly into the cold, her breath visible in the air.

I am.

Tears filled her eyes. "Why? Why would You want me?"

For God so loved the world.

"I know You love the world. They say that You are love so of course You love the world, but why me?"

I am not willing that any should perish.

"So I'm just one of 'any'?" Amy sighed.

No, you are a unique individual, and I love you because I formed you.

Amy stood still. "You didn't form me. My parents DNA formed me."

Did it? Who formed their DNA or their parents' DNA? Where did it come from?

"Chance?" She shook her head in frustration. "You know what? I'm done with this. Stop pursuing me? It'll never work. I don't need anyone. I certainly don't need You."

You don't need Me? Or you don't want Me?

"What does it matter?" Amy was yelling by now. If someone was down on the porch, they probably thought a crazy woman was up on the balcony arguing with herself. Yet somehow this was the most real conversation she'd ever had in her life. "What matters is that I'm fine on my own."

Are you? It doesn't seem like it to Me. You may not need a lot of things, but everyone needs love – My love. You want to prove you can do it all on your own, but you can't. You need others. Most of all, you need Me.

The tears fell down Amy's cheeks. "I don't want to need You. Why can't I just go on the way I was?" she whispered.

Because you're not the same. You've been changed. You now know what true love is. It's not romance and roses. It's not physical passion. It's Me. I am love. I love you unconditionally.

"No one has ever loved me unconditionally. There was always something in it for them."

I know. That's how humans have twisted love. They love themselves more than anyone else.

Amy wiped her cheeks. "I'm not ready. I can't do it. It seems like a big leap of faith to me, and I just can't jump."

It's not a leap. It's a step. And I'll be with you all the way.

But, I know you're not ready. I'll still be here when you are ready, though. I'm waiting, and I love you, always, no matter what.

Amy almost felt as if God had walked away. She stood on the balcony, and she knew she was all alone. Shivering, she turned to go inside. She had never felt as lonely as she did when she felt God leave.

Immediately, she moved to the verses. Maybe in reading them, she'd feel Him again. "Love is patient and kind;" she read aloud, "love does not envy or boast; it is not arrogant or rude. It does not insist on its own way; it is not irritable or resentful; It does not rejoice at wrongdoing, but rejoices with the truth. Love bears all things, believes all thins, hopes all things, endures all things. Love never ends."

Taking a deep breath she thought about what she knew about God. She hadn't really thought about Him until coming here, but not only had she learned about Him, but she had experienced Him. He was no longer an entity that didn't exist. She couldn't claim that anymore. Instead it was as if she believed that He was who He said He was.

"He's been patient with me, and the pastor today read a verse that talked about Him being patient because He doesn't want anyone to die without Him. He is kind. I can't imagine an all-powerful God being envious of anything or anyone. And although He could boast about His power, His riches, or pretty much anything else, I don't think He does. The pastor talked about Him giving us free will to believe in Him or not so I guess He doesn't insist on His own way. I've given Him plenty to be irritable or resentful about, but He's not. I know that He doesn't rejoice in wrongdoings. It was wrongdoings that separated us from Him in the first place. So He must rejoice in truth. He sent His Son to die for people who hated Him so that would mean He can bear all things. If He could bear that, what couldn't He bear?" Amy paused reading over the rest of the verse and fixating on the final sentence. "Love never ends. God is eternal and God is love."

Amy felt her head spin at the revelation. These verses aren't just about love. They were a description of God. To show real love, one had to imitate God. No wonder Tristan, Carmen, and Carol were her best examples of love. They knew God and tried to live their lives for Him.

Curling up on the couch, she grabbed her sketch pad. She still didn't feel like God was with her, but she felt a warmth that she couldn't explain settle over her. The pieces were coming together. She had confidence that eventually she would fit the final piece in, and it would all make sense.

Her fingers deftly moved over the paper and the landscape from the balcony appeared. Snow was falling, the lake covered in ice, a white covering over the ground, trees heavy with snow on their branches. At the edge of the lake, a woman stood. Somehow Amy knew it was her. She looked so lonely in the bleakness of the winter day. Yet there was no one that she could sketch in beside her. Carol belonged in the house. Tristan and Carmen belonged together. Katie belonged in the city. Her family – well, they didn't belong to her. She sighed. A month ago, the woman would have looked fiercely independent, solid, a force to be reckoned with. Today, she looked lost.

I once was lost, but now I'm found.

The corners of Amy's mouth tipped up in a soft smile. The words brought a comfort to her that nothing else could. She may be lost now, but Someone was looking for her, and she had confidence that He would find her.

23

Amy had never seen Carol so frantic before. She rushed about the kitchen like a whirlwind. She stirred a pot, checked the oven, chopped some vegetables, then moved on to some other task. Amy stepped closer and placed a hand on Carol's shoulder, causing the woman to jump in surprise.

"Oh my goodness! I didn't even hear you come it."

"Why did you agree to the field trip today if it was going to double your load?"

"Because I wanted to. These children need to know that they're loved. Some of them don't even know what love is."

Amy closed her eyes. "Yeah, I know."

Carol pulled her into a hug. "Oh, my dear. You were one of those little ones weren't you? I'm so sorry." Tears slipped down Carol's face, and Amy was amazed at the love she felt from this woman who had known her such a short time.

"Hey, I turned out okay," she tried to lighten the mood. "So what needs to be done? Where can I help?"

"The cookies on the counter need frosted and put on trays." Carol moved on to rushing around, and Amy was glad for a task that she could accomplish that would help Carol get things ready.

The women chatted as they worked, and before they knew it the doorbell rang. Since none of the guests rang the doorbell, the women knew that the kindergarteners had arrived. Carol took off her apron and ran her hands over her hair. "Do I look all right?"

"Just one second." Amy wiped a bit of flour off of Carol's cheek. "Perfect."

Carol smiled and headed to the front door. Soon the sound of excited children's voices flooded the house. A sign had been posted announcing to the guests that the living room was reserved for a field trip, and Amy was sure that the guests were relieved to have the advanced notice, because the room was empty. Amy followed the group and went to stand in a far corner. She wanted to be there to help Carol, but not be spotted by the children – or any of the adults for that matter.

The kids were seated on the floor while the adults took the chairs and when they finally got the children calmed down enough, Carol read a book to the children. Amy's eyes scanned the room, and finally rested on a little girl who tugged at her heart. The girl's brown hair was tangled and her clothes were too small and covered with stains. Freckles covered her face, and she sat slightly apart from the rest of the class. Her arms were tightly folded across her chest and her face had a hardened look that dared anyone to approach her.

Although Amy had always looked like she was taken care of (her mom wouldn't have people talk about them), she had sat with that same expression, that same body language. This little one was a child who didn't know love. Her heart ached when she watched the girl. The little girl tried so hard to pretend that everything was fine, but Amy could see that she was well aware that she was different from the other kids.

Her eyes were riveted on Carol during the reading of the story, though. Amy had a feeling that while she had escaped into art, this little girl escaped into books. The teacher, a woman with shoulder length strawberry blonde hair, sat down next to the girl. For the first time, the girl's face lit up as she looked at her teacher with almost hero worship.

Amy smiled. At that young age, Amy still was looking for the person who would love her, too. She hoped that this little girl didn't end up as cold and cynical as she had. Maybe her teacher would be the person who showed her that there was a reason to care.

The story was over and the children were led to a table covered with construction paper hearts, glitter, stickers, and glue. The happy chatter started back up as the kids designed their valentines.

Each one could give their card to whomever they wished. Amy's heart clenched as she watched the little girl. What would happen to her when all the pretty girls gave their cards to each other and left her out.

Amy found herself at the teacher's side. "I'm Amy Juliette. I'm helping Mrs. Holliday," she introduced herself.

"Oh, Carol's told me about you. I'm Willa Newman – I mean Willa Coburn." She blushed. "Sorry. It's still a new name."

"Congratulations."

"Thanks. We actually met and married here, so Holliday Hotel is very special to us."

"I've been watching the little girl on the end there. She reminds me a lot of myself at that age."

Willa looked over to where the little girl was sitting. Her head was bent low over her work, as if she could ignore the rest of the class if she just concentrated hard enough. Willa smiled softly. "That's Ava Reilly. She's in foster care right now. She's had a rough life for someone so young."

"Aren't you concerned that she won't receive any valentines when they're all passed out?"

Willa shook her head. "She keeps the kids at a distance, but that doesn't necessarily mean that they stay at a distance." Willa pointed out a group of girls giggling at the same table that Ava was sitting at. "The girl with the long dark hair will most likely give her valentine to Ava. She's always trying to get her to play with her group, and since she's the ring leader of that group, the rest try to include her too."

"Wow. That's impressive at this age."

Willa smiled. "It is. But she's an impressive little girl. She's a Christian who's very strong for someone so young. She's always looking for the child who is hurting, in need, or lonely, and doing something about it. And the other girls love her for it, because they've been the recipient of her attentions at one point or another."

"I wish I'd known someone like her."

"I think you do now." Willa nodded to where Carol was

kneeling next to Ava. Her little face lit up as Carol began speaking to her. "Carol is another one who shows God's love to everyone around her. I think it's been the key to her success. She genuinely loves her guests and it shows."

"I think you're right." Amy looked at the rest of the kids. Each of them was hard at work, finishing the final detail of their cards. Soon they began to exchange them. True to Willa's word, the girl with dark hair calmly walked over to Ava and handed her a valentine. Ava's face showed a shy delight and then she slowly handed her card to the dark haired girl. The girl hugged Ava tightly which was an obvious shock to her.

"Lupe Garcia is Carol's best friend's granddaughter." Willa looked up Amy. "That might explain why she's such a sweet girl."

Lupe ran over and gave Carol a hug. Carol whispered in her ear which caused a broad smile to brighten her face. When Carol straightened, she nodded at Amy which was their signal that it was time for snacks.

Amy excused herself and rushed to the kitchen and grabbed a tray of cookies and a pitcher of fruit punch. She set them on a table that already had plates, napkins and cups. She immediately started filling the cups as the kids lined up and took their snacks from her. Each one said a polite thank you as they passed, a testament to their teacher's training. As Ava passed, she barely glanced up and her words were difficult to understand, they were spoken so softly.

When the last one had received their snack, Amy picked up a cookie and a cup of punch and went to sit next to Ava. "Can I sit with you?" Ava shrugged, but Amy could see that she was pleased. "My name is Amy."

"I'm Ava," she glanced up shyly. "I can spell it. A-V-A."

"That's impressive. Our names both begin with A and both have three letters. My name is A-M-Y."

Ava smiled and took a big bite of her cookie. "I'm learning to read," she mumbled around the tasty treat.

"Do you like to read?"

Ava nodded enthusiastically. "When I read, I get to pretend that I'm in the story."

"That's one of the best parts about reading."

"Then I can be anyone I want to be."

"When I was your age, I liked to draw for a similar reason, too. When I drew, I could make my world into anything I wanted it to be. If I wanted pink trees, I could make them pink. Or if I wanted to be taller, I just drew myself that way." Amy didn't mention that she also used to draw pictures of a happy family, because she wished that her family looked that way.

"That sounds nice, too, but I don't draw very good."

"I probably didn't either at first. It was something I had to learn."

Ava nodded. "Like when I learned to write my name."

"Exactly."

Willa stood up near the fireplace. "Okay, children. It's time for us to head back to school. What do we say to Mrs. Holliday?"

Together the class chimed, "Thank you, Mrs. Holliday."

"We have one more thing to do. Do you remember what it is?" Hurriedly, the children stood up and rushed over to the parents. One by one they gave a pink rose to Carol and wished her a Happy Valentine's Day. Carol's cheeks were flushed with pleasure as she accepted the children's gifts. "Make sure you've put your trash in the trash can before we leave and line up at the door." The students rushed to comply with their teacher's wishes and soon they were lined up neatly at the living room door.

Carol stood next to the door clutching a large red gift bag with glitter covered hearts all over it. As the children passed by her, she handed them each a small heart-shaped box of chocolates. The kids all beamed as she handed them their gift.

The house grew quiet as the final child exited and the last adult closed the front door. Carol collapsed on the couch. "Whew! That was a busy morning."

Amy joined her on the couch. "I know. You did a great job with them. They definitely enjoyed their trip here."

Carol smiled broadly. "Children easily join in the excitement of holidays. It was only when my own girls were teenagers that their enthusiasm began to wane. Even then, I could tell they really enjoyed it. It just wasn't 'cool' to show it." Carol sighed and pushed herself up from the couch. "I suppose I should get these in water." She cradled the pink roses and inhaled their aroma. "Willa knows me so well."

As Carol headed for the kitchen the doorbell rang. "Could you get that?" she hollered over her shoulder. Amy stood up shaking her head at how she had become a part of Carol's family without even knowing it.

A florist delivery person handed Amy a beautiful arrangement of red roses with one yellow rose, wished her a Happy Valentine's Day and headed off. Amy looked at the card and saw Carol's name, so she took it to the kitchen. "This just came for you."

Carol turned from the sink where she was filling a vase with water. "Oh, Libbie's flowers." Amy set the arrangement on the counter. Carol began placing the pink roses in the vase. "Every year my daughter sends me this arrangement. The red roses are because that's what Gabe gave me every year for Valentine's Day and the yellow rose is to remind me to be happy."

"That's very sweet." Amy touched the roses gently. "It must have been hard for you after Gabe passed away."

Carol's eyes misted. "It was, but Libbie and May got me through." She stepped back to look at her handiwork. "That and I knew that God was with me, so I wasn't really alone."

"He's really real to you, isn't He?"

"Oh, yes. I don't think I could have coped without Him. Because of Him, I know that I'll see Gabe again, and God's always with me. That first year especially would have been much lonelier without God."

Amy nodded though she wasn't sure she really understood. "I think I've been lonely my whole life." She couldn't believe that the words had escaped her mouth.

Carol wrapped her arms around her. "Just because that's the way it's always been doesn't mean that it can't change. You have me, Tristan and Carmen now if nothing else. And I can guarantee you that God would love to be with you as well."

Amy's eyes filled with tears. "I think I pushed Him away. We were talking," she paused. "Is it weird that I talked to God – or at least I felt like I was? I didn't hear a voice, but it was as real as if I had."

"That's not weird at all," Carol assured her with a smile.

"Anyway, after I went to church with you, God and I argued. I finally told Him that I wasn't ready, and He said He knew, but He was waiting. Then it was almost as if I saw Him walk away from me. And I have never felt lonelier."

Carol leaned her head against Amy's. "You don't know how happy that makes me." Amy looked at her strangely, and Carol clarified. "Not that you felt lonely, but that you talked with God. I don't think He left for good. I think if you look, you'll see that He's nearby waiting for you to be ready to accept Him."

"Maybe. I sort of hope so."

"I know so."

The front door opened and closed. "Mom, we're here!"

"I'll let you go spend time with your daughters. Thanks for everything."

Carol grabbed her hand as she turned away. "Just remember that I'm always here if you need to talk about it some more."

Amy nodded and left quickly. She didn't want to intrude on Carol's family time. Besides, she had a lot to think about.

24

Amy opened up her laptop as soon as she got to her room. When the Google page came up, she paused, her eyes caught by the artwork done for Valentine's Day on the Google logo. Her eyes widened and she gasped. Of course! Why hadn't she realized that what her logo was missing was holidays? But to smash all of the holidays into one logo was too much. So why not make it a monthly change? The answer was so simple.

Quickly, she put away her laptop and pulled out her sketch pad. Using her original design, she made the 'o' in both Holliday and Hotel into clocks about to strike midnight. The next sketch she made the o's into hearts. She continued in this way for quite some time, becoming unaware of the time passing. Her pencil flew over the page. Her face glowed as she drew. She had been concerned about getting the logo finished before she had to leave and with her departure coming the next day, she hadn't expected to finish. Thankfully, inspiration had come at just the right time.

A knock startled her from her work. She jumped up and answered the door. One of Carol's daughters was standing there holding a small package. "I'm May Holliday," she greeted her with a bright smile. The woman reminded Amy so much of Carol that she eagerly returned her smile. "This just arrived for you." She handed Amy the package.

Looking through the clear package, Amy could see it was a corsage of red roses. A note was attached that read, *Hope you can join us tonight. Carmen.* She smiled, knowing that she wouldn't miss this dinner now. She had so much to share with Tristan.

"Thank you so much! It's so nice that you can come and help your mom out."

"This was one of the hardest holidays for my mom after Dad passed away. But we didn't even know she wanted us to come until last year or so. Now, we come take her to a tea room in town, help with her dinner, and then we go watch chick flicks in her apartment."

"Sounds like a nice Valentine's Day."

"I think so. I better get back. The dinner crowd is going to start arriving soon." With that May headed back downstairs. Her comment made Amy glance at the clock. If she was going to make dinner with the Romeros she should start getting ready. Before she started getting ready, she sent a text to Tristan letting him know that she would be eating with them.

An hour later, she stood in front of the mirror putting the finishing touches on her lipstick. Her short, dark hair was shiny and in place. The black dress was both attractive and professional. The red roses gave her outfit a festive look. Her make-up was carefully done and she felt like she had the right look – both elegant and professional. She slipped on her heels, grabbed her sketchpad and headed down the stairs.

The downstairs was bustling, and Amy got her first experience at Carol's famous holiday celebrations. In the living room came the sound of a harpist. She stuck her head in and glanced around. Couples snacked on hors d'oeuvres set around the room and talked quietly. The roses from the field trip and from Carol's daughter were placed on the mantle. Amy smiled as she remembered her first idea of what Holliday Hotel would be like. She had pictured the room filled with cheap cardboard hearts and cupids. Instead, it was tasteful and exquisite.

Looking around she didn't see Tristan or Carmen. She stepped back into the entryway right as the door opened and the people she was looking for arrived. With a welcoming smile, she met them.

"I'm so glad you chose to join us," Carmen said as she greeted Amy with a kiss on her cheek.

"Thank you for inviting me and for the roses. They're lovely."

"You're very welcome." Carmen leaned on Amy's arm as they headed towards the dining room. Carol's daughter, May, met them at the entrance.

The room was nearly full. Amy had heard that reservations were made months in advance and only a limited number of guests were served. Each table was draped with a white tablecloth and had a bud vase with a single rose in it. China and crystal gleamed in the soft light. Tristan gave May their names and she led them immediately to a table in the corner.

"If people have reservations, why are there people in the living room waiting?"

"Some people arrive early to enjoy the hors d'oeuvres and music," Tristan explained. "I've heard that some come before their reservations at other restaurants to enjoy the atmosphere that Carol provides."

Libbie came and set some salads in front of each of them. She filled their goblets with water and asked if they wanted coffee, tea or cider as well. After getting their drink orders, she moved off to the kitchen. To make things easier, Carol only served one meal and everyone got the same thing. Since it was basically only her in the kitchen, this allowed her to prepare the exact amount of food and do a lot of the preparations beforehand. Libbie came back with their drinks and then went to help another guest.

"I'm glad Carol has help," Amy pointed out. "This would be a big undertaking on her own."

"At the beginning, I think she did do a lot of it on her own," Carmen said. "As her dinner became popular, she recognized that she needed help. So her daughters come to help, and she hires some teenagers as well."

With the salad completed, Libbie came by to take away the plates and put their dinners in front of them. Filet mignon was cooked perfectly and paired with new potatoes and roasted asparagus. A bread basket was put on the center of the table. "Everything is so wonderful! Does she make this same meal every year?" Amy asked.

"No, it's different every year, but it's always wonderful," Tristan explained. "Carol is very talented."

"I'm realizing that," Amy said with a smile. "I finally got the logo figured out by the way." She reached for the sketchpad, but Carmen placed her hand on top of it first.

"After dinner," she said. "Pleasure before business."

Amy laughed. "I think that's backwards, but I like it better."

They chatted through dinner, and Amy found herself sorry that she was leaving this place and these people who had become so dear to her. For someone who prided herself on her aloofness, she had become close friends awfully fast.

Soon dinner was replaced by a cheesecake drizzled with fudge and strawberry sauce. Amy enjoyed every bite of it although she did wonder how many calories she had consumed. Pushing that thought away, she decided that every last one was worth it.

"Now that we're finished, why don't you take me to enjoy the harpist. Then the two of you can conduct your business out on the porch," Carmen suggested.

Tristan helped his grandma to her feet and led her into the living room. He sat her in an empty armchair and made sure she was comfortable before leaving with Amy through the French doors onto the back porch. Amy was glad she had grabbed her coat before coming out. The backyard was crisscrossed with white lights, and heaters and fire pits were arranged around the yard. Couples strolled hand in hand or sat cuddled together on benches.

"I bet this would be lovely from my balcony." Amy knew that the view from her room was going to be one that stuck with her for a long time. She almost wished she could stay throughout the year so she could see it in all its different looks through the year.

"I'm sure it would," Tristan agreed.

Amy decided it was time to get down to business. "So I was on Google today, and it struck me that what was missing was the holidays. I didn't want to make it busy by putting all of the holidays around it, so I made several different ones." She handed him the sketchpad at the page where she began with New Year's. He studied each one carefully and she enjoyed seeing the pleasure on his face.

"This is perfect. It's simple, dignified, and lovely. It's the very reason I asked you to do the artwork for me."

Amy felt her face flush with pleasure. She didn't know why his praise meant so much to her. "I'm so glad I got it finished before I left."

"I wasn't too worried about it." Tristan handed her back the sketches. "Whenever it got done, it got done."

"You're very low key about this. Most of my clients are pushing me to get it done by a certain time."

Tristan shrugged. "I've never felt like it accomplished anything to push an artist to complete a project on a timeline. Usually it just got me bad artwork."

"I've definitely submitted some sub-par artwork because it had to be done by a certain time before." Amy sighed. "I hate to leave tomorrow."

Tristan's mouth twitched in a half-smile. "This from the woman who came to Willow Creek kicking and screaming."

Amy joined in his mirth. "I know, I know. But it's been so restful here. I've met some amazing people. I've seen that love exists." She paused and added in a lower voice, "I've talked with God."

Tristan looked at her quickly, his eyebrows raised. "You have?"

Amy nodded. "Do you think I'm weird?"

"Not at all. I'm just surprised. My grandma was sure that God was working on you though, so I shouldn't be surprised."

"Really?" For some reason the thought of Carmen seeing that God was working on her made her feel warm inside.

"Really. So what did you and God talk about?"

"He's been showing me what love is and that He is love. I've never experienced love before."

Tristan frowned. "Not even from your family?"

Amy shook her head. "My mom and dad had their own issues. They've both been married multiple times and had multiple divorces. They don't know what love is."

"A grandparent? Sibling?"

"My grandma I think loved me in a way, but she was aggravated at my mom for always leaving me with her. I heard her complaining about it, and that sort of stuck with me. I have half-siblings, but we aren't close." Amy looked over at Tristan. "By the time they came along, I had started keeping people at arm's length to avoid getting hurt."

Tristan put his arm around her shoulders and gave her a brotherly squeeze. "I'm so sorry."

"Maybe I had to see what love wasn't before God could teach me what it was." Amy stood up and walked over to the porch railing. With her back to the railing, she faced Tristan who remained seated on the bench. "I know He's real. I just don't know if I'm ready to take the leap of faith that I need to."

"It's not really a leap. It's more of a step of faith."

Amy's eyes widened. "That's what He said, too." Her voice was barely a whisper.

Tristan smiled and stood up. "See? It must be true." He joined her at the railing and leaned his forearms on the top. "I think there's more to it. You're afraid that God will let you down just like everyone else has."

Amy's heart beat fast. How could this man that she had only known a short time see through her so easily?

"He won't, you know." Tristan looked up at her. "He's never let me down."

"Just because He's never let you down, doesn't mean He won't let me down." Tears started to fill her eyes.

Tristan stood up and placed his hand on her shoulder. "It wasn't your fault. Your parents, your grandparents – they chose their path, and it wasn't because you were unlovable, or you were a disappointment. It was because they were only focused on themselves."

"I want to believe," she whispered, the tears began falling down her cheeks.

"I want you to believe, too, but I can't do it for you. You have to do it yourself." Tristan reached in his pocket and pulled out a packet of tissues. He handed one to Amy which she gratefully took.

For a long while, she stood at the railing and stared up at the stars. She could feel Tristan's gaze, but was thankful that he remained quiet.

I will never leave you or forsake you.

Amy smiled softly. God was back. "Does the Bible say something about God not leaving His people?"

"Sure. Hebrews 13:5 says, 'I will never leave you nor forsake you.'" Tristan watched her for a moment. "Are you ready?" She nodded enthusiastically. Oh, yes! She was ready. She needed Someone in her life who would always be there for her. Tristan's smile was broad as he took her hand and led her over to the bench. Sitting down, he kept her hand clasped in his own. "Why don't you just tell Him what you're feeling?"

Amy bowed her head like she'd seen others do. "Lord, I'm scared, but You know that. I know I don't deserve Your love, yet You give it to me anyway. I'm sorry for all the wrong things I've done. Please forgive me. Most of all, Lord, I believe. I believe that You came, died and rose again, and paid the penalty I deserved. Thank You for Your love. Help me as I go home to stay faithful to You." She raised her head, then quickly bowed it again as she remembered how she was supposed to end a prayer. "Amen."

Tristan squeezed her hands, joy clearly expressed on his face. "This is the best Valentine's Day ever!"

Amy's smile was so broad her cheeks hurt. "Absolutely! I feel – I don't know how to describe it – clean, I guess."

"You are clean. You'll never be alone again. I'm very grateful for that. I hated to have you go back home all alone."

"That will be a change." Amy hesitated for a moment, not sure if she should ask the question on her mind. Taking a deep breath, she asked, "Does God always talk to people like He's been talking to me? Like a thought in my head that I know isn't mine?"

"Not always. A lot of times, He'll speak through the Bible, or another believer. Sometimes He simply talks through the situation – like not letting you get a job He doesn't want you to have. Things like that."

"So I shouldn't expect to hear Him talk to me all the time." Amy felt disappointed. How was she going to know He was still there?

"The best thing to do is get a Bible and read it. Pray every day. Join a church. Those will help you know that God is still there, and He's still talking to you."

Amy nodded. Impulsively, she gave Tristan a hug. "I'm going to miss you."

His arms tightened around her. "I'm going to miss you, too. But you need to know that I'm here for you as well. Always."

Amy pulled back. "You may regret telling me that. I may harass you incessantly."

"Somehow I doubt that you could bother me too much." There was a look in Tristan's eyes that Amy couldn't decipher. It was as if he was questioning something, or maybe as if he had just come to a realization.

Amy stood up. "I should get packing, and you should probably get Carmen home."

"Yeah, I definitely should go home now. Get my grandma first, obviously." His voice sounded strained as well.

Amy gave him one more hug. "Thanks for everything Tristan." Then she was gone.

25

Tristan was quiet on the way home. He had hoped that Carmen would just think he was tired, but there was no such luck. As soon as they got inside, she began to question him.

"What happened out on the porch?"

"What do you mean?" Tristan led her over to her bedroom, knowing that she would want to go to bed soon.

"I mean that when you came back in you were more introspective than normal. Something happened. What was it?" Carmen sat on the edge of her bed while Tristan got out her nightgown.

"She showed me her designs which were fantastic. She hit just the right balance. Then we began talking about her visit here, and she introduced God to the conversation. After a little bit, she decided that she was ready to believe."

Carmen clasped her hands together. "Oh, thank You, Lord!" Her eyes lifted to the ceiling. "You've answered my prayers. Thank You!"

Tristan smiled. "You took to Amy right away, didn't you?"

"I did. There was something about her that made me want to wrap her in my arms and make everything all better." Carmen's eyes sparkled. "The first part of my prayer came true. Now I just need to see if the second one will."

Tristan averted his gaze and became busy putting Carmen's jewelry away. "What was the second prayer?" Not that he needed the reminder. He just didn't want her to know that he remembered.

Carmen scoffed. "You know what I'm talking about. I think she's the girl for you."

"She's leaving tomorrow," he reminded her. "It's not likely

that anything will come from it. Besides I have you. I don't need another girl." He tenderly kissed her forehead.

"I won't be around forever. It'd be nice for me to leave here knowing that you won't be alone."

"God will bring me a wife in His time. Not in yours or mine. When it happens, I'll be happy to share my joy with you, but until then, this is a waste of time."

Carmen rubbed her foot as she stared at her grandson. "Okay," she finally said. "I won't say a word more."

"Thank you." Tristan headed towards the door. "Do you have everything you need?"

"We should get her a Bible."

"What?"

"Amy. She needs a Bible. You should go get one tomorrow and give it to her before she leaves."

Tristan's face softened. "That's a great idea, Grandma. I'll be sure to do that. Now do you have everything you need?" Carmen assured him that she would be fine for the night. Tristan closed the door, then did his nightly routine before heading to his own bedroom next door to Carmen's.

As he lay in bed, his mind went over and over the events of that evening. Amy's face had positively glowed after she had prayed. She had always been lovely, but in that moment she was absolutely beautiful. Something had changed not only in her, but in him as well. Suddenly, she wasn't a woman who was a business associate, but now she was a fellow believer. The taboo that was on her was lifted, and when she hugged him, he was very aware that he no longer had to keep her at a distance.

It was what happened during the hug that stunned him though. God rarely spoke to him clearly. Usually it was through a sermon, or his devotions, or one of the ways he had described to Amy earlier that night. But in that moment, he had heard, *This is your bride.* It had absolutely stunned him. Surely it was simply because he was caught up in the moment. It couldn't be real.

Yet when he had pulled back and looked at her, he felt a certainty that one day she would be his wife. He hoped that he had finished their conversation in an understandable manner, but from the way she looked at him, he had a feeling that there was something strange about his behavior.

He ran his hand over his face and turned onto his side. "Lord," he prayed quietly, "I don't know if what I thought was from you, or from my own selfish desires. Maybe I've just been lonely, too, or maybe Grandma's prayers have gotten to me. The good thing is that I have to give it to You, because she won't be here. If You do want Amy to be my wife, You're going to have to work it out, because I don't see a way for it to work." Feeling better after putting it in God's hand, Tristan sighed, and fell asleep.

******

The next morning Tristan got breakfast for Carmen and then left her to run to the bookstore. She had reminded him of the Bible first thing when she woke up and not knowing how late Amy planned to stay before checking out, Tristan decided that he should get going right away. Worst case scenario, he would ship it to her, but he would much rather give it to her in person if he could.

As he walked into Holliday Hotel, Amy was coming down the stairs. It reminded him of the first time he saw her. Even then he had thought she was beautiful, but now with the voice he heard in his head last night, he saw her in a new light. Maybe it was his imagination, but there seemed to be a new glow about her.

The smile that lit her face when she saw Tristan was vastly different from the haughty look she wore when they first met. She was a changed person. Tristan knew that the source of her change went deep. With God in her life, she had a new focus, a new purpose, and a new life.

"I'm so glad that I get to see you before I leave," she said as she reached the bottom of the stairs.

"Yeah, me, too. I wanted to give you something." Tristan held out the package that he had gift wrapped at the bookstore.

"I was going to grab some breakfast. Do you want to join me?"

"That would be nice." Together they went into the dining room.

Amy went over to the buffet and began to fill her plate with a hash brown casserole, fruit, and sausage. She filled a cup with orange juice and found a table. Tristan only grabbed a mug of coffee since he'd already eaten with his grandma.

"Have you told Carol about what happened last night?" Tristan took a sip of his coffee.

"No, I haven't seen her. She was a little busy when I came in, finishing up with her Valentine crowd. Then I didn't want to intrude on her time with her daughters." Amy took a bite of her breakfast. "Besides, I sort of wanted to be alone last night. It was all kind of new to me."

"I can understand that." Tristan nudged the gift. "Why don't you open up your gift? It's from both my grandma and me."

Amy eagerly began to unwrap the gift. It was only then that Tristan really noticed the paper. It was red with white hearts covering it. He smiled to himself thinking about how fitting it was. Not only had she been saved on Valentine's Day, but the blood of Jesus had washed her heart white as snow.

"My own Bible." She tenderly ran her hand over the cover. "Thank you so much!"

"We figured it would be something that you could use."

Amy chuckled. "When I came here, the last thing I would have wanted was a Bible. Now it's the best gift I could receive."

"It's amazing how things change when you believe in God."

Carol came in carrying a tray of muffins. Her face lit up when she saw Tristan and Amy. After depositing the muffins on the buffet, she joined the two of them. "It's so good to see the two of you. I didn't see you hardly at all last evening. I was so busy!"

"I came by to give Amy a gift before she left, and she invited me to join her for breakfast."

"I'm going to miss you when you leave," Carol stated. "You've become very special to me."

"I didn't think that I would miss this place when I first arrived. I was counting down to when I could leave, but now I don't know how I'm going to leave." Amy blinked hard and took a sip of her orange juice to compose herself. "You guys have become my friends in such a short amount of time."

"I know I've said it before, but I have lots of guests come and go who just pass through my life and don't leave any impact on it. But I cherish the ones who visit, and my life is changed because of it."

"My life was certainly changed because of staying here." Amy looked at Tristan nervously. He nodded encouragement. "Last night, I decided that it was time to believe in God."

Carol shot out of her chair, tipping it over in her excitement with a crash. She rushed around the table and pulled Amy into a big hug. "That's the best news I could have gotten this morning! I'm so happy!"

Amy laughed happily. "I feel so different. Life seems brighter somehow. Tristan and Carmen got me a Bible as a going away present."

Carol admired the gift and resumed her seat next to Tristan. "Make sure you find a church when you get back home. I'll ask Pastor Aaron if he knows of any good ones, and I'll let you know."

"That would be great."

"And don't believe everything you hear. Look it up in the Bible, and study it for yourself. There are plenty of wolves in sheep's clothing out there," Carol warned. She wrung her hands. "Oh, now I hate for you to leave even more."

"Me, too. I have a feeling I'll be back though," Amy said with a smile. "There's something about this place that I love. After last night, it's become even more special to me."

"And we'll keep in touch," Tristan added. "With email, text, and phone calls, we can talk everyday if we wanted."

"I'd like that," Amy agreed. "Oh, I almost forgot. I finally finished the logo, Carol! I have it up in my room, but I'll make sure you see it before I leave."

"I don't know if I'm pleased that it's done or not," Carol stated. "If it wasn't done, it would at least give me an excuse to contact you, and maybe force you to visit again soon."

Amy stood up and put her arm around Carol. "You don't need an excuse to contact me, and I can visit without being forced into it." She looked around the dining room almost wistfully. "I should go finish packing."

Tristan seemed reluctant to part. "Would you like some help?"

"I don't need any help, but I wouldn't mind the company," Amy admitted. Carol quietly went back to work, and the couple headed up the stairs.

Tristan whistled as he entered the room. "I never realized what a nice suite this was."

"I've been more than comfortable," Amy said with a smile. "I'll just be a minute." She went into the bedroom, and Tristan sat on the couch to wait for her. Picking up the sketchpad off the end table, he started flipping through the sketches. He smiled at her logo designs, thankful that she had finally found something that worked. He nearly laughed out loud at her failed attempts. Pausing, he studied a drawing of the lake. It must be from her balcony. She had mentioned how much she liked that view. A solitary woman stood by the edge of the icy water, and Tristan somehow knew it was Amy. She looked cold, isolated, and lonely.

Amy came back in dragging her suitcase behind her. "I think I've got just about everything from there." She stopped as she saw what he was looking at. Suddenly Tristan felt as if he was caught reading her middle school diary. "You found my sketchpad."

"Sorry. I was just – sorry." He didn't even know what excuse, or explanation to give.

"It's fine. I don't think there's anything in there that you couldn't see. I was just surprised you'd even be interested." Amy came over and joined him on the couch.

He pointed to the woman in the drawing. "Is that you?" She nodded. "You look lonely."

"I was lonely and hid it behind independence." She smiled up at him. "But I don't ever have to be lonely again."

"That's right. You'll always have Someone with you now." He had never relished a promise of God for someone else more than in that moment. To know that as Amy went back to her job, her apartment, her old life that God would be with her every step of the way comforted him as well. He wished he could keep her close, to help her as she went on her new journey in life, to get to know her on a personal level, but knowing that she now had Jesus made it a much easier separation. He went to hand the sketchpad to her, but it dropped from his grasp and fell to the floor. As he bent to pick it up, he paused. The pages had flipped to a sketch of his own face. It was well done, and he felt that it was a flattering portrait as well. He looked up at her to see and found that she was blushing and looking at him with a mixture of embarrassment and fear.

"I guess there was one picture I didn't really want you to see," she finally said in a low voice.

He picked up the pad, carefully closed it, and handed it to her. "It was very good. I think you were a little too generous and made me look too nice."

"I just drew what I saw. Actually when I did that I wasn't even thinking, my fingers just did what they wanted while my mind was occupied with other matters. So I guess that's how you look in my mind's eye."

Tristan adjusted his glasses awkwardly. "Well, that's – nice."

Amy put the sketchpad in her bag and began to put away her laptop as well. Suddenly she wheeled around. "Do you want it? The picture I mean."

"Uh, no. I don't need to stare at a more handsome version of myself every day." He smiled. "But if you want to give me the sketch of you by the lake, I wouldn't mind having that." He knew it was brave to ask an artist for one of their pieces. He watched the indecision on her face and could tell the instant she made up her mind about it.

"No. That's how I was, not who I am now. But I'll give you something later."

He wondered what she had in mind, but before he could ask anything else she moved in front of the needlework. "I wish I could take this with me," she said wistfully. He came and stood behind her. He understood her desire to take it with her. The verses had come to mean something very special to her. Before he could say anything though, she gasped and darted to her purse. Pulling out her phone, she took a picture of the verses. "Now I have them forever."

Tristan chuckled. "That's a brilliant solution."

Amy glanced around the room one more time, but didn't see any stray articles that belonged to her. "Want to see my view? I have to go out one more time before I leave."

Tristan followed her out and then stood in awe. No wonder she liked sitting out here. It was incredible. She leaned against the railing. "Even with the snow trampled from all the guests last night, it's lovely," she pointed out.

"It certainly is." Tristan came and stood next to her. "No wonder Carol picked this to be the honeymoon suite. It'd be the perfect place to sit and relax with a loved one. It feels private, and it's beautiful."

"Carol's done such a great job with this place. It's been such a pleasure to get to help her with it even a little bit." Amy pushed away from the rail. "As much as I hate to leave, I really need to get on the road."

Tristan followed her back inside and grabbed her suitcase as she took her bag and purse. With one last glance around the room, she closed the door behind her. Tristan glanced back at the closed door. *You'll both be back.* He stifled a gasp and turned forward. What was going on with him?

Carol was at the front desk helping another guest check out when they got down the stairs. Tristan set the suitcase near the door, and then began to pace the entryway. Something was happening, and he wasn't completely sure he liked it.

The guests left, and Tristan opened the door for them. He hoped he didn't seem as distracted as he was. He heard the two women chatting and knew it would be time for him to tell Amy farewell soon.

How is she going to be my wife when we won't be near each other? This is ridiculous!

As ridiculous as a virgin giving birth or a dead man coming to life? Trust Me.

Tristan stared out the window holding his breath. Had that just happened?

"These are wonderful!" Carol's exclamation pierced his thoughts. He turned to find her studying the logos that Amy had developed. "You're right. They give it just the right touch."

"I'm so glad you like them. I'll get them finished up when I get home and send them to Tristan." Amy beamed under Carol's praise. She took the pad back and flipped to a page. Pulling it out, she handed it to Carol. "I want you to have this. It's not much, but I wanted to thank you for being patient with me, and talking with me when I really needed someone to talk to. You were one of the people who showed me what real love looks like, and I know now it's because you've experience God's love and so it comes through you."

Carol's eyes misted as she looked at the picture. Holliday Hotel sat in the middle of the page with snow covering the ground around it. A woman stood on the porch, her hand lifted as if waving, and a broad smile on her welcoming face. Carol looked at her likeness much like Tristan felt he had looked at his own. "It's beautiful. Thank you." Carol came around the desk and threw her arms around Amy. "Keep in touch. I'm going to miss you."

"I will absolutely keep in touch." Amy squeezed Carol tightly. Tristan wondered how a woman who by her own admission had never received love could demonstrate it so wonderfully. Maybe it was because she now had God's love reflecting from her.

Amy grabbed her bags and headed out the door. Tristan followed behind with her suitcase. After loading it into her trunk, he turned to find her soaking in the view of Holliday Hotel one last time. He put his hands on her shoulders. "You'll be back."

"I know," she said with a tear slipping down one cheek. "But I'll miss it while I'm gone." She turned and buried her face in his chest. He held her tightly and marveled at how natural and right it felt to hold her. "I'm going to miss you, too," she whispered.

On impulse, he kissed the top of her head. "Same here," he said almost gruffly. "Just promise that you won't forget me."

"I could never forget you." Amy's smile up at him was radiant. "You helped show me Christ, and you were with me when I gave Him my life. You'll always be someone who is special to me." She reached up and kissed his cheek in a sisterly fashion. "Good-bye, Tristan." And with that she was gone.

Tristan told himself that a sisterly kiss shouldn't affect his heart rate so much. He justified that it had been a long time since he'd been out on a date since his grandma needed him. Still his heart raced as he watched her tail lights disappear. He trudged back through the snow to the hotel, thinking that somehow the sky seemed to be more overcast all of a sudden. When he opened the door, he saw Carol wiping her eyes.

"Oh good! You came back. Let's go eat cookies!" Tristan laughed, but agreed that cookies seemed to be the best solution right now.

26

It was dark by the time Amy arrived home. She was weary as she entered her apartment, dragging her suitcase behind her. Leaving Willow Creek had been even more difficult than she had anticipated. Carol had become a mother figure to her, and Tristan had become – she had spent the better part of her journey home to trying to figure that out. A friend? A brother? Something more? All she knew was that she felt safe in his arms, and when she was with him she somehow felt a mixture of contentment and excitement. It was the strangest thing.

She collapsed on her couch not bothering to remove her coat or shoes, or even turn on a light. Too exhausted to do anything more than absolutely necessary. Putting her arm over her eyes, she sighed deeply.

And then her phone rang. Groaning, she fished it out of her purse and saw her sister, Angela's number. "Hey, Ang," she said stifling a yawn. "What's going on?"

"It's Dad. He's in the hospital."

Amy sat straight up, immediately wide awake. "What? Why? What happened?" Sure, she'd never been close to her dad, but he was still her dad. He was so healthy and strong. It didn't seem right that he was in the hospital.

"He collapsed. They're not sure why." Angela sobbed. "Amy, they're saying it was a possible overdose, that he might have tried to harm himself."

Amy jumped off the couch. "Where are you?" After Angela gave her all the details, Amy grabbed her purse and jumped back in the car that she had been so happy to get out of. She wasn't sure if her dad would be glad to see her or not, but Angela needed her.

Angela sat in the waiting room, her hands were clenched together, eyes were closed, and her mouth was moving silently. Amy instinctively knew that she was praying. She moved near her half-sister and sat in the empty chair next to her. Angela looked up then and threw her arms around Amy sobbing on her shoulder. "I'm so glad you came! April said that Dad wouldn't visit her when she had her appendectomy, and Craig just laughed and said something about karma."

"You are by far the most forgiving and compassionate of all of us," Amy pointed out. "All of us have emotional scars from Dad, but you love him anyway."

Angela looked up questioningly. "Of course. No matter what he's done, he's still my dad."

Amy smiled, but said nothing. Angela couldn't understand why anyone wouldn't love their own father. She had a tender heart which Amy guessed must have been inherited from Ruthie, because heaven knew Larry had a heart of stone and ice.

Except maybe he wasn't as hard-hearted as she had thought. Maybe something had finally penetrated his heart. Why else would he do this to himself?

"So tell me everything you know," Amy said firmly. She needed Angela to pull herself together, and Amy had found in the past that being tough was a good way to achieve that.

"He was supposed to meet me for dinner, but he didn't show. I thought that maybe he had forgotten so I went to his house. He's staying in a cheap rental home right now until the divorce is final. I let myself in since sometimes Dad's not – himself when I go visit."

"In other words, Dad's been drinking again." Amy rolled her eyes. "Go on."

"He was laying on the floor in the living room. His breath was shallow and his pulse was faint so I called 9-1-1." She paused. "There was a note," she added softly.

"Oh man, Ang! You found him? I'm so sorry." Amy pulled her little sister closer. "What did the note say?"

Angela reached in her pocket and pulled out a wadded up piece of paper. "I didn't even remember that I was clutching it when the paramedics came. I stuck it in my pocket when I discovered it was still in my hand," she explained.

Amy opened the paper and read the words her father had written. "I know there will be few tears shed when I'm found. I've reaped what I've sown. I have no one left. Tell my children I'm sorry I wasn't a better dad. I should have tried harder." Amy looked up at Angela. "He knew he was having dinner with you tonight, and yet he could say he had no one left?"

Angela shook her head. "I should have checked on him more often. I knew he wasn't doing well since the divorce."

Amy bit back a sarcastic remark and took a breath. "Honey, this isn't your fault. Dad made his choices."

"Did you check on him after I talked to you?" The question was innocent, without accusation. Amy froze. With everything else going on, she had completely forgotten the conversation she had with Angela while at Willow Creek.

"Angela, I'm so sorry. I completely forgot." Angela nodded sadly, but Amy could tell that she was hurting even more. "Maybe things would have been different if I had called him sooner, but I think things happened the way they were supposed to."

"How can you say that?" Tears slid down Angela's cheeks. "Are you just trying to alleviate your conscience? Make yourself feel better?"

Amy pulled her sister close once more. Squeezing her eyes shut tight, she prayed for the first time since she became a Christian. *Lord, I don't know how to handle this. Could You please help me?* A peace came over Amy that she couldn't explain. "I know you believe in God, but you don't know that now I do, too. While I was on my trip, God put some people in my life that demonstrated His love. I could feel God pulling me to Him. I fought it, believe me! I didn't want Him, but I found Him irresistible. I don't know what would have happened if I had taken time to call Dad, but I know that I can't regret a single moment of my trip, because through it, I came to Christ."

Angela studied her sister's face for a long moment then squeezed her so tightly Amy wondered if her ribs would crack. "I thought there was something different about you. I just couldn't figure out what it was. I'm so happy."

A woman in scrubs came into the waiting room at that point and heard the last sentence that Angela had said. She looked confused for a moment. "Did someone already come talk to you? You already know that your father is out of danger and awake?"

The women stood to their feet and shook their heads. "No, we were talking about something else. Can we go see him?" Amy asked.

"Follow me." The woman led them to a room and then discreetly left.

Amy and Angela slowly went into the room not knowing what to expect. Larry was sitting up and staring at the wall. His face was completely emotionless in a way that frightened Amy. Her dad had always been full of spirit, but now he looked broken. His face had new lines that hadn't been there the last time she had seen him, his hair was grayer, and he suddenly seemed very old.

Angela immediately went to her dad's side and clasped his hand in her own. "Daddy, you scared us! I'm so glad you're going to be okay." She rested her head on his shoulder, but he didn't move or respond.

Amy stepped to the foot of the bed. Larry's face changed when he saw his oldest daughter. His eyes widened and his face softened slightly. "You came?" His voice was raspy and low.

Eyes damp with tears, Amy nodded. "I love you, Dad." The words surprised her as much as they did Larry, but what shocked her even more was knowing that it was true. Somehow in this process, she had forgiven her dad without even intending to. Maybe it was because God had forgiven her so much or maybe it was knowing that she came close to missing the opportunity to have a relationship with him.

Tears rolled down Larry's cheeks and he shook his head violently. "No, you can't possibly love me."

Amy went to his other side and placed her hand on his shoulder. "You're my father. You certainly weren't perfect, but you're the only one I have. Do you think that your death wouldn't have affected me?"

Larry's shoulders heaved as he began to sob. "My death would have been better for everyone. I've done nothing in my life except cause pain. I didn't realize how bad it felt until my wife left me. After the divorce, I sat at home and kept thinking about how my actions affected everyone in my life. You all would have been so much better without me."

"Without you, none of us would be here," Angela pointed out softly. "You've made mistakes. We all have. But maybe instead of it being the end, it should be a new beginning."

Amy's heart pounded. She knew what she needed to say, but it scared her. "I recently made a new beginning. I realized that I needed God, and He's changed my life."

Larry sniffed. "God." He spit the word out derisively. "That's just a fairy tale. I need reality."

Amy looked pointedly around the hospital room. "This is reality. You nearly died, and now you're stuck here for a while. Of your four children, two came when you needed them most."

"Amy," Angela said with a sound of warning. "I'm not sure that's helpful."

"You've had four failed marriages and more affairs than we will probably ever know. And none of that has made you happy, none of that has satisfied. You want reality? You're living it. And it's messy and ugly and sad."

"Amy, stop!" Angela cried.

"Now for the 'fairy tale'. There is a God, and He's so much bigger and better than you can imagine. He loves you even though He knows every bad thing you've done, every mean word that came out of your mouth, and every evil thought that has crossed your mind. He loves you so much that He took the death penalty you deserved, and He's offering you life." Amy grabbed Larry's hand. "Reality has given you death. God is offering you life. And He's more real than anything this world can give. The world has offered you fairy tales. It's told you that you would be happy if you had that woman. That person would finally satisfy you. The next drink would be what you needed. Has it been what it told you it would be? No. It's all been lies."

"Dad, Amy's right," Angela added. "You've gone through life believing the next woman, the next drink, the next adventure would be everything you needed to be satisfied. But all it did was leave you depressed and facing death. God wants to satisfy you in a way that nothing on earth can. All you have to do is believe."

Larry looked back and forth between his two daughters. Finally his gaze found Amy's. "I expected this from her." He nodded in Angela's direction. "But what happened to you? You were my strong one. You never needed anyone or anything."

Amy's eyes filled with tears. "Except I did. I was so lonely, and I masked it with independence. I learned young that people hurt you, abandon you, and use you, so I determined to never rely on anyone, but myself. It was what I felt I had to do. But then I realized that while people might let me down, God never would. I didn't have to be alone anymore."

"I did that to you, didn't I?" Larry reached out his hand and cupped Amy's cheek. "I made you a lonely person."

"You weren't the only one," Amy whispered as she pressed her face into her father's hand. She couldn't remember the last time Larry had shown any type of affection for her.

He turned to Angela. "What about you? What turned you to God?"

Angela's face whitened, and she seemed scared to answer. Taking a deep breath, she finally said, "I needed a Father I could trust."

Larry nodded and closed his eyes. "See. You both would have been better off without me."

"But we're not without you. You are a big part of our lives, and to lose you would be painful, too," Amy explained. "While you're alive, it's not too late. You can change. You can be the father, the man, the husband that you want to be, but once you're dead, it's over."

"You can still choose God now," Angela added, "but it's an offer only available in this life. God's given you another chance by saving you now. Will you accept Him?"

Larry was silent so long the girls wondered if he'd fallen asleep. "I have nothing left to lose," he finally said.

"And everything to gain," Angela stated.

"I don't know how to do – this." He gestured vaguely.

"Just pray, talk to God like you would talk to us," Angela explained. "Tell Him that you know you've sinned and that you're sorry, and then let Him know that you believe."

"That's what I did," Amy added, "and I've never felt better in my entire life."

Larry looked between his two daughters. Each of them clasped his hand in their own. Amy found herself holding her breath as she waited for her dad to make a decision. Finally, he closed his eyes and with a voice full of unshed tears began to pray. "Dear God, I've made a mess of my life. I don't even feel like I should be able to come to You, but my daughters say that I can. I'm sorry for everything I've done. Could you ever forgive me? I believe that You can save me. Please help me. Change me. Amen." He looked up at his daughters with wonder shining in his eyes. "I feel – clean."

Amy laughed. "Isn't it wonderful?"

"The Bible says that you're a new creation. You can start fresh now," Angela pointed out.

"I want to start with the two of you." He turned to Amy first. "I can't even count the number of things that I need to ask you to forgive me for. I've never been the dad you needed or deserved. I'm sure you heard things that a child shouldn't have to hear. I'm sorry for all I've done to hurt you."

Tears ran down her cheek and splashed onto Larry's hand. "I forgive you," she whispered.

He turned to Angela. "You were my soft-hearted one, and the only one that I'm certain has forgiven me even though I've never asked for it. But it's time for me to apologize. I'm sorry for all I put you through. Thank you for not giving up on me."

"It's okay. I love you, Daddy." Angela's face was beaming through her tears. She finally had what she'd always wanted.

"I love you, too," he answered, causing her to break down

completely and sob on his shoulder.

Amy wasn't sure she'd heard her dad proclaim love to anyone. Of all the children, Angela was the one who had craved it the most. Amy was absolutely astounded. What were the chances that only one day after she had given her life to Christ, her dad of all people would do the same?

"Dad, I'm so glad you made this decision, but some friends of mine told me that it's not over. You need to find a church and read the Bible so you can know what this new life is all about."

"Why don't you guys come to church with me?" Angela was on the very edge of her chair in excitement. "I'd love to have you with me."

"Sure, honey. If you're sure you'd like to have me there."

"I would love it." Angela's face softened as she looked at her father's face.

"I'd like to come, too," Amy said. "We'll make it a family event."

"And then we can have lunch together." The eagerness on Angela's face nearly broke Amy's heart. Angela had been attending church alone since she was a child, getting rides from friends or from the church van. She had probably watched her friends sit with their parents and siblings all her life and longed for the same thing. "Oh, this is such an awesome answer to prayer!"

27

The phone rang the moment Amy stepped out of the hospital doors. Recognizing Tristan's number, she answered immediately.

"You haven't answered my texts so I decided to call," he explained. "I wanted to make sure you made it home safely."

"I'm so sorry. I got home and immediately found out my dad was in the hospital so I've been there. I've been ignoring my phone." Amy climbed into her car to get out of the wind, but didn't start it yet.

"I'm so sorry to hear about your dad. Is he going to be okay?" Even over the phone Amy could hear the genuine concern in Tristan's voice, and it made her smile.

"Yeah, he's going to be better than he's ever been. He made a decision to believe in Jesus tonight." Saying it out loud made Amy want to laugh for joy. She would have never guessed that would be the outcome of his trip to the hospital.

"That's fantastic! What happened?"

"I don't know how much I told you about my childhood, but my dad has always been the love 'em and leave 'em type." She thought for a moment. "And a 'love the one your with' type. So he's been in and out of marriages, and relationships my whole life. But while I was in Willow Creek, his latest wife left him, and he found out that she had been unfaithful. It got him thinking about his life, and he was in a state of depression. He took too many pills and ended up in the hospital. My half-sister, who is also a Christian, and I talked to him, and he gave his life to Christ."

"Wow. That's incredible! It's so great that God was working on both of you at the same time. Now you can start your Christian walk together."

"We're going to church with Angela on Sunday, and she is positively beside herself with excitement." Amy couldn't wipe the smile off her face. She was so blessed.

"I'm sure. She's probably been praying for that for a long time."

"I know she has," Amy answered softly. "Tristan, I'm sitting in the hospital parking lot right now. Can I call you back when I get home?"

"You don't have to do that. I just wanted to make sure you made it home safely." He hesitated. "If you want to call me back though, you can. I like talking to you."

For some reason, his simple statement made her heart race. "Okay. I'll call you back in a little bit."

The drive home passed in a flash with her mind whirling. It was hard to believe that only that morning she had been in Willow Creek having breakfast with Tristan and Carol. She had received her first Bible. Her exhaustion had been removed by the news about her dad, and then she was amazed at his transformation. It had been a memorable and difficult day. She should feel completely wiped out, but instead, felt energized.

Her mind rushed back to her parting with Tristan. There had been something different then, something she couldn't yet describe. Or maybe that she wasn't yet ready to put a name to. It had occurred to her that of her three friends in Willow Creek, Tristan was the one that she would miss the most. And now her heart fluttered with anticipation of calling him and talking to him when she got home. She almost felt like a teenager with her first crush.

She slammed on her brakes at the thought. Looking in the rearview mirror, she gave thanks that no one had been behind her. Pulling into her apartment's parking lot, she sat in the space for a little while. What good was an attraction to a man who lived so far away? No, this wasn't attraction, it was gratitude. She was thankful that he had helped guide her to Christ. That was all. There was no other reason for her heart to feel so light.

Still she had barely gotten inside her apartment when she dialed Tristan's number, and the sound of his voice when he answered made her heart pick up its pace once again.

"You're going to be on cloud nine for a while," he told her. "I know I'm still excited about your decision last night! But to have your father join you so shortly afterward has got to be amazing."

"It is. I don't know who was happier; me, Angela, or him." Amy curled up in her favorite chair. "He went from this desperate, heart-sick man to a joyful, new being. Was that what it was like when I made my decision last night?"

Tristan cleared his throat. "There was definitely a change – in a completely different and unexpected way." Amy felt like there was something deeper than his words, but wasn't sure if she was ready to know what it was. "You weren't desperate though. It was more like you were exhausted, tired of running from God, tired of fighting Him. When you gave your life to Him it was like you were re-energized. You had new life."

"That seems right. I couldn't believe how different I felt, but I couldn't really put my finger on what it was that had changed."

"Carol and my grandma are excited, too. Can I tell them about your dad?"

"Of course. I'm sure we'll need your prayers, too. After all, we both have so much to learn, and Dad has a lot of bridges to mend. I'm not sure my other half-siblings will be as willing to forgive as Angela and I were."

"It's hard when there's been a lot of hurt. Sometimes it feels like if we forgive them we're setting ourselves up to be hurt all over again. I wouldn't be surprised if they were skeptical that this 'new dad' was going to last."

Amy leaned her head against the chair. "I know. I probably would have been, too, if I hadn't experienced the same change in my own life. I know it's real."

"You've had a long day. Are you going into work tomorrow?"

"No, I'm waiting until Monday, but you're right. It has been a long day."

"I'll let you go then. Thanks for calling me back. We'll keep you and your family in our prayers."

"Thank you. We're going to need it."

28

Sunday morning was chilly, but sunny. Amy woke up with a sense of excitement that she hadn't expected to feel. She got ready with a spring in her step ready for her first visit to church as a new believer. It was even better going with her half-sister and father. Her father! She was still amazed at his transformation.

Angela was waiting outside the church for her, anticipation visibly evident on her smiling face. She ran up to Amy and embraced her tightly. "I have wanted this for so long. I can't wait to show you around."

"I didn't think I would be so excited to be here, but I'm really looking forward to it."

Amy didn't think Angela's face could get any brighter, but it did when she saw their dad walking up. "Daddy!" She ran up and gave him a big hug as well. Then with Amy on one side and Larry on the other, she marched them proudly into the church building and then to a pew. She introduced them to a few of the people around her, and Amy could tell by the surprised looks on their faces that they had heard about them.

One lady when she heard who they were quickly wrapped Amy up in a warm hug and with tears running down her cheeks gushed, "Oh, we've been praying for you for so long!"

"Thank you," was all Amy could think to say.

Larry looked at the woman quizzically. "You've been praying for us? What have you been praying for?"

"That the Lord would draw you to Him and save you," she said cheerfully. "Angela has wanted her family to come to Christ for so long. Now we'll pray that since two of you have come to Him that the rest of the family will follow." She headed back to her own pew, but Larry sat down with a thoughtful expression on his face.

"What are you thinking about?" Angela asked, studying Larry's face.

"I didn't know that this was an answer to prayer for people who have never met us. I sort of knew that you were praying for me, but I never expected strangers to care."

Amy really hadn't thought about that either. It seemed odd that people who had never met her would care enough to pray for her and rejoice in her salvation.

"We're family," Angela explained to her dad. "We pray for each other's burdens whether we've met those involved or not. We care about each other, because we love each other."

Amy looked at Angela. Love was apparently a common thing for Christians. "With an unconditional love?"

"Well, that's the goal. I'm afraid that sometimes our humanness gets in the way, and we don't always demonstrate God's love. But we're only capable of showing that kind of love, because of the Spirit in us." Angela put her hand on Amy's. "I don't want you to be disillusioned when you discover that Christians make mistakes, too. We still sin, although we should be trying to be more like Jesus every day. Don't think that life will be all sunshine and rainbows now that you're a Christian."

Amy nodded, but the service began and ended their conversation. Angela's church was different from Carol's. It was bigger, louder, and more modern, yet when the pastor got up to preach there was a familiarity in the way he explained the Scriptures. Amy remembered how the last time she'd been in church she had felt like God was speaking directly to her, and how she had been fighting Him. Now, she listened eagerly, with her Bible in front of her and took notes. She was attentively soaking in every word.

Down the pew a little ways Amy could see her dad eagerly leaning forward as if straining to catch every syllable before it fell to the ground. He also had a brand new Bible on his lap, a gift from Angela.

When the service ended, both Larry and Amy sat for a second

longer than everyone else almost reluctant to leave. Angela seemed ready to burst with joy. Amy was certain that if her sister had any doubts about the sincerity of their decisions, she was fully convinced now.

They left the church together and decided quickly on a restaurant to eat at before separating. As they sat down to eat together, Amy couldn't help but marvel at the change a week made. Last week she was in Willow Creek, sitting next to Carol, but pushing away from God as hard as she could. Her sister was someone whom she kept at a distance, and her father was someone she came close to hating. Now she was eager to know God better and eating lunch with her estranged family members.

As if she could read Amy's thoughts, Angela said, "I can't believe you're both here." She looked at them happily. "This has been the best day of my life."

"It's a little unreal to me, too," Larry admitted. "I really have wanted a better relationship with my children. I just didn't know how to do it. The past few years I've been particularly aware that I was getting older and all of you guys were grown or close to it. I was afraid it was too late." He drummed his fingers on the table. "It may still be too late for my chances with April and Craig."

"Have you talked to them?" Angela asked.

"I left messages for both of them, but I haven't heard from either one. I wouldn't be surprised if they both deleted them without listening to it." Their food arrived and they took a moment to pray before digging in. "I called your moms, too. I called all my ex-wives."

Both Amy and Angela stopped with their silverware halfway to their mouths. Amy could just imagine what Rhonda would have felt. She didn't really know how Ruthie would have reacted, but imagined they would both be incredulous at the change in their ex-husband. "How did they respond?" Amy finally asked.

"Parker laughed. Coral hung up on me. Ruthie cried and wanted to know why I was opening old wounds. And Rhonda yelled at me for fifteen minutes before she began to sob. She said that she wished I had been like this years ago."

"What did you say to them?" Angela voiced the question that was running through Amy's mind.

"I simply apologized for everything I had done to them and told them that I was a new man." Larry looked at Amy. "It kind of surprised me, but I think your mom is the only one that believed me."

"That surprises me, too," Amy admitted.

"My mom is probably too afraid to let down the walls she's built to protect herself," Angela added.

"I think you're probably right. I know they talk to each other – call themselves the ex-wives club – so I'm hoping that when they see I've tried to make amends with each of them they'll realize it was a real change, not just a ploy to get something out of them."

Larry began eating his lunch and something in his intensity let the girls know that he was done discussing this part with them. The conversation shifted, and Amy realized that it was the first time that she had talked with her family and it didn't feel forced or fake somehow.

When she went home, Amy realized that she hadn't told her mom about her own change. Larry had been eager to apologize to his children and former wives, but she still tried to keep her family at a distance. For that matter, she could try to make up with her half-siblings as well.

She made a pot of tea to calm herself before calling her mom. Before she could get out more than a greeting, Rhonda started in on her most interesting piece of gossip.

"Did you hear that Larry tried to kill himself? Couldn't do it right though. Then he had some sort of mid-life crisis or something and called me to apologize. He said he found *God*! Can you believe? Anyway, I just got off the phone with the other wives, and they each got phone calls from him, too. What do you think of that?"

Amy was pretty sure her mom hadn't taken a single breath as she tried to get out her news as quickly as possible. "Well, I think he really did find God."

"Did he call you, too?" Her mom's voice rose in surprise.

"No, I was at the hospital when it happened."

"When what happened? Why were you there?"

Amy explained how she had found out and what had happened at the hospital. "Mom, it's true. Dad really did change in that moment."

Rhonda scoffed. "Believe me, if Larry changed it's only because he wants something. He'll be back to his old self soon enough."

"I hope you're wrong, and deep down I think you hope that you're wrong, too." Amy had always had the feeling that Rhonda still loved Larry deep down. She felt like it was why Rhonda's other marriages had failed, too, and why she was always so gleeful when Larry's marriages ended.

"Maybe I do," Rhonda surprised her by admitting. "I'd love to know that your dad has finally become the man I thought he was when I married him."

"I think you'll be pleasantly surprised. As it is, it took courage for him to call all of you and apologize. He also apologized to each of us kids." Amy paused, but only for a moment. She wanted to get in the next sentence before her mom could change the subject. "I think it's real, because I found God, too."

Silence reigned for a while. "How did that happen?" Rhonda's voice was soft and hesitant.

Amy reminded her about her trip to Willow Creek and told her about Carol, Carmen, and Tristan. She explained about how God had pursued her, and how she had learned what true love was. "I found that I finally had the opportunity to experience love in a way I never had and had always wanted. I had to take my chance, and it's been the best thing I've ever done."

"So now you and Larry have something in common?" Amy realized that her mom was worried about their relationship.

"Yes, and it probably will give us a better relationship than we've ever experienced before. But it won't change our relationship." Amy didn't feel particularly close to her mom, but now she wondered if her mom was lonely. She had no family except for her daughter.

"So you and Larry will get closer through this God thing, and you and I get to keep our half-hearted distant mother/daughter relationship. Well, I feel much better."

"Mom." Amy sighed. "I think that our relationship will improve as well. I want it to at least."

Rhonda was quiet for a long moment. "Thank you, but somehow I think your charity will be short lived. I hope you and your dad are happy." With that she ended the call.

Amy leaned her head back against her chair. It seemed like the best way to convince her mom that the change was real would be for it to last. She hoped that she would be able to show her mom what a difference God made in her life.

29

It felt strange to walk into work on Monday morning. The office looked the same, but somehow it no longer seemed as welcoming as it always had before. There was a coldness and formality that she had never noticed. She went to her desk and sorted through the notes that Katie had left. Most people probably felt a reluctance to go back to work after vacation, but Amy had always been energized by her job. This time it seemed unimportant, and she found her mind wandering to what her friends in Willow Creek might be doing.

Katie smiled brightly when she came in. "I know it was my idea that you turn your business trip into a vacation, but I'm so glad you're back."

Amy's smile didn't quite match Katie's, but it was passable. "I'm glad you forced me into that vacation. I had a wonderful time and met some amazing people. Plus I got that logo finally figured out." She showed her work to Katie who frowned in confusion.

"It doesn't seem – cute enough for a B-and-B," she said hesitantly.

"You have to see this inn to get it. This is perfect. Both Tristan and Carol loved it."

"Who are Tristan and Carol?"

"Tristan is the one who contacted me to do the logo, and Carol is the owner of Holliday Hotel."

"Well, if the client is happy then that's all that matters." Katie stood by Amy's desk shifting her weight from foot to foot as if unsure of her next move. "I got a call from Wright Shepard."

Amy frowned. Wright had been her third boyfriend, but she had quickly learned that he wasn't the right one for her. He was persistent though and had kept calling or dropping by. Wright had been arrogant of his own good looks and enjoyed flirting with any woman who would let him. It had reminded Amy too much of her dad, and she hadn't wanted to go down that road. She supposed that it bothered Wright to have a woman who he hadn't conquered still in the city. He had always hoped she would be jealous of any girl who crossed his path, but she only felt sorry for them.

She sighed. "What did he want?"

"He wants you to do some work for him. I wasn't sure if you would feel comfortable with it, so I told him to call back today." Katie wrung her hands nervously. "I hope you're not upset."

"I'm not upset."

"Oh good. Because he said that he'd drop in instead of calling."

Amy looked at Katie carefully. Tilting her head to one side she realized that Katie had taken more care than usual in her appearance. Her hair was styled a little more carefully, make-up was a little brighter, outfit was crisp and new. "And you're happy that he's dropping by?"

Katie rubbed her hands nervously on her pants. "No, of course not. I mean, he only ever has eyes for you whenever he's here, and he's your ex-boyfriend so that would be weird."

"Katie, if you want him you're welcome to him. I don't have any feelings for Wright." Katie's face brightened immediately. "I just want to caution you about being with a guy who still likes to check out other options. It's a difficult life. I've seen what it does to people, to families. Be careful."

"Yeah, sure. It'll be fine. I'm sure of it. I think he just needs the right girl." Katie smiled dreamily and went to her own desk. Amy sighed and reminded herself that Katie was a grown woman, capable of making her own choices. She didn't want to see her hurt though.

Not surprisingly, Wright showed up right before lunch. Katie's voice dripped with honey when she greeted him. "Good afternoon, Mr. Shepard. It's so good to see you again."

Wright leaned on Katie's desk and looked her over appreciatively. "You're looking nice today Miss Miller. How's the boss doing?" He looked past Katie to where Amy's desk was.

Amy saw Katie's shoulders slump as Wright's focus quickly turned away from her. "The boss is doing better than ever," Amy answered for herself as she moved to the front of the office. "I had a wonderful vacation and am rested and ready to get back to work." Wright's smug smile made Amy want to slap it off his handsome face. "What can I do for you?"

"Why don't we discuss it over lunch?"

"Fine. Just give me a moment." She went back to her desk to gather her jacket and purse.

"Wow. I was expecting to have to try harder to get you to come with me." His smirk showed that he considered her quick assent as a tribute to his charm. "I like what a vacation does for you."

Amy thought back to when she had assumed that Tristan's request for a dinner meeting was a proposition for more. It was men like Wright who had made her so skeptical. In this case, she *knew* that Wright was looking for more than a business lunch. However, she had also learned that it was better to go with him and let him say his piece. He would stick around forever and pester her until she gave in. After she let him explain himself, then she would turn him down, and he would go sulk for a few months.

As they left the office, he put a proprietary hand on her back. She shrugged away from his touch by putting on her jacket. Her distance made him smile more. "There's my little prude. I was wondering if vacation had altered you in other ways as well." Amy had always put off his physical contact knowing that she was just another conquest for him, instinctively knowing that he would lose interest as soon as she gave in to him.

"It did change me in other ways, but somehow I doubt you'd approve."

They walked to a nearby restaurant, one that was well out of Amy's price range. She watched Wright as he talked to the hostess. She had to admit that he was good looking with blond hair, twinkling blue eyes, and a smile that lit up the room. His features were better looking than most models. Everything about him oozed success; from the cut of his suit to the Rolex watch to his confident posture. He turned on his charm with the hostess, and the poor girl was left a blushing, giggling mess. She immediately took them to a table in spite of the crowd waiting for a seat.

"How did you do that?" Amy wondered as she sat down across from him.

"There are still places that take reservations," was all he replied, but Amy wondered what sort of strings he had pulled to get those reservations.

"Katie said that you have some work you wanted me to do."

"Let's order first. I highly recommend the lobster. It's excellent." His allusion to having eaten at this establishment before was yet another way that he let people know he had arrived at the top.

Amy ended up choosing a salad with grilled shrimp while Wright went with his favorite lobster meal. When the waiter left, Amy leaned on the table. "Now can we talk business?"

"I always loved your ambition," he said with a patronizing smile.

"You don't know what love is." The words slipped from Amy's mouth before she could check them.

Wright laughed. "I know you haven't liked competing with other women for my attention, but I can be a one woman man."

Amy's eyes narrowed. "First off, I'm not competing with any woman for your attention, because I don't want it. Second, you can't even be a one woman man through lunch. I doubt you'd be able to make it for a lifetime. Third, love is more than claiming to be a faithful man."

"Okay smarty. What is love?"

"Love is patient and kind."

"I am the epitome of patience and kindness."

"Love does not envy or boast; it is not arrogant or rude. It does not insist on its own way; it is not irritable or resentful," Amy continued. "It does not rejoice at wrongdoing, but rejoices with the truth. Love bears all things, believes all things, hopes all things, endures all things. Love never ends."

Wright sighed and shook his head. "If that's your idea of love, you'll never find it."

"I already have," she said softly.

Suddenly Wright's face became serious. "Who is he?"

"That description of love is from the Bible, and it's a description of God's love."

Wright's face showed his condescension. "Oh, you found religion. I can live with that." The waiter brought their food, and Amy bowed her head and prayed silently. When she opened her eyes she found Wright looking at her in amusement. "You are really playing this up. It's not going to make me uninterested in you just because you're playing like you're a Christian."

"I'm not playing at it. I am a Christian now. I met some wonderful people on vacation and they showed me the truth."

"Okay, baby. I'm fine with your life choices."

Amy gritted her teeth together. "I'm not your baby, and I really don't care what you think about my life choices." She took a deep breath to calm down. "Now, what about the job you have for me?"

"I want you to update the logo of my dealership. I want it to say Wright Shepard Car Sales: The Wright choice for all your automotive needs."

Amy put a note in her phone. "I think I can do that. Who came up with the slogan?"

"I did."

Amy looked at him skeptically. "You did?"

"You don't think I could come up something like that?" He looked offended that she didn't believe him, but then the façade cracked as he laughed. "Of course I didn't. It was my advertising guys."

"Clever." Amy took a bite of her salad. She didn't know what she had seen in Wright to date him in the first place. She supposed her head had been turned like every other woman by his looks.

"So where were you when you went on vacation? Finally take that trip to Hawaii?"

"I went to a small town called Willow Creek. A client was there that I needed to see so I combined business with pleasure."

"You went on vacation with a client?"

"I was designing a logo for a bed and breakfast, but I was having trouble so I went up there to stay and figure it out."

Wright smiled. "Oh, your client was some little, old lady. That makes sense. It would have been out of character for you to go on a trip with a man."

Amy couldn't resist teasing him a bit. "Actually, my client was Tristan Romero. He owns a web design company and brought me in to help."

Wright pushed his plate away. "So you did go with a man. How does that fit with your new 'religion'?"

Shaking her head, Amy explained. "He lives in the town with his grandma. I stayed at the inn. It was partly because of his influence that I became a Christian though."

The check came and Wright grabbed it before she could. He seemed agitated. It amused her that he wanted to make women jealous, but didn't like the feeling when he had it. When they were walking back to her office he finally spoke his thoughts out loud. "You like this guy? He's a client and a Christian. It seems like a bad idea to me." It was the first time Wright had seemed discomposed around her.

"It doesn't feel good does it?"

"What?" His stride was long as he hurried down the street. Amy had to take two steps to each step he took.

"Jealousy."

He stopped abruptly and stuck a finger in her face. "I am not jealous. Wright Shepard does not need to be jealous of some small town hick, some *Christian*. I'm the man other men envy and women want."

Without warning Amy saw something new in Wright. He was insecure. All of his arrogance, posturing, and spurring others to jealousy was compensating for his own low self-esteem. She placed a hand on his shoulder. "You don't need to be jealous of Tristan – not because he's a hick or a Christian – but because you don't need to be jealous of anyone."

Wright straightened up and his shoulders relaxed. "That's what I was saying."

"It's not because you're so wonderful that you don't need to be jealous though. It's because you are exactly who God created you to be, and that's all you need."

Wright smirked. "Sure. Whatever you say." With his hands thrust into his pockets he strode down the street. The rest of their walk back to the office was silent.

He laid a hand on her shoulder before she entered the office. "There's no chance for me with you, is there?"

Amy slowly shook her head. "Not the way things are now. I don't want to be with someone who is always looking for someone who's better than me to be with. I don't want to have to doubt your faithfulness to me. I don't want to feel like every woman who passes is potential competition for your affection. If something were to change, it might be different."

"If I were to become a Christian," he suggested.

"Posssibly. I don't know, Wright. I'm not sure that we're meant to be together."

"Because of that guy you met?"

"No, because I think the only reason you're interested in me is because I'm a challenge." Amy paused and studied his face for a moment. "You don't love me."

"According to you I don't know what love is." Wright's mouth twisted bitterly.

"None of us do without God." Amy grabbed his hand. "He wants to show you what true love is. Only then will you be able to experience it with humans."

"I'll think about it." He dropped her hand, and Amy knew that he wasn't going to accept God at that moment.

"Do you still want me to do the drawings for you?" Knowing that there was no chance between them, Wright may want to take his business to someplace with more possibilities.

"Absolutely. You may not be interested in me, but you are the best graphic artist I know. Business is business." Impulsively Amy gave him a hug.

"Thanks. If you want to talk, I'm always available."

Wright looked at her curiously. "You are different – in a good way, I think." He took a step back and lifted his hand. "I'll see you around."

Amy watched him leave and sighed. She had finally gotten through to Wright that she wasn't interested, and yet in a way, felt terrible. She didn't worry about his ego - that would survive anything. Now, she was concerned for his soul. She hoped that he would take her up on her offer to talk, but somehow felt like all of their interactions would be strictly business now.

30

The day went downhill from there. Katie was downhearted the rest of the day because Wright hadn't seemed to notice her beyond that first glance. A client pulled their account claiming that Amy hadn't fulfilled the promised delivery time even though they kept altering what they wanted so she had to keep changing her designs. Another client called to yell at Amy for having the audacity to go on vacation and not be at their beck and call at all times. Amy's computer froze in the middle of a design and when she rebooted she had to start from the beginning. And to top everything off, it began to rain just as it was time to leave. The cold February rain penetrated through every layer of clothing quickly, leaving Amy a shivering drenched mess.

As she entered her apartment she had just two thoughts on her mind – dry clothes and hot soup for dinner. She grabbed the warmest pajamas she had and put them on. After making herself a bowl of soup, she went to the living room to eat with her television to keep her company.

After a while though, she began to long for the company of humans. It was a shock to discover this since she had always enjoyed her alone time before. She had felt safe in her fortress of solitude. But she longed for a person to talk with, to tell about her day, to get advice from. Without really thinking it through, she pulled out her phone and called Tristan.

As she waited for him to answer, she wondered why she had instinctively called him. Why hadn't she called Carol or Angela? She could have called her mom or dad, too. Why him? She hadn't come up with an answer when his voice came through. She smiled hearing the sound and felt warmer than she had when eating her soup.

"It's so good to hear your voice," she admitted without stopping to think.

"It's good to hear yours too." She could hear his amusement. "What's wrong?"

"How did you know something was wrong?"

"I could hear it in your tone of voice." How was it possible that they had known each other such a short time and yet he could read her so well without even seeing her face?

"Oh, I had a rough day." She went through everything that had occurred. "I felt like I needed to talk to someone."

"I can understand why. Anyone would need someone to talk to after a day like that. What was the absolute worst part of the day?"

Amy thought back over everything. "The client who left can be replaced and the one who was upset can be dealt with. Even though I hate it that Katie was hurt, I think it's better for her to realize what Wright is now than to suffer through a relationship where she was constantly wondering if he was thinking of someone else. And now that I'm warm and dry, the rain wasn't that big of a deal. I think it was Wright. I saw him differently today for the first time, and I ache for him."

"How so?" Unlike Wright, Tristan's voice showed no signs of jealousy or displeasure at her reference to the other man.

"I always saw him as arrogant before and someone who always wanted more. Don't get me wrong, he's still those things, but when I looked at him, it seemed like what I saw was someone who is insecure. He needs women's attention to convince himself that he's attractive. He needs the newest, best car, house, toy, whatever to show others that he's a success, because he doesn't feel like one. It's sad." Amy sighed. She wondered how she had missed it before. She supposed she had been too wrapped up in her own emotions to see how he was feeling.

"That's very discerning of you. You know what would help him, right?"

"Yeah, God. He's the only one who can give Wright the confidence he needs." Amy got up and began to pace the living room. "I think that's what bothers me most. He so quickly shut down when I brought up God. He doesn't want anything to do with him."

"Well, that's not entirely out of the ordinary. Think back on when you first came to Holliday Hotel. Remember how uncomfortable it made you when Carol or Grandma or I would talk about the Lord to you?"

Amy sank into a chair. "Yeah, you're right. I wanted nothing to do with Him."

"You were so fortunate that the first person you talked to about Jesus was ready to believe. Your dad had hit the bottom and knew he needed God. Wright is at the top – or at least he thinks he is. He doesn't need any help."

"So there's no hope for him?" Amy felt her stomach clench at the thought.

"As long as he's alive, there is hope. He may not even have to hit the bottom to find God. Here's what you need to know. The Bible says that one plants, another waters, but God gives the increase. You've planted the seed. Someone else may come along and water it, but if Wright comes to God it will be because God gave the increase.

Another thing is that even though you may never know if that seed bears fruit, you can always pray for Wright. What you are doing is the right thing. God wants us to tell others about Him. Pray for opportunities and for the Spirit to help you. Keep studying the Bible so you'll be ready to give answers. It may feel like you've failed because Wright didn't immediately accept Jesus, but you did what you were supposed to do. The rest is up to God."

Amy curled her feet up under her and felt the weight on her chest lifted. It wasn't her job to save Wright or her mother or anyone else. It was simply her job to share God with others.

"Thank you. I needed to hear that. I think I was discouraged because Wright was the second person to shut down when I talked about God. My mom didn't want to hear about it either. She doesn't believe that Dad, or I have really changed." Amy thought for a moment then added, "I also think she's afraid that Dad and I are going to have this really close relationship through God, and she'll be left out."

"That's definitely a possibility. Christians have a bond like no one else. When you went to church on Sunday with your sister, you were surrounded by strangers, but did it feel that way?"

Amy thought back. "No," she said with surprise. "It felt like I belonged."

"Exactly." Amy could picture Tristan's smile. "There is a family bond between Christians that is unique to the Church. Like any family we have our quarrels, and there are people we like better than others, but our love for each other ought to go deeper than those issues."

"So Mom could have a reason to be nervous." Amy chewed her lip. "How do you think I can help her?"

"It was finding out what real love looks like that drew you to God. I think your mom has also never experienced that kind of love and has been searching for it in all the wrong places. Show her what it looks like."

Tristan's reminder brought the needlework to focus in her mind. The first time she had sat down with her Bible she had found those verses and highlighted them. Her second highlight was John 3:16. She now had those verses memorized.

"That's a great idea." She made a mental note to try to find ways to show love to her mother. "That's enough about me though. How's Carmen doing?"

Tristan paused a long moment. "She's fine, but I get the feeling that she won't be with me much longer. She seems a little more tired, a little slower, a little weaker."

Amy put her hand on her chest, her heart aching for both Tristan and herself. It was going to be hard when Tristan had to say good-bye to Carmen. Taking care of his grandma had been his life for several years now. "I'm so sorry. If there's anything I can do to help let me know."

"I will. It feels so selfish of me to want her to stay here when she could be in heaven, free from all her health issues and struggles, but I'm going to miss her when she goes." Tristan's voice wavered and then she heard him take a deep breath. "God is in control of when that happens. There's no sense in worrying about it." He seemed to be almost talking to himself, reminding him of what he already knew.

"I think God understands the pain of the separation of death," Amy said softly.

"He absolutely does. He experienced when Jesus died on the cross. It's why He hates sin and death so much." Tristan chuckled. "It's good for me to see life through a new believer's eyes."

"It's good for me to have an experienced believer to get advice from." Amy smiled feeling the warmth of their friendship all over again.

"Can I ask you a personal question?"

"Sure." Amy's heart picked up pace wondering where the conversation was going.

"If Wright became a Christian, would you be interested in dating him?"

Amy felt like Tristan was holding his breath as he waited for her answer, the line was so silent. She hadn't really thought about it. "I don't know," she finally answered cautiously. "He's definitely good looking, but I'm not sure I could easily get over his flirtatious ways. Maybe if that changed, but if not, then no."

She heard him take a deep breath. "Do you think you could be interested in dating someone like me?"

Amy sat motionless in her chair. She heard the sound of the furnace kicking on. Her heart thudded in her chest. "I could definitely be interested in dating someone like you."

31

The walk up to her mother's house had never seemed longer to Amy. Tristan's conversation was still replaying over and over in her head, and she was determined to show Rhonda love. In one hand she held her mom's favorite drink from Starbucks, a hot caramel macchiato, and in the other she had a bag of Chinese food.

Rhonda answered the door and grudgingly opened it wide enough for her daughter to enter. "I suppose you've come to convert me. Do you get points towards your ticket to heaven with every new conversion?"

"I don't need any points. My ticket was bought and paid for by Someone far more precious. And I didn't come to convert you or talk religion. I simply came to have dinner with my mom." Amy went to the dining room and began setting out the dinner on the table. Her mother followed with her arms folded across her chest.

"Why?"

"Do I need a reason to have dinner with my mom?"

"You do, yes. You've never just dropped by before. In fact, normally I only have the honor of your company when you absolutely have to come over." Rhonda's voice dripped with sarcasm.

Amy began dishing up what she knew were her mom's favorites and set the plate down at the chair her mom was standing behind. Reluctantly, her mom took the chair and grabbed a pair of chopsticks. Amy smiled slightly at the small victory and then filled her own plate.

Sitting across from her mom, she began to explain, praying for wisdom while she spoke. "I've recently come to the understanding that what I always saw as independence and solitude was actually masking a deep loneliness. I decided to make some changes."

"You decided to get some religion." Rhonda pointed her chopsticks at her daughter. "And now you're going to preach at me every chance you get."

Amy sighed. "Even before I 'got religion', I was recognizing how alone I was. Maybe part of that drew me towards Jesus, but the biggest thing that got my attention was that true love does exist. It just doesn't look the way I thought it did. God shows us true love, and without Him we can't experience it."

"Preaching," Rhonda murmured around a mouthful of chow mein.

"Sorry. I don't want to preach at you. I want to get to know you."

Rhonda's eyes narrowed. "You know me. You brought my favorite dinner and favorite coffee. If you're easing your conscience, consider it eased."

"I know about you. I know what you like and dislike. But I don't know *you*. I've purposefully kept you at arm's length my whole life, and I'd like to change that."

Rhonda's mouth curled. "I suppose I should feel guilty now. I made my daughter into a lonely hermit and now she needs me to love her. Like a bad Hallmark movie."

"You love those bad Hallmark movies though," Amy said with a smile. "And I'm not trying to make you feel guilty. Look at all of Dad's kids. If anyone should feel guilty about parenting, it's him. Of the four of us, Angela was the only one who didn't push him away, even when he pushed her away. We all dealt with the same grief, the same issues, but one of us reacted differently. I chose my path. That's not your fault or Dad's. It was my doing, and I'm accountable for it."

Rhonda grunted and pushed back her chair. Without speaking the two women cleaned up the dinner and then went to the living room. Rhonda sat on the couch while Amy chose a rocking chair. "I do love those Hallmark movies," Rhonda said breaking the silence.

Amy laughed. "I know you do."

"What do you want to know about me?" When Amy's expression showed her confusion, Rhonda explained, "You said you want to know me. What do you want to know?"

Amy's mind raced. She hadn't actually thought her mom would be willing to talk. She had always been a very private person. "Why weren't you and Grandma close?"

"She didn't want me to marry your dad, and she never forgave me for going against her wishes. When our marriage ended, I called her up crying, and she told me that I had gotten what I deserved, and she hung up on me." Rhonda's face had softened as she spoke. There was a look of regret on her features.

"That's why she didn't like taking care of me, wasn't it?"

Rhonda pursed her lips. "I know she loved you in her own way, but you were the product of my marriage so you reminded her of that every time she saw you." Rhonda shrugged. "Plus, she was never a kid person. And the very fact that I needed her help was because my marriage had failed just like she had predicted."

"Were you ever close to her?"

Rhonda smiled tenderly. "When I became a teenager, my mom and I would sit out on the porch swing and talk for hours. I could tell her anything. She said that she loved when I became old enough to have intelligent conversations with her."

"It's nice that you have some fond memories of her." Rhonda looked sharply at Amy as if trying to figure out if it was an insult in disguise. "I remember when I was little you would come in and sing to me before bed. That was my favorite time of the day."

"Mine, too." Rhonda's eyes welled with tears. "I should have kept doing that."

Amy shrugged. "You had responsibilities."

The silence between them now was comfortable. Amy couldn't remember a recent time when she had so enjoyed being with her mom.

"I wanted to be an architect." Amy was surprised out of her thoughts by her mom's admission.

"What happened?"

"Larry happened." Rhonda sighed. "He was so handsome and

every girl wanted his attention, but he chose me." Her voice turned bitter as she added, "I just didn't realize at the time that he didn't choose *only* me." She looked at Amy. "I was so proud of you for going after your goals and achieving them. You didn't let anything stand in your way, and now you're doing what you love."

Amy's pushed the tears away. "Thanks, Mom."

"I know I didn't do everything right, in fact, I'm lucky you turned out so well. I can't really take any credit for your success, but I did care about you."

Amy thought back to what life was like with her mom, but for the first time saw it from her mom's perspective. Rhonda was often tired and stressed from working long hours to provide for her. Her relationships took a toll on her emotionally as well, but she never allowed Amy to be in an unsafe situation. Although she had always seemed to need a man, she never pushed Amy to date or marry. Her mom had loved her, but she hadn't seen it.

"I think I'm realizing that for the first time." Amy put her hand on her mom's arm. "I love you, Mom. I always have, even if I haven't always shown it."

Rhonda nodded, and Amy saw her swallow hard and knew that she was fighting emotions.

Amy decided it was time to lighten the mood. "I saw Wright Shepard yesterday." Her mom had never liked Wright. She, too, had seen the similarity between Wright and Larry.

"Ugh, what did he want?"

"He had some business for me to do for him."

Rhonda snorted. "I'm sure he did."

Amy laughed. "I don't think he'll be pursuing me for a relationship anymore. He doesn't care for religious girls."

"Well, that's one good thing about getting religion I guess. I'm so glad you're smarter about men than I was." Amy had never noticed the lines on her mom's face until that moment. Her life choices had taken a toll on her.

"Maybe you taught me that, too."

Rhonda chuckled. "I showed you what not to do."

"Something like that." Amy wiped her palms on her pants.

"There is a guy I think I might be interested in. I don't know if it'll work out though because it'd be a long distance relationship."

Rhonda searched Amy's face. "Is it that guy you mentioned while you were on vacation?"

"Yeah, Tristan Romero."

"I knew there was more to it than you were letting on." Rhonda's eyes gleamed as she leaned forward on the couch.

"At the time, there really wasn't anything going on besides business. It's been sort of recent." She set the rocking chair going with the toe of her foot unaware of the dreamy expression on her face.

"So what's he like?"

"He's got dark hair and eyes, wears glasses, and owns his own company. He's – nice. It doesn't seem adequate to describe him. He's been caring for his grandmother for years, and he's just so sweet to her."

"I've heard that you can tell a lot about how a man will treat his wife by how he treats his mom – or I guess grandma in this case. I should have listened to that advice before I married your dad." Rhonda curled into the corner of the couch. "So where do you go from here?"

"I don't know. Last night he asked me if I thought I could be interested in him, and I said yes, and then – nothing. But he also has told me that as long as his grandma needs him that he wouldn't date or marry since his time and energy is focused on her. He didn't think it'd be fair to a woman to have to be second to his grandma." Amy thought for a moment. "Mom, what do you think I should do? Should I pursue him, or wait to see if he makes the next move?"

"I'm not sure I'm your best choice for relationship advice." Even with that statement, Amy could see that Rhonda was pleased that she had asked her. "I'd say that you've told him you're interested, and now the ball is in his court."

Amy nodded. "That's kind of what I thought, too."

Again they were quiet, each lost in their own thoughts. "Amy Romero," Rhonda said softly. "It sounds nice."

Amy giggled. “Oh mom. We haven’t even gone on a date or anything yet.” Rhonda joined her in her laughter, and Amy thought that this was the type of relationship she had always hoped to have with her mom. Looking at her watch, she groaned. “I need to get going.”

Both of them stood up and Rhonda walked Amy to the door. “This was nice, Mom. Thanks for not pushing me away.”

“Thanks for not preaching at me.” Awkwardly Rhonda hugged her only child. “As long as you aren’t trying to convert me or anything, I think we can maybe work on that getting to know each other thing.”

Amy smiled softly. “I love you, Mom.”

She wasn’t sure, but as she walked out the door, she thought she heard her mom whisper, “I love you, too.”

32

Tristan helped Carmen out of the car and back to the house. The doctor's appointment had been disappointing to him, but it hadn't altered Carmen's mood. If anything she seemed even more cheerful than normal.

"Don't be such a gloomy Gus," she teased as she mounted the stairs. Her breathing was erratic with the effort of climbing. Tristan had tried to convince her to put in a ramp, but she insisted she could manage.

"I'm glad you can keep your sense of humor at a time like this." Tristan held the door open for her and patiently waited as she slowly entered their home.

"Come sit with me," she invited. Tristan wouldn't have turned down the invitation if he were to lose every client he had. Who knew how many more times he would get to sit down with his grandma? He wanted to cherish every moment he had left with her.

She rested a few minutes after sitting down, trying to catch her breath. "You realize that someday soon, I'll be able to run, and dance, and not get tired." Her mouth stretched into a big smile. "That will be wonderful."

"I know. I'm being selfish wanting to keep you here with me. I'm going to miss you." He swallowed hard. His life had revolved around his grandma for such a long time that he didn't even know what he'd do without her. He'd have to rethink his plans and purpose.

"I know you will. You'll sorrow, but as the Apostle Paul wrote, you will 'not grieve as others do who have no hope'. We'll meet again." She placed her hand on his cheek. "As much as I have loved having you with me, I have hated that you had uproot yourself and come take care of me. I've hated that you had to put your life on hold. I'm looking forward to you getting on with your life."

"I don't even know what that looks like," Tristan admitted. He rubbed his hands over his face.

"The possibilities are endless. You can move back to Los Angeles, have a social life, get a girlfriend." She smiled up at him slyly.

"I don't know that I want to move back. I've grown to love it here. As for your very subtle hint about a girlfriend, I'm not sure about that either."

"Not sure about the idea of a girlfriend or a specific girlfriend?"

Tristan smiled at his grandma's probing. "Specific girlfriend." He shifted in his seat so he could look at Carmen's face. "I asked Amy the last time we talked if she thought she might be able to date someone like me, and she said yes. But since then I've been trying to picture how this would work, and I don't think anything will come of it."

"Why not?"

"Distance for one thing."

"Fear for another," Carmen responded nudging him lightly. "You're finding excuses, because you're afraid. I don't know if you're more afraid it won't work out, or more afraid that it will."

"That's not – that's ridiculous. I'm not scared of it. I just don't see how it could work."

"And so why even bother?"

Tristan let her words sink in for a moment. "We could both end up hurt."

"You could both end up in a wonderful relationship. Life isn't without risk, but you'll miss so much if you stand on the sidelines too afraid of getting hurt to dive in and experience it." Carmen sighed. "Don't miss out on something wonderful because you're scared of the risk."

"She's such a new believer. What if it doesn't work and it affects her walk with God?"

"That's for her and God to work on. You aren't responsible for her relationship with God."

Tristan sighed. "You're right. I know it."

"Are you nervous that she'll influence your own walk?"

Tristan gave the question some consideration. "I don't think so."

"So why are you concerned that you would negatively influence hers?"

Tristan smiled. "Good question. And one I can't answer."

Carmen laid her hand on his arm. "Tristan, I love you dearly. You were so quick and willing to come to me when I needed you. But it's time for you to get your own life back, and I think that it includes letting Amy in." She grinned at him teasingly. "You know that I picked her for you, so that means she's perfect."

Tristan laughed. "She's only perfect if God picked her for me."

Carmen grew serious. "I think He has, and I think you know it. You just aren't ready to admit it yet." After a few moments of silence, Carmen added, "I know that we don't have any idea how much longer I have. The doctor doesn't think I'll see summer. If it's a slow process, and we can tell my time is growing short, would you please ask Amy to come see me one more time? If it's possible, I'd like to talk to her once more before I go home."

"Of course, Grandma." Tristan took a deep breath. "I hope I don't have to call her for a while yet."

Carmen smiled sadly. "I'm ready to go, Tristan. Don't try to hold onto me too tightly."

Tristan felt his chest tighten with emotion, but simply nodded. He knew that she would be better off in heaven, but selfishly he wanted to keep her with him. He tried to picture her running and healthy, meeting her beloved Savior, and reuniting with her husband. "You're right. I'll be praying that when the time comes, I'll be ready to let go."

"And I'll be praying that God won't take me until you're ready." Carmen used her walker to get to her feet. "I think I'll go lie down now. The doctor's visit has made me sleepy."

Tristan watched his grandma make her slow progress to her room. He leaned his head against the couch. "Lord, you know how much I love my grandma, but I know You love her even more. Help prepare my heart for the time when You take her home." He took a few breaths trying to ease the weight on his chest. "And Lord, guide me in my relationship with Amy. If You really want me to pursue a deeper relationship would You make it so clear that I can't ignore it?" He thought back to the voice he had heard when she had become a Christian. What was clearer than that? "Help me to trust You."

It wasn't going to be easy, but the time was coming. He had to be prepared, and he needed to be ready to make some changes to his life.

As if on cue, his phone chirped with a text message alert.

Thanks for your advice. I showed my mom some of God's love and we had a wonderful visit.

I'm so glad it worked. Was she more receptive to hearing about God?

Not yet, but maybe someday soon. Just got to keep praying.

Tristan smiled. Amy was already growing. *I'll be praying, too. Could you also pray for my Grandma? We didn't get a very good report at the doctor's today.*

Oh no! I'll keep her in my prayers.

She's ready to go, but I'm the one who's not quite ready to let her go.

Understandable. You'll miss her.

Yes, I will.

Tristan held his phone for a while staring at the screen in indecision. *I'm so glad I have you as my friend.*

Me, too. You're a good friend.

Tristan stared at the word 'friend'. Suddenly he felt like it wasn't enough, but what could he do so far away? He needed to talk to her. Dialing her number he didn't have to wait long before she answered.

"I wanted to hear your voice," he admitted.

"Sometimes texting isn't enough," she agreed.

He got up and started to pace. "About our conversation the other night," he paused.

"Yes?"

"I want to be more than your friend, but I don't know what that looks like long distance." He rushed the sentence out before he could change his mind about saying it.

The silence on the phone was so long that he checked his phone to make sure they were still connected. "I don't know what that looks like either."

"So what do we do?" Tristan stood at the window and gazed at the winter scene on his street. Bare trees stretched their skeletal limbs to the sky. Snowmen decorated the yards of homes with children. The snow was turning gray and dingy. It was bleak and dismal – rather befitting of his mood now that he thought about it.

"Why don't we leave it as it is for now? We both know that we want more so let's just see what happens. I won't date anyone while we're figuring this out, but if I think God has someone here for me, I'll let you know. You can do the same for me."

"Yeah, okay. Like serious friendship."

Amy's laugh made him smile. "Exclusive friends. For now." She stopped laughing and her voice was low as she continued. "But maybe someday. . ."

"Someday." Tristan liked the sound of that.

33

Throughout the next few weeks, Amy found little reasons to stop by her mom's house or invite her to lunch. Rhonda began opening up to Amy in ways she never had before, and Amy started to understand her mother better than ever. They started to mend their broken relationship, and although it was still fragile, it was growing stronger day by day.

Amy had also contacted April and Craig which had gone better than she had expected. Because she had never really hurt them, but had instead been a non-entity in their lives, they were willing to forgive. Both teenagers agreed that it might be okay to have a big sister, but made sure that she understood that she couldn't embarrass them in any way. Amy had already gone shopping with April and had gone to see Craig play basketball.

Larry had completely changed. The arrogance that had been so hurtful was tempered. He had been single for longer than Amy could ever remember. The biggest change was that there was a peace and contentment that hadn't been there before. Amy had never imagined having a good relationship with her dad, but every Sunday they met at church then together with Angela they would go to lunch. Larry was excited about God's Word and always had something to share that he had learned at Bible study or reading a devotion.

Perhaps what most surprised Amy was Larry's commitment to atoning for the hurt he had caused others. He went to one of Craig's game and convinced his son to at least hear him out. He hadn't offered any excuses, simply a sincere apology and a desire to mend the relationship if possible. Craig had forgiven, but didn't want anything more to do with his dad. Larry had been disappointed, but had respected his son's wish. April had reluctantly agreed to meet him for lunch, but had been more ready to hear him out and give him a shot. Since April had seen Angela's relationship with Larry flourish recently she was more apt to try it for herself.

Amy walked past shops in the mall with Angela and April. The girls were shopping for Easter dresses, particularly for April since she had agreed to go to church with them that day. "We won't be able to have lunch together that Sunday," Angela explained. "Mom wants us to have lunch with her, and she doesn't trust Dad still."

"That's understandable. It's a holiday. You should be with your mom," Amy agreed.

"I think she'd be fine with you coming if I asked," Angela suggested. "She never had anything against you, except that she said you had the warmth and personality of a robot."

Amy laughed out loud at the description. She had always known that her self-protection had made her come across as cold and proud. "I've already told my mom that I would be having lunch with her."

"Our mom is so not happy that we're spending time with Dad," April put in. "She says that we shouldn't come crying to her when he breaks our hearts."

"After what Ruthie experienced with Dad, I'm not terribly surprised. What does surprise me is that Angela has had a relationship with Dad for a while, and I didn't think your mom cared."

"Oh she cared," Angela said, "But I was an adult by that time so she felt she had to let me make my own choices."

"Technically I'm an adult, too," April said, proud of being eighteen. "That's why she hasn't forbidden me from seeing Dad."

They went into a popular store for teenagers and began sorting through the racks of dresses. After gathering several for April to try on, they went to the fitting rooms. With April inside, Angela and Amy sat on a couch near the fitting rooms.

"Has Dad tried to contact your mom anymore?" Amy asked.

"Yes, but mom's being stubborn. She refuses to answer his

calls," Angela told her, "but she always listens to the voice mails he leaves. Then she cries. At least, that's what April's told me."

April came out of the dressing room and showed off her first dress. They all agreed that it wasn't quite right for her.

"How's your mom doing?" Angela asked.

"I think she's coming around. At least my relationship with her has improved. I don't know if Dad has talked to her any more or not. I wouldn't be surprised if he's tried." Amy worked hard to not hope for a reconciliation between her parents.

She knew that Angela would like to see their Dad back with Ruthie. Still her six year old self still wanted that happy family picture to be true. It was too much to hope for though. Her parents had too much history and too much drama to ever fully trust one another again. Besides with their different world views now, it would only create new arguments. The most she could hope for was that they could be civil to each other. Then maybe they could at least spend holidays together.

That thought led her to think about Carol and Holliday Hotel, which inevitably led her thoughts to Tristan.

"What's that smile about?" Angela nudged her just as April emerged with a new dress.

"That one is nice," Amy told April trying to switch Angela's attention.

"Ooh, very pretty," Angela agreed. April smiled brightly and then headed back to the dressing room. "Now about that smile. . ."

"What smile?"

"You got this goofy looking smile on your face – the kind you get when you're thinking about a guy you like." She gasped. "You *like* someone!" She laughed at the blush that spread across Amy's face.

"It's really nothing, and I mean nothing. He's a friend, but he doesn't live here so there's not much chance of anything ever happening."

"Oh, it's that guy you met on vacation! Does he like you?" Angela's eyes sparkled as she teased her big sister. Amy marveled that not long ago she wouldn't be grilled by her sister about her love life, because she had kept them at a distance, but now it seemed so normal.

She laughed. "Yeah, I think he likes me, too." April came out and did a pirouette. "I like that, but not as much as the other." She turned back to Angela. "I know he likes me, but we both have agreed that for now we'll just be long distance friends who don't date anyone else."

"Sounds like you're in a relationship to me." Angela smiled at her teasingly. "When you can't date anyone because of a certain person, I think that means you're a couple."

"Well, if I found someone that I was interested in here I could let him know, and he'd be fine with letting me date. The same goes for him."

"Um-hm. I'd like to see that happen. You'd call him and say, 'Hey! I found this amazing guy that I want to date.' And he'd be like, 'Oh that's great. I'm so happy for you.' But deep down inside he'll be crushed because essentially his girlfriend just dumped him." Angela stood up as April came out with the clothes she tried on draped over her arm.

"I think I'll get this one," April said, showing the one that they had all liked. She placed the rest on the rack to be returned by the employees and went to purchase her dress. "Did I miss anything while I was trying on clothes?" she asked as she picked up her bag to leave the store.

"Amy's got a boyfriend," Angela said.

"Shut up!" Amy laughed as she gave her a small shove.

"Oh man! I knew I'd miss something juicy while I was in there trying on dresses." April bounced up to Amy's side and linked her arm in hers. "Who is he? Is he cute?"

Amy sighed and shook her head. "He's just a friend. And yes, he's cute."

"Ooh. What does he look like?" April practically skipped beside Amy as she enjoyed teasing her new big sister.

"He's got dark hair and eyes and wears glasses."

"Wow. You sound as excited as you would talking about your computer. I guess there really isn't anything to it." April drooped in disappointment.

"He has a really sweet smile and when he hugged me, I felt like I fit just right in his arms," Amy added. Her sisters squealed with joy at the new revelation.

Amy couldn't believe how much she had missed out before by keeping her half-sisters out of her life. She was so thankful that things had worked out now. She was enjoying the sister time and the bond they were developing. Before they parted they made plans to meet up for a chick flick night, and Amy felt light on her feet as she went to her car.

Soon after she got home, her phone rang. Seeing her mom's name on her caller ID, she answered quickly. "What's going on, Mom?"

"Can we meet for coffee?" Rhonda's voice had tears in it.

"Yeah, sure. Just tell me where." After setting a location, Amy grabbed her stuff and headed out again. A million thoughts went through her mind on the way to the coffee shop. Did her mom have more boyfriend troubles? Or was it something more serious? Did she have financial problems? Or health issues? Maybe her mom had been diagnosed with cancer just as they were becoming close. As the worry began to creep in, Amy simply prayed, "Lord help me with whatever is to come."

She rushed into the little café. Her mom wasn't there yet so she ordered for both of them. When her mom did come in, her eyes were red and swollen from crying. She looked so upset that Amy jumped out of her chair and hurried to give her a big hug. "What's wrong?" She sat her mom on one side of the table and handed her a coffee while she took her own place on the other side. Her face was lined with concern.

"It's your dad."

"Dad? What has he done?" Amy's heart sank. Had Larry gone back to his old ways and hurt Rhonda? That would be such a disappointment.

Rhonda burst into tears, and it took some minutes before she could compose herself to talk. "He came over to talk to me today." She sniffed loudly and searched her purse for a tissue. "He brought me flowers, red roses because he remembered they were my favorite. We talked for hours. He said that he had always hated it when he heard I was with someone new. I guess he kept track of me." Rhonda gave her a watery smile. "He told me that of all his wives I was the one he most regretted losing."

"That upsets you?" Amy was having trouble following her mom's story.

"Not upsets per se. More like," she sighed as she tried to think of how she was feeling, "confuses me."

"I see." Not really, but she was sure Rhonda would explain further.

"I thought I was doing okay. I had moved on. Larry was a lying, cheating, arrogant, pig who didn't deserve me. He had killed my love for him – or so I thought."

"Mom," Amy took a deep breath. "What are you saying?"

Rhonda laughed shakily. "I don't know. I think, maybe, your dad and I might – get back together, sometime, possibly."

Amy's eyes widened and she took a sip of her coffee while she tried to think things through. "Do you want that to happen?"

"I don't know. I didn't know who to talk to about it, but I needed to tell someone. Talk it through. It affects you, too, so I thought maybe we could discuss it."

"Like work out the pros and cons?"

Rhonda shrugged and played with her coffee cup. "Something like that. It felt so nice to spend the day with him again. It was like when we were first together."

"You know that his change is because of his religion, and you have to accept both of them together. You can't take God away from him."

Rhonda pursed her lips. "Yeah, I know." She sighed. "If he doesn't preach at me, we could probably work something out."

"He's going to want to share what he's learning with you. Most of all, he'll want you to believe like him because he knows what it's done for him, and he wants you to have that too – especially if he loves you." Amy didn't want to ruin her mother's happiness, but she wanted her to think this through.

After a sip of her coffee, Rhonda said, “Well, we’ll just have to deal with it when we get there.” Amy sighed knowing that she had closed the door on any more ‘religious talk’. “Would you be upset if we got back together? I know your life wasn’t fantastic when we were together.”

Amy laughed. “My dream was always to have a loving family. To have you and Dad together and happy together would be the answer to a little girl’s deepest hopes.” Amy reached across the table and grabbed her mom’s hand. “But for all of our sakes, I want you to go slowly. Make sure that this is really what you want, that you are in love with Larry as he is now, not as he was. You have both been through a lot since you were married. You’re different people. You don’t need another heartbreak.”

Rhonda nodded thoughtfully. “You’re right. I rushed in the first time against my mom’s wishes. I’ll listen to my daughter this time, and I’ll make sure it’s the right thing for both – for all of us.”

“I am happy that you are giving him the opportunity to talk to you,” Amy said. “It means so much to him to be able to try to make amends for what he’s done.”

Rhonda looked unhappy for a moment. “I think I’ve probably hurt his chances for that with the other women. My ex-wives club has created a lot of hard feelings against him.”

“I think Dad did enough on his own to create hard feelings. The other wives need to make decisions for themselves where Dad is concerned. It’s up to them to decide if they’ll forgive him or not.”

“Still, we might have all forgiven him long ago if we didn’t get together to relive everything he did and celebrate every divorce he went through.” Rhonda wiped her eyes with her tissue again.

“In some ways I think you guys probably needed the support at the time. But now, you could encourage them to at least hear Dad out.” Amy knew that the other wives looked to Rhonda as their leader, and they took a lot of cues from her.

Rhonda bit her lip. “What if he still has some feelings for them, too, and when they forgive him he turns to them instead?”

“Don’t you want to know that now and not a few years down the road?” Amy watched the indecision cross her mom’s face. “It seems like your past is still haunting your present. You don't trust Dad with these other women. You need to make sure you can trust him one hundred per cent before you move forward."

Rhonda tapped her nails on the table. "You're right of course. I need to know that the others aren't a potential rival." She stood up. "Thanks, Amy. You've been so much help."

Amy embraced her. "I'm happy to help. I'll be praying for you guys."

Rhonda laughed. "You do whatever you need to, but I don't need prayer."

She walked out the door with a spring in her step. Amy threw her cup away and moved more slowly. As she exited she murmured under her breath, "I wish you knew just how much you do need prayer."

34

Amy didn't even wait until she got home before calling her dad. "What are you doing?" she asked roughly. "You had better not be toying with Mom's emotions!"

"What are you talking about?" He sounded as if he had been asleep, his voice rough and unfocused.

"Mom. She called me tonight in tears because you came over with roses, and you talked, and now she's falling in love with you all over again, and you'd better not hurt her!" Her words came pouring out in a torrent. She knew that she probably didn't make any sense, but her concern over her family was too great to put it off.

"Your mom talked to you?"

"Yes. What are you doing?" Her voice was quieter now. She was so confused about her own feelings. On the one hand, she would love for her parents to get together and be the happy family she always wanted. On the other hand, Larry and Rhonda were even further apart than ever because of their beliefs. She didn't know which one would sway the other, but knew that they couldn't exist together as they were.

Larry sighed. "It was nice talking to your mom again. You know what I was like so I won't lie to you and say that your mom was the only woman for me, but in some ways she was my first real love. When we married, I really did have every intention of being faithful and making it last, but I was weak. I got such an ego boost from every conquest I made, and that's what they were, conquests. I didn't have feelings for any of them, it was just physical. When your mom had enough, I was angry, but not surprised." He took a deep breath. "I've thought about Rhonda more than any woman I've been with. Being with her today reminded me of when we were first together."

"That's what she said, too." Amy had reached her apartment by now. She turned on the lights and sat on the couch, leaving her jacket on. She felt emotionally exhausted. "Dad – I don't really know how to say this, I'm certainly new to this whole Christianity thing, but I'm not sure getting back together with Mom is a good idea."

"Why not?"

"You don't have the same belief system. She's still very opposed to God. You guys would fight all the time just like before except instead of women it would be about God." She rubbed her forehead with her hand, feeling the beginning of a headache forming.

Larry was quiet for a while. "You may be right."

"Also, what happens if and when you reconcile with your other wives? Didn't you have feelings for them, too? Will you want to try to get back together with them?"

"No, it was different with them. I married them because I had gotten them pregnant and felt I ought to marry them. I didn't have a connection with them other than physical."

"What about Parker?" Amy hated to bring it up knowing that it was her infidelity and divorce that had left her dad depressed and eventually fighting for his life, but if he had cared that much, it was possible that he would go back to her if she so much as crooked her little finger.

"Even though you know what I was like, it's not easy for me to admit exactly how bad I was," Larry admitted. "Parker was so young and beautiful. It made me feel like I had accomplished something to have her as my wife. I was proud to show her off. But I never really enjoyed being with her. She always wanted more things - nagging me, asking me to get her this and that , demanding."

"Then why were you so heartbroken when she left?"

"Because being on the other side of things made me see myself in a new light, and I didn't like what I saw. I had become a person

I despised, and if I hated myself so much, who would love me? I could only picture the rest of my life spent in loneliness since I had pushed my children away from me, and no longer had anything to offer a woman – or I felt like I had nothing left. It was a bleak picture for me."

Amy stood up and went to the window looking out over the street. "So what now? Mom thinks there's something between the two of you. She was walking on air tonight."

"I don't know, Amy." He was starting to sound irritable. "I'm still trying to figure everything out."

"I know you are. I am, too, but rushing into a relationship seems like your old habits coming to life again. You never could stand to be alone. Are you wanting her just so that you have someone in your life?"

"It's hard to believe, but I'm not alone anymore. Not like I once was anyway. I have you, Angela, and April. I'm still praying that the Lord with heal my relationship with Craig as well. I don't feel like I need a woman in my life, but it was so nice to be with her again."

"If you don't need her, please go slowly. I'm not going to tell you that you should never even entertain the notion of getting back together with Mom, because heaven knows I would love it if you did. But there are things that worry me. Mom could pull you away from your walk, because she doesn't want anything to do with God right now. She's going to be watching you like a hawk, and if you stumble or fall – and we all do – it may make her never want to be a Christian." Amy leaned against the wall by the window and wrapped one arm around her middle. "I'm scared, Dad."

Larry was quiet for so long that Amy was beginning to think their call had been dropped. "Okay, Amy. I'll take it slow. In the meantime, let's pray about this – both of us. You're right that I haven't really been thinking this through. I was basing everything on my emotions. I'll talk to Pastor about it as well and get his advice."

Amy sighed and closed her eyes. "Thank you, Dad. You know that I love you and Mom, right? I don't want to see either of you hurt through this."

"I know, Sweetie. I love you, too." They said their good nights and disconnected the call.

With a sigh, she took off her jacket and sat down on the couch. What a day.

35

Tristan listened to Carmen coughing and sighed. His computer was on, and he was supposed to be working on a website design, but he couldn't stop worrying about his grandma. He saved his work and mounted the stairs.

"Are you okay, Grandma?" He walked into the living room and found Carmen on the ground. He rushed over and helped her up.

"I'm okay. I was only reaching for the remote, and I fell," she explained.

The concern didn't get any better. "Are you sure you didn't hurt yourself when you fell? Your hip, back, everything's good?" His eyes looked her over to see if he saw any bruising or bleeding.

"I'm a bit sore, but I don't think anything's broken." Carmen looked at Tristan intently. "I think it's time though."

"Time for what?" He looked at his watch wondering if he had forgotten to give her one of her medications.

"Time to call Amy." His startled gaze met his grandma's. She had promised to let him know when she was concerned about Amy not making it in time to see her before she passed on.

Heaviness settled on his chest. He had been preparing for this, but it was still hard to hear. He nodded. Gently making sure that Carmen was comfortable, he tucked a blanket around her and got the remote that she had been reaching for before she had fallen. Heading out to the back porch he sat down on the porch swing and gazed over the backyard. Spring was coming. The trees were starting to show signs of green. A symbol of new life. Yet an old life was fading in the home behind him. He sighed heavily. "Lord, help me through this."

Pulling out his phone, he made the call that he had been

dreading. He knew she would be at work, but he hoped that she wasn't in a meeting so that she would answer. Relief filled him as he heard her voice.

"Amy," his voice cracked. He cleared his throat.

"What is it? What's wrong?"

"Grandma's not doing so well. She'd like for you to come see her one last time."

There was no sound for a long time. "Of course." In that simple statement he heard so much emotion. He knew that in just a short amount of time Carmen had become a very special person in Amy's life. He had never realized how quickly someone can become dear until he met Amy – and Carol, too, for that matter. "I'll be there are soon as I can. I need to get some things rearranged here first."

"Of course." He pushed the swing with his toe. Closing his eyes, he said, "Thank you so much for doing this."

"I love your grandma. She's taught me so much in such a short time. I would hate to not get to see her again in this life." Tristan smiled at the affection Amy had for Carmen. "I've got to go, but I'll see you soon. I love you." And the call was disconnected.

Tristan pulled the phone away slowly and stared at it. Had she just said she loved him? He probably heard wrong. Or maybe she had still been talking about Carmen. That was probably it. She meant 'I love your grandma'. Still the heaviness that had settled on his chest lifted and was replaced with warmth he couldn't describe. His heart felt much lighter as he went back inside the house.

******

Amy's eyes widened as she realized what she had said when she had ended her call with Tristan. Had she really told him that she loved him? Maybe he hadn't heard her. Oh, she hoped that was the case.

Shaking herself, she got busy on making her plans to leave. She first went to Carol's new website and made a reservation. She smiled as she saw that Sweetheart Suite was available and reserved it. Somehow she viewed that room as her own personal spot. She couldn't wait to see the view from the balcony in spring and made a mental note to bring her sketch pad.

The next thing to do was clear her calendar as much as possible. She began making phone calls and sending out emails. Distantly she was aware of Katie standing by her desk watching her curiously. As soon as she hung up, Katie jumped in. "What's going on?"

"A dear friend of mine isn't doing well right now. I'm going to go visit her before she passes away." Amy kept typing as she talked.

"I thought I heard you mention Willow Creek. You can't possibly be close to someone from there. It's only been a couple months since you visited for the first time."

Amy met her assistant's gaze. "I've discovered recently that relationships can develop, be repaired, and fall apart in a much shorter time than I ever thought possible." She turned back to her work.

"You're going to lose clients over this," Katie kept on.

"So far everyone has been very understanding. Besides most of them I deal with through email and nothing will change there."

"Wright won't be happy." Katie's eyes widened as she met Amy's.

"Ah, that's the reason you're upset about this." Amy drummed her fingers on her desk. "I'll tell you what. All he's coming to do is look over the proofs. I'll keep his appointment and you can take my place."

"I can't do that!" Katie exclaimed in fear. "He's expecting you. It's not my place, not my job. I can't – I just can't."

Amy laughed at her panic. "It's not rocket science. You just have to show him the proofs and make note of which one he likes and what kind of changes he'd like done if any." Amy turned back to the computer as if the matter was done.

"He's not going to be happy." Katie was actually wringing her hands in worry.

"Fine. I'll call him and make sure he's good with it. Stop

worrying." She picked up her phone and dialed Wright's number.

"I was hoping to hear from you," he answered.

"Yeah, you say that to any female who calls you." She heard him chuckle before she continued. "I have a friend who isn't doing well, and I need to go see her before she passes away. Unfortunately this affects our meeting, but I don't think it should delay anything for you."

"How's that?" Wright didn't sound upset at all which was a good sign.

"This meeting was simply to look at proofs. You can still come down to the office and meet with my assistant, Katie. Tell her which one you like and any changes you want made, and she'll get that information back to me." Katie looked like she was about to sink into the floor with mortification. "Another option would be for me to simply email you the proofs and converse that way."

"Katie's that cute girl in your office, right?"

Amy rolled her eyes. Wright was always ready to please a lady – one of the reasons she could never trust him. "Yes, she's cute." Katie blushed brightly.

"I can come in. I've already got it on the schedule anyway. I was going to try to persuade you to come to lunch with me afterwards. Do you let her lock up the office and slip away while you're gone, or do you keep her chained to her desk?"

"She'd be free to go to lunch with you if she'd like." Katie stifled a squeal of delight.

"You know I'd rather it be you, baby, but I'm flexible."

"And that's exactly why I'm not your 'baby'. Thanks for being flexible professionally though." Wright chuckled again, and Amy was glad that his spirits were back after their last meeting. She was certain that all it took was a few girls fawning over him to get his ego at its normal level. Any further damage to his arrogance would certainly be repaired by Katie who was as giddy as a teenager at a boy band concert. She disconnected and looked up at Katie. "Happy now?"

Katie's giggle was all the answer Amy needed.

36

Carol rushed out front when she heard the door open. She had been anxiously waiting for Amy's arrival all day. Tristan had confided why Amy was coming back to Willow Creek so soon after her first visit, and although Carol was saddened by the reason, she was pleased to see her new friend again so soon.

"I was hoping it was you!" Carol cried as she hurried forward to give Amy a hug. "I'm so glad to see you, although I'm sorry you're here for such a sad occasion."

"Sad, but sweet," Amy said with a wistful smile. Carol was amazed at the maturity Amy was showing in her faith. Already she understood that death was viewed differently on the other side of the cross.

"I see you're in the Sweetheart Suite again." Carol smiled at her. "I'm so glad you like that room. I think it's one of the prettiest rooms I have."

"It's got a special place in my heart."

Carol finished all the check-in paperwork, and then came around the desk. "I know you know the way, but I'd like to escort you to the room anyway, if you don't mind."

"Of course. I would be disappointed if you didn't." Amy grabbed her small suitcase and followed Carol up the stairs.

"Tristan's been by to see me often since you left. He keeps me up to date on what's going on with you" Carol turned around to grin at her. "I like that you're exclusive friends. I think that was a smart decision."

"It's been nice to have him in my life, but it's hard to classify our relationship as anything else."

Carol shrugged. "And maybe it will never develop into

something else. Too often people ruin a good friendship by trying to force something that's not there." They reached the door and Carol opened it wide for her guest.

"Can a friendship be ruined by not pursuing something further?" Amy asked. "I guess what I really mean is what if God wants us to be more, but we're too afraid of ruining our friendship, and so we miss out on something even better?"

"I guess you need to be praying about it, watching closely, and following where you think He's leading." Carol patted her on the arm. "I have a feeling you'll know one way or another after this trip though."

"I don't know. It doesn't really seem like a great time to get romantic." Amy shrugged off her jacket and laid it on a chair.

"Probably not, but sometimes it takes emotional events for us to truly understand our feelings. It was at my father's funeral that I knew I would marry Gabe someday. He was so sweet and helpful without being intrusive. I remember going home, lying on my bed completely emotionally exhausted, but feeling like there was a bright future just ahead." Carol picked up a package that was on the mantle and handed it to Amy. "When I heard you were coming, I had May make this for you. I wished I had thought to do it before you left the first time."

"That's so sweet." Amy opened the package and found a frame with a lovely watercolor inside. "It's 1 Corinthians 13:4-8. My favorite verses." She gave Carol a hug. "Thank you so much. Your daughter is so talented."

"I'm proud of her. She helped me a lot when I was getting Holliday Hotel ready to go."

"I memorized these verses as soon as I got home. I wanted them with me all the time." Amy ran her hand tenderly over the letters of the painting. "If it hadn't been for these verses, I'm not sure I would have ever seen God's love."

"Perhaps. Either way, I'm glad He used them to bring you to Him." Carol headed for the door. "I'd better get back to work, but feel free to stop by and see me whenever you can."

Carol had a feeling her inn would be used for another wedding in the near future. She loved seeing romance unfold under its roof.

******

Amy immediately went to the balcony after Carol left. The lake had thawed and was now sparkling in the warm sunlight. What had been blanketed in snow was now the bright green of fresh growth. Along the edges of the woods, wildflowers were beginning to bloom. The trees were budding with new life. Birds chased each other in the sky as they prepared their nests. She had been right. The view from the balcony was lovely in more seasons than winter.

She longed to sit down and sketch the view, but knew she had to contact Tristan first. Going back inside, she grabbed her phone and sent him a text saying that she was at Holliday Hotel. *Can I visit Carmen tonight, or would tomorrow be better?*

It didn't take long before she got a response. *Can you join us for dinner?*

Absolutely. When? Where?

After setting up the time, Amy got freshened up and headed down to the kitchen. "I'm going to the Romeros for dinner tonight," she informed Carol.

"Oh good. I'm glad you'll get to see them right away."

Amy sat down at a stool at the island. "Is she doing very badly?"

Carol clasped Amy's hands in her own. "I'd be surprised if Carmen makes it through the week you're here, but it's in God's hands. If He wants He can allow her to live many more years."

Amy nodded. "I wish I'd known her sooner."

"I'm sure she feels the same way about you. Don't focus on that though. Focus on enjoying the time you have with her." Carol gave her hands a squeeze before releasing them. "Sometimes it's a blessing to have some forewarning." She smiled sadly.

Amy knew she was thinking about Gabe's passing by the watery look to her eyes. Every time Carol spoke of Gabe, she got that same look. "I'd better get going. I'll keep your advice in mind while I'm visiting."

When she arrived at the house, she hesitated before heading to the door. Life had happened in this house, and now death was lingering outside. She took a deep breath and forced herself forward. Pasting on a bright smile, she rang the doorbell.

As soon as she saw Tristan her heart melted. His face bore lines of worry and strain. His brown eyes reflected sadness even as he smiled at her. Instantly she threw herself into his arms. Holding each other tightly for a moment, she realized that they were both fortifying each other before heading in.

"I'm so glad you came," Tristan told her. "She's been asking for you." He sighed. "And I could use a friend right now, too."

Amy smiled. "Me, too. We'll help each other through."

She entered the house and found Carmen sleeping in her usual spot in the living room. The television was off this time. "Has she been sleeping often?" she asked.

Tristan nodded. "I feel like she's awake less and less every day."

Amy went and sat near Carmen, placing a hand on the heavily veined hand of the older woman. Carmen blinked and looked to see her guest. Amy's smile wasn't forced when she saw the joy on Carmen's face as she saw her.

"You're here!" She turned her hand over and squeezed Amy's. "Let's eat."

It was so like Carmen to skip the emotional for the prosaic that Amy had to laugh. "I'm ready for dinner, too," she admitted as she helped Carmen to her feet. Tristan had already gone to the kitchen to grab the dinner, so Amy let Carmen lean on her as they made slow progress towards the dining room.

A bowl of chicken and dumplings and a salad sat at each place along with a glass of water. Carmen inhaled the scent happily. "My favorite. I'm so glad I don't have to watch my weight anymore."

Tristan chuckled. "You always were an optimist."

Despite Carmen's raptures, Amy noticed that she ate very little of the delicious meal. Tristan watched each small bite with concern, but they both kept up cheerful banter throughout the meal. When Tristan began to clean up the dishes, Amy felt like his shoulders were slumped in resignation. Or perhaps it was defeat. Death was coming. It loomed over the table as palpable as the utensils they were holding in their hands.

Amy started to help clean up, but Tristan shooed her off to spend time with Carmen. "She needs you right now," he said, as he took the bowl from her hand.

Amy got to the living room just as Carmen reached her recliner. She hurried over to help her sit, and then took the seat on the couch nearest her. "I'm glad I got to see you once more," Carmen said.

"I hope it's more than once more. I'm here for a week. I plan on visiting you every day while I'm in town." Amy's heart felt heavy as she realized that Carmen's words could very well be true. This could be the last time she saw her.

Carmen shook her head. "It'll be good for Tristan to have you near as he goes through this. Don't get me wrong. I wanted to see you for my own sake, because I love you, but I really wanted you here to comfort Tristan. When the time comes, I'll be fine." A lovely light shown on her face as she spoke. "But Tristan is going to be grieving and lonely. He'll need a friend."

"I'll be with him as long as I can," Amy promised.

"Good girl." Carmen studied her carefully. "I probably shouldn't say anything, but I feel like God brought you here for a specific purpose."

Amy smiled. "I feel the same way. If I hadn't come here, I don't think I would have ever become a Christian."

"Even though I rejoice that you are a believer now, that's not what I meant." The confusion Amy felt must have been visible on her face, because Carmen laughed. "I've been praying for God to bring Tristan a wife. I knew he didn't want to marry because of me, but God brought the right girl at the right time, and I'm so thankful." She clasped her hands together at her chest. "He was faithful to answer my prayers just when I needed it most. He didn't have to let me see it, but He did."

"I don't know . . . we're just . . . it's not," Amy stammered.

"I know, dear, but I believe that you'll see it soon yourself."

She laughed softly. "God's timing is so good. Tristan couldn't marry while he was caring for me so God brings you along at the end of my life. He lets you two become friends first, but I believe it won't be long before you both realize that you're more than that." She sighed. "I prayed. God answered. Oh He is good."

"Have you told Tristan any of this?" Amy wasn't sure she could face him if he knew about his grandma's hopes for them.

"Of course I did!" Amy barely repressed the groan that threatened to escape. "He needed a little push and encouragement to begin thinking about girls again. It's been a while since he was free to go out with anyone seriously because of me." She leaned her head back on her chair. "It'll be so nice not to be a burden anymore."

"I don't think Tristan saw you as a burden. He loves caring for you."

"I know he does. He's a good boy, but he put his life on hold for me. I'm so glad he can resume living again when I'm gone." Carmen's eyes twinkled as she touched Amy's cheek. "I've thought of you as a granddaughter since I met you. I hope it won't be long before you're really my granddaughter. I wonder if I'll get to see it happen from Heaven." She gazed dreamily at Amy's face. "Do you think God lets us see what's going on down here?"

Amy shrugged helplessly. "I'm afraid all my education on that subject has come from Hollywood. I doubt it's very Scriptural."

Carmen laughed. "Probably not. Well, either way, I'm content."

Tristan joined them at that moment, and Amy found that she couldn't even look at him. He pulled up a chair next to Carmen and sat down. "What have you ladies been discussing?"

"Whether or not I'll get to see you two get married from heaven," Carmen said quickly, her eyes lively and young.

Tristan flushed a deep red, and if her mortification was any indication, Amy's color was close to his. "Well, that's an interesting – and awkward – conversation."

Carmen chuckled again. "I think Amy agrees." She sighed. "Maybe I am just a foolish old woman, but I pray my hopes and dreams are right. You two both mean so much to me. I'd love to know you're taking care of each other."

"We can promise that we'll look out for each other regardless," Tristan suggested.

Carmen shrugged. "You can promise that, but if you marry someone else, they may object to your attachment to each other." Carmen reached out and grabbed each of their hands. "I'm leaving you in God's hands in any case. I know that He has better plans than I could ever come up with." She sighed again. "I'm so tired. I'm ready for God to take me." She closed her eyes and leaned back in her chair.

Amy and Tristan exchanged glances. Carmen was fading before their eyes. Amy sighed heavily and got down on her knees by Carmen. She laid her head on her lap. "I'm going to miss you," she whispered.

Carmen placed her hand on her head. "I'm glad you and Tristan will have each other when you get lonely. And of course, God is always with you as well."

A tear slipped down Amy's cheek. She laughed shakily. "To think that before I came here loneliness was my life. I embraced it, but now I don't want to go back to my solitary existence – even if sometimes it brings pain."

"God didn't intend for us to be alone. It's why He created us women in the first place, so man wouldn't be alone." Carmen laughed softly. "You see why I want Tristan to find a woman."

"Okay, Grandma, that's enough," Tristan spoke up with slight smile. "Let Amy be."

"All right, all right." She smiled at her grandson. "You can't blame me for trying." She yawned. "I think it's time for me to lie down. I really am weary."

"I'll help you to your room," Tristan said, as he held his hand out to help her up. Amy went back to the couch as she watched Carmen lean heavily on Tristan as she went to her room. When he came back, Tristan sat next to Amy. For a while they stared at the floor each lost in their own thoughts.

"How long do you think she has left?" Amy finally asked softly.

Tristan shook his head helplessly. "I don't know. I'm at the point that I'm hoping it comes soon. It's hard to watch her fade a little bit more every day." He leaned back on the couch. "I'll miss her, but she's ready to go, and I'm finally at the point where I'm ready to let her go."

Amy reached out and held his hand. "I've been praying for both of you."

"Thank you." Amy searched Tristan's face. He looked tired and worn. She knew this had been hard on him.

"I should go so you can rest," Amy said.

Tristan simply nodded, and Amy wasn't even sure if her words had pierced his consciousness. She slipped out the door quietly leaving Tristan sitting in the same place with his eyes staring unseeingly in space.

Tears slipped down her cheeks as she drove back to Holliday Hotel. Carmen was still so full of life and spirit, yet her body was failing. She seemed ready to leave this earth, and Amy didn't blame her. She'd leave behind all her pain, her weakness, her fatigue, and wake up whole, and well in the presence of her Savior. But she'd also leave a hole in the hearts of those nearest her. Amy knew she would miss this woman, but she also knew that she had to be ready for her to go, because the end was drawing near.

37

The balcony of Sweetheart Suite was tinged pink as the sun began to rise. Amy sat with her sketchpad on her lap drawing the scene that had so charmed her in winter, and now comforted her in spring. Tears rolled down her face, and she often had to stop what she was doing in order to wipe them away. For some reason she couldn't sleep. She had awoken suddenly and had felt an urge to pray for Tristan and Carmen. She had prayed for an hour, and then a peace had filled her. Still she couldn't sleep. Even though she had peace, the sadness was nearly overwhelming.

A familiar figure emerged under her skilled hand. Standing along the shore was a young woman, not lonely this time though. She looked stronger than she had in the winter, although there was a sorrow about her. Beside her another woman stood. The other woman was older and seemed to be saying good-bye. A ray of sunlight fell on her head giving her an angelic appearance.

Amy sighed as she finished the sketch. It was her farewell to Carmen. She wondered if she would be able to give it to her before she died. If not, she would give it to Tristan.

The sun was now above the horizon and shining cheerfully on the lake. Amy stood up and stretched. Surely Carol would be up by now. No sense in brooding by herself. She went inside and got dressed. As she reached for the doorknob to go downstairs, her phone let her know she had a text.

Grandma went home peacefully in her sleep early this morning.

Amy clutched the phone tightly as her breath caught in her throat. *What time this morning?* She wondered if God had woken her up just as Carmen was passing.

Just before sunrise.

Amy laughed a little even as her eyes filled with tears. Carmen would have gone about the time Amy had felt peace settle on her. She shook her head in wonder. Even though she hadn't been at Carmen's side, she felt as if she had somehow taken part in her home going.

I was up and praying at that time. Couldn't sleep.

I couldn't sleep either, so I was sitting near her bed and praying.

Are you okay? She remembered how down Tristan had been the night before.

Yeah, I'm okay. I probably won't be able to see you today. Gotta get the plans in order and talk to the family.

That's fine. I can find things to do. If you need anything let me know.

I will.

Amy leaned against the door and took a deep breath. For a moment she contemplated staying in her room and wallowing in her grief. It didn't take long for her to shake off that idea. She needed comfort from someone who cared about her.

With resolve she descended into the kitchen. Carol turned around in surprise when the door swung open. "Oh, Amy! I never have guests down this early. You surprised me." After another look at her young guest, Carol put down the pan she had been getting out of the oven, and rushed over to pull Amy into her arms. "What happened? Are you alright?"

Amy nodded and then burst into tears. Carol held her tightly as she cried, not attempting to talk, simply being a comforter. When Amy was calm enough to speak, she whispered, "Carmen's gone."

"Oh no. I'm so sorry." She rubbed her back, then led her to one of the stools. "Sit here. Don't move." With a burst of energy, Carol moved around the room. She brought back a mug of coffee, a serving of quiche, fresh fruit, and a muffin still warm from the oven. "Eat. Things will brighten a bit with food in your stomach."

Amy's smile was pathetic, but she obeyed. She doubted that Carol's prescription would work, but it was worth a shot. Carol finished getting breakfast ready for her other guests, but once it was out on the buffet, she sat down next to Amy.

"How are you feeling?" Carol asked when Amy had finished her plate.

"Not as miserable as I thought I would," Amy admitted. "She was ready to go when I saw her last night. It was almost as if she hung on until I got here."

"It's good to know that she's better off now than she was."

Amy nodded. "I know I'll miss her," she smiled at Carol, "but for the first time I have comfort that I'll see her again."

"Paul wrote that Christians grieve, but not like those without hope." Carol pulled Amy close. "That's exactly what you're experiencing now."

"I like that. Hopeful grief." Amy toyed with her coffee mug. "I drew a picture this morning from the balcony. I was standing by the lake, and Carmen was next to me waving good-bye. She looked so eager to leave."

"What a lovely farewell. I'd like to see your drawing if it's all right with you."

"I'll bring it down later. I think I'll give it to Tristan."

"That's a great idea." Carol patted her shoulder. "I need to go check on things in the dining room, but don't go away." Amy put her dishes in the sink while Carol was gone and refilled her coffee mug. She was surprised that her grief was less than she had expected. More than that, there was even a sense of joy in her grief. She wouldn't have guessed it was possible, but knowing that there was life after death made such a difference.

Carol bustled back in. "Now, how was your time with her last night?"

Amy laughed. "It was wonderful. She was so funny and lighthearted. You'd never guess she was staring death in the face except for the weariness that hung over her. She was more than ready."

"I'm glad you have such a good final memory of her."

Amy chuckled and shook her head. "She spent most of the night trying to convince me to marry Tristan."

Carol smiled mischievously. "Maybe she was onto something.

I don't think that would be such a bad idea. Tristan will be lonely now without his grandma."

"I hardly think that's a reason to marry someone," Amy said dryly.

"I can still hope," Carol murmured as she took a sip of coffee. "You would live in Willow Creek, and I'd get to see you more often." She looked at Amy slyly. "It worked for Willa and Owen."

Amy hugged Carol. "I would love living near you. I'll let you be for now. I know this is a busy time of day for you." She waved her hand as she slipped out the door.

Back in her room, she got caught up on work emails, did a design for one of her best customers, and called Katie to make sure everything was going well on her end. She thought about Carol's idea of living in Willow Creek. She had grown to love the small town. But her clients were all in the city. An image of Tristan's workspace came to mind. Working from home wasn't so rare anymore. In her line of work, it wouldn't be completely impossible to do everything online.

She went back out onto the porch and stared at the lake. Leaving her family behind might be an issue, especially with their relationships just beginning to mend. She shook her head. What was she thinking? She couldn't leave. Katie depended on her for a job, and she'd never agree to move to a small town. Her family would grow distant again. It was a terrible idea.

Grabbing her jacket, Amy decided to pass the time by going for a walk. She headed out and walked beside the lake. She hadn't explored the area around the lake yet. Most of her excursions had led her into town.

She loved how the lake looked from different areas. Unlike most lake fronts where houses were built as tightly together as possible to capitalize on the premium space, these houses were spread out with mature trees on the property. The houses were as interesting to her as the views of the lake. Each had its own personality. Some were stone cottages while others were wood cabins and still others were more traditional in design. Modern homes with straight lines and large windows sat next to historic homes. It was so diverse and interesting.

All of sudden, one house caught her attention and she came to a stop. Amid all the lovely homes, this one was an eyesore. The lines of the house were good, but it had been sadly neglected. Windows were broken. The paint was peeling badly. The back door was swinging awkwardly on its hinges. The porch was sagging. The house looked sad and lonely.

Amy's steps took her right up to the house. The appearance spoke plainly of abandonment so she wasn't afraid of trespassing. She looked in the windows and from what she could make out through the dirt on them the inside had been almost completely stripped. She walked around to the front and found that even though it was dilapidated as well, the house was on a nice lot. The yard was overgrown and the picket fence had pieces missing, but she still found the house charming. The traditional lines of the house were charming with peaked eaves and a large porch.

On impulse she called a local realtor and asked who owned the house and if it was for sale. The realtor was surprised at her interest, but let her know that the house was indeed available. She agreed to meet Amy there and show her the inside.

Amy walked around the property a couple of times noting things that she liked as well as things that needed repaired. A car pulled up and a woman stepped out. She had dark skin, nearly black eyes, and her hair was braided. She was tall and curvy. Her slacks and blouse were crisp and neat, and Amy immediately felt comfortable with her. She greeted her with a handshake.

"I'm Amy Juliette."

"It's nice to meet you. I'm Concordia Hill, but most people around here call me Connie." The woman looked over at the house. "It's even worse than I remembered." She laughed as she looked back at Amy. "Probably not the best sales tactic to say something like that."

"I'd have to be blind to not see that there are issues. What's the story behind this house? Why is it in this condition?"

"It was bought by an investor before the housing market crash. He had gutted it before the money ran out, but never got a chance to finish it. He let it go back to the bank, but there was so much work to be done that even at a great price no one was interested." Connie looked at Amy with interest. "Willow Creek isn't really a booming town with people moving here so the real estate market isn't always great. Right after the crash it was worse than ever."

"You'd think that another investor would have swooped in when the price was low and flipped it."

"I don't think the other lake house owners were too happy about an investor being here in the first place to be honest. They pride themselves on being a family community. I think they were afraid it'd be a summer home or a vacation rental property." She eyed Amy suspiciously. "You wouldn't be trying to do that would you?"

Amy turned and looked at the house. "I don't know what I want. This house kind of spoke to me." She laughed self-consciously. "Sounds stupid, I know."

Connie smiled. "Not to me. Houses speak to me all the time. It's why I got into real estate. Sometimes I think I should have become an architect, but we didn't have money for that kind of education. Let's go see your house." She led Amy inside. As they had thought the inside was pretty bare. The flooring was all torn up, the kitchen was completely ripped out, studs were visible in places, and the bathrooms were gutted. "It's pretty rough."

"Yes, it is." Amy's eyes sparkled as she looked around. "There's still a lot that I like though. I love that fireplace, and the floor plan is nice."

"Beauty is in the eye of the beholder," Connie said with a smile. "All I see is work."

"There's definitely plenty of that, too, but I can make it exactly what I want it to be." She stepped out onto the back porch and gasped. "And that view can make the work worth it all."

"It is a good view," Connie agreed. The lake was beautiful with large trees near the shore, a couple of which were close enough that Amy could see a hammock strung between them. There was a short dock for a small boat or swimming. "What do you think? Is it worth it?"

Amy sighed indecisively. "I don't know. What's the asking price?"

Connie gave her a number that surprised Amy. "But we could probably get them to go lower since it's been on the market for so long."

"The property is worth so much more than that," Amy stated.

"Worth more when the house is in shape," Connie explained.

"Is there someone in town that I can get an estimate on how much the work would cost?"

"Sure." Connie reached in the folder she carried with her and pulled out a business card. It read "Coburn & Son".

"I think I've met Mrs. Coburn," Amy said thoughtfully.

"They're newlyweds. Got married at Holliday Hotel."

"I've definitely met her then. Carol Holliday speaks highly of them."

"Owen Coburn, the son of Coburn & Son, did all the repairs on Holliday Hotel," Connie mentioned.

"Then he does great work. I'll give him a call."

Connie handed her another business card, this one with her own information on it. "Give me a call when you've made a decision. Even if you decide not to take it, I'm curious how much it would cost to get that house in shape, too."

38

When Amy got back to the inn, she ran up and got her drawing to show Carol. She found her cleaning up the dining room. Carol greeted her with a smile and stopped working to take a look at the picture.

"This is beautiful, Amy. It's going to be so meaningful to Tristan." Amy beamed at Carol's praise. "So where did you end up going this morning?" Carol resumed wiping off the tables.

"I took a walk along the lake. There's this house that I just fell in love with."

Carol smiled at Amy. "There are so many beautiful homes along the lake. Is it the stone house with the ivy on it?"

"I don't think you'll ever guess," Amy answered with a laugh.

Carol thought for a minute, turning her head to the side and studying Amy. "The white home with the bay window?"

Amy just laughed harder.

Carol shrugged. "Which one is it?"

"The abandoned home." Carol's expression was even more humorous to Amy. "I told you that you wouldn't guess."

"Why that one?"

"I'm not sure. I like the traditional style, and I see so much potential. Maybe it's my artistic side that sees what it could be." Amy sat down at one of the tables. She grabbed a napkin and started shredding it. "I called a realtor."

Carol sat down across from Amy, her eyes wide. "Are you considering buying it?"

"I don't know." Amy looked up at Carol. "A part of me would love it. I really enjoy it here and I could do my job here as well as I could back home." She sighed. "But I'm just starting to reconnect with my family, and I'm not sure I should leave them."

"Which realtor did you call?"

"Her name was Concordia Hill, but she goes by Connie. Do you know her?"

Carol nodded. "My best friend, Elena, is a realtor, and Connie works in her office."

"She gave me the name of Owen Coburn to give me an estimate on the renovations."

Carol smiled broadly. "One of my favorite people," she stated. "He did my renovations, and he was very reasonable. His estimate wasn't perfect, of course, since it seems like they always find something that they didn't expect, but it was close enough. He and I became close during the project. I view him almost as if he were my son."

"Well, seeing what a great job he did here, I know I can trust him." Amy's gaze took in the small room. He had either left or reintroduced some of the character that gave old homes their charm. "What should I do?"

Carol shook her head. "I can't tell you what to do. You know that I would love to have you just down the way from me, but this is a decision that you have to make." Amy lowered her head in discouragement. "I will give you some advice though." Amy raised her head in anticipation. "Pray about it. Get the estimate from Owen. Pray about it. Talk to your bank about loan information. Pray about it. Talk to people you trust, and especially your family. And most importantly, pray about it."

Amy chuckled. "I think I get what the most important advice you have for me is. How will I know what God answers?"

"I think you'll know one way or another. Sometimes it's through circumstances like financing falling through. Sometimes it's through a gut feeling. Sometimes it's through others who tell you that they think this is where you belong. Sometimes it's a still small voice that speaks to you. But somehow you'll know."

Amy nodded and stood up. "I think I'll go call Tristan and see how he's doing. Then I'll do some research."

Carol patted her shoulder. "I know you'll make the right

decision, and regardless of whether God tells you to come here or stay where you are, you'll always have Tristan and I as friends."

Amy went back to her room, her heart racing with indecision. When she got to her room, she immediately fell to her knees by the couch. "Lord, I don't know what to do. I like this house and the idea of living here excites me. But I hate to leave my family and friends behind especially since we're recently growing close." She sighed. "Then again, Tristan could use a friend nearby right about now. See what I mean, Lord? I have no idea what to do. Will You help me by making it very clear what I'm supposed to do?"

Feeling more at ease, Amy stood up and called Tristan. "Hey. I just wanted to see how things were going."

Sadness tinged every tone of Tristan's voice. "It's okay. Since we'd been preparing for it, Grandma had all her final plans in order so that makes it easier in some ways. My parents should get here tonight, and my brother and sister should be here tomorrow or the day after. The service is going to be on Saturday."

Amy offered a silent prayer of gratitude. She was leaving on Sunday and had been afraid that she would miss the service. "I'm glad you'll have your family soon."

"Me, too. I'd better go now. I'm meeting with Pastor Westley in ten minutes to go over the service." He paused. "Could you meet me for dinner?"

"Sure. When and where?" He gave her the name of a deli downtown and set a time, then ended the call.

It must be hard to be alone when something like this happened. She was certain that Tristan's outlook would be better once his family got there. He needed their help and support now. He had borne Carmen's burdens for years on his own. It was time he had others to help him.

She prayed for Tristan before getting online and checking out some loan information. Her credit was good, and she even had quite a bit saved up. Buying the house wouldn't be a problem, but the repairs might be. She made a call to Owen and set up a time for the following day to meet him at the house. Making a mental note to take pictures of the house next time, she got her sketchpad out.

Her fingers moved quickly across the page as she sketched the house from memory, but as she drew she fixed it up to what she wanted it to be. She flipped pages and sketched the floor plan as best she could and drew what she wanted that to look like as well. She continued doing each room of the house until she had everything exactly as she pictured it. It wouldn't hurt to have her ideas on paper when she met Owen so he'd have a better idea of the cost. As she closed the notebook, her mind went to the basement. Connie hadn't taken her down there because there was no electricity in the home so they wouldn't have been able to see much anyway. Amy wondered if it would be possible to make the basement into a guest suite for her family when they came to visit. A living room, a nice bathroom, and a couple of bedrooms would make a nice space for guests.

Smiling softly to herself, Amy knew suddenly that she was going to pursue this until she got a definitive 'no' answer from God. For the time being she would assume that God had led her to this home and given her this plan.

39

Tristan walked slowly into the deli. Looking around he saw that Amy was already at a small table near the back. He wasn't sure he felt much like eating, but he knew his grandma would tell him he needed to eat something if she were still with him. Joining Amy he felt the sorrow ease slightly. Her eyes reflected his own grief, but there was a twinkle of joy in hers as well. Carmen would have been happy to see that Amy wasn't mired in grief. That thought gave him a small jolt. She wouldn't want him to be drowning in grief either. After all, she was in the best place she could be.

He smiled slightly as he took the seat opposite Amy. "Thanks for meeting me for dinner."

"How did the meeting with the pastor go?" she asked softly.

"Aaron had already talked with Grandma so he understood most of what she wanted already." He rubbed his hands over his face. "It's been a long day."

"I would imagine so. You were up before dawn and have been busy all day. It'll be good for you to have your family here so they can bear some of the burden, too."

Tristan nodded. A girl came to take their order. Tristan ordered a bowl of chicken noodle soup while Amy got half a turkey sandwich with a side salad. When the waitress left, Tristan said, "Thanks again for meeting me. I needed to get out of the house."

"Of course. I would have been happy to have spent the day helping you if you had wanted."

"You would?"

"Absolutely! This isn't a good time to be alone. This is the time for people who care about you to be by your side. Which is why I'm so glad you won't be alone tonight."

The waitress brought their food, and they paused their conversation to pray before eating. "I wish I had known you would have gone with me," Tristan said. "I didn't want to burden you, but it would have been nice to have some company."

Amy shrugged. "All you had to do was ask."

Tristan laughed softly. "You're right." He took a bite of soup and immediately realized that he was hungry. He hadn't eaten hardly anything all day. "What did you do all day?" he asked before digging into his soup eagerly.

Amy's eyes twinkled. She put down her sandwich and wiped her hands on her napkin. Leaning forward, she said, "I found a house."

"Here?" Tristan stopped eating and looked at her.

"Yeah, beside the lake. It's adorable, and I love it, but it needs a lot of work. I'm looking into what everything is going to cost." She picked her sandwich back up. "Obviously it's a decision that I would have to consider carefully before making." She smiled. "And Carol drove home the point that I should be praying about it as well."

"Wow. That was not what I expected at all." He felt a little bit of excitement – a welcome relief from the weight of mourning. Having Amy close by would be great. He could use a friend when his family left. Not that he didn't have other friends in Willow Creek, but Amy was different. She had loved Carmen, too. "I'll be praying for you, too. Can I see the house?"

She looked up at him indecisively. "I don't want to take you away from your family while they're here, and I leave on Sunday."

Tristan hadn't thought about his family being here. While he was sitting with Amy, she was all he needed. "Well, I can see what plans are made once everyone gets here. I might be able to get away from things for a little while."

Amy smiled. "I'd be happy to show it to you if you have time. Just be prepared. It needs a ton of work so it's not pretty right now, but the way it looks in my mind, it's gorgeous."

Tristan chuckled. He had needed this. Amy understood his emotional state, the obligations he was under right now, and yet was able to lift his spirits.

They finished dinner and stood up to leave. "I have something for you in my car," Amy told him. They stepped outside and the fading sunlight tinged everything in shades of pink. Opening the car, Amy pulled out a gift bag and handed it to him. He pulled out a framed and matted sketch of Harper Lake. As he stared at the two figures by the lake, he had to swallow hard. The picture showed how much Carmen had meant to Amy. It touched him that she wanted him to have it.

"Thank you. This is very special," he whispered.

"I drew that as the sun was rising this morning." Tears made her eyes shimmer. Tristan simply nodded, unable to speak. "I think she was telling me good-bye." Amy stood close to Tristan's shoulder looking over at the drawing.

"Maybe you should keep it then," he offered.

"No," she said looking up at him. "It was meant for you." Almost on impulse, she reached up and kissed his cheek. "Let me know if I can help at all."

Tristan wasn't sure what he answered or even if he answered anything. All he knew was that he was standing alone on the sidewalk with the picture in his hands watching Amy's taillights as they disappeared into the distance. He roused himself and headed home. His steps that were sluggish an hour ago had acquired a spring to them. His heart had lightened with only a few minutes in Amy's company.

As soon as he got home, he hung the drawing above Carmen's favorite chair. He stared at it for a moment, then whispered, "I'm going to miss you, Grandma." Even as he said it, he realized that though it was true, the loneliness wasn't as oppressive as it had been. He thought that it probably began lightening when Amy had announced that she had found a house she loved in Willow Creek.

A car's lights penetrated the front window as it entered the driveway. Knowing it could only be his mom and dad, Tristan went out to help them with their luggage. Kurt and Liana Romero met their son with embraces and tears.

"I'm so sorry we didn't get here before she passed," Liana

cried. "You told us that she was fading fast, but we couldn't seem to get away. Now I wish we'd tried harder."

"It's okay, Ma. She understood." Tristan patted Liana's back as she cried on his shoulder.

Kurt stood looking at the house with sadness in his eyes. "It doesn't seem real to walk into that house and not find her there," he finally said.

Tristan sighed. "I know. Fortunately, I've been busy today, but I know in the coming days I'll go check on her out of habit."

"We shouldn't have let you carry this alone for so long," Liana said.

"I was fine," Tristan replied honestly, as he helped his dad with the suitcases. "Grandma and I had a great time together. And when it happened you guys couldn't leave. Let's not spend time thinking about what should have been or might have been."

Liana nodded as she held the door open for her men to enter the house. Tristan took the suitcases to the guest bedroom. When he returned to the living room, he took a moment to study his parents. He knew he looked like a younger version of his dad whose dark hair was mostly gray now. His brown eyes had lines fanning out from them and his glasses were wire rimmed instead of the black plastic frames that Tristan wore. Liana was petite, barely over five feet tall. Her hair had come back all gray after the chemo and she kept it short in a pixie cut that fit her diminutive frame nicely. Tristan noticed that white was beginning to replace the gray in her hair, but her face still had a youthful appearance. Her eyes were red rimmed now from crying, but the green seemed brighter because of it.

Liana came over and took Tristan's shoulders – not an easy feat with her small stature. "Well, at least you look like you've taken care of yourself, too. You've grown into a handsome man."

"Of course, he has. He looks like me," Kurt teased. Sobering, he gestured towards the couch. "We should talk about what needs to be done before the service."

Liana nodded and sighed. Heading over to the seating area, her eyes were arrested by Amy's drawing. "When did you get that?"

"Just this evening." Tristan's heart warmed whenever he looked at it. "A friend of mine drew it this morning."

"I recognize your grandma, but who's the young lady with her?"

"That's Amy Juliette, the artist who drew it."

Liana looked over at her son inquisitively. "She lives here?"

"No, she's from San Francisco, but she came back to visit, because Grandma asked her to." Tristan put an arm around his mom's shoulders and gently propelled her towards the couch. "She came in February this year, and became special to Grandma."

"And is she special to you?" Liana asked, not so subtly.

"We're not dating if that's what you're asking, but yes, she is special to me. I was able to lead her to the Lord while she was down here earlier, and we've become friends."

He could tell his mom wanted to ask more questions, but his dad brought her attention back to the decisions that still needed made. Tristan was thankful for the reprieve because the truth was he wasn't really sure how to answer questions about Amy.

40

The next day Tristan's siblings arrived. Both had caught red eye flights into San Francisco and as it happened that their arrival times weren't too far apart, they rented a car together to drive to Willow Creek. Tristan's brother, Brendan, was tall and broad. His hair was a shade lighter than Tristan's and his eyes were the same green as their mom's. His sister, Kylee, was only a little taller than Liana. She had dark brown eyes and hair. Her husband, Jordan, was average height with his blonde hair cut in a short military style and friendly blue eyes that could become steely if he was crossed.

Kylee was the first out of the car as she ran up and hugged Tristan tightly. "I'm sorry we weren't able to help more." Tristan smiled at the greeting that was so similar to Liana's.

"You had to travel the nation with Jordan and take care of the munchkins. By the way, where are the kiddos?"

"Air fare was too much with the kids, too, so Jordan's parents came to watch them while we're gone," Kylee explained.

Brendan and Jordan walked past carrying the suitcases. "Don't worry, Ky-Ky, we've got the bags," Brendan teased.

Kylee slapped his arm as he passed. "He's been a pest the whole way here."

"I've been a pest my whole life. Don't sell me short." Brendan smiled broadly as he entered the house.

Tristan went inside with his sister. "I've got Kylee and Jordan in the basement. Brendan, would you rather share my room or sleep on the couch?"

"Uh, couch. You snore." Brendan took his suitcase to the living room, while Jordan took his and Kylee's downstairs.

"Okay, first things first," Kylee said pulling out her phone.

"Sibling selfie." Brendan groaned, but joined the other two as Kylee took the picture. "We don't get together often enough to waste the opportunity."

Kurt and Liana came in at that moment carrying grocery bags. Brendan and Tristan immediately relieved their mom of her burden while Kylee hugged her mom tightly. "Come help me unload," Liana told Kylee as soon as she could breathe again.

"Ugh, it's just like being at home. Work, work, work."

Tristan couldn't stop smiling as Kylee and Brendan teased each other, and Kurt and Liana stepped right back into their parenting roles from when they had all lived under the same roof. Jordan came back up and soon joined in the banter as well. Who knew there could be so much happiness in the middle of sadness?

Tristan's phone dinged letting him know he had a text. *I'm meeting Owen Coburn at the house I'm looking at. He's going to give me an estimate. If you're free, you could join me. If not, I'll see if I can show you later.*

Looking around at the chaos in the kitchen, Tristan decided he wouldn't be missed. Liana and Kylee were discussing what food to make for family meals while they were there. They insisted that any food that was brought from friends to help out could be put in the freezer for Tristan to have later. He hated to remind them that he had been the sole cook for quite some time now. Brenda, Jordan, and Kurt were talking about travel. It seemed like a good time to duck out.

"I'm going to go do something real quick," he told his dad, knowing he wouldn't ask questions. "I'll be back in about half an hour or so."

"Okay, we'll be here."

Before the front door closed behind him he could hear Liana start asking Kurt twenty questions about where he was headed. He smiled at the familiarity of the scene. He sent a text to Amy letting her know that he'd be coming and then headed towards Harper Lake.

One side of the lake had the log cabins of Cozy Haven, a bed-and-breakfast owned by Harry and Sandy Barton so Tristan went to the side that he knew was more residential. Driving slowly he looked for a house that needed 'a ton of work'. It was easy to find. Every house around it was meticulously cared for. But this house looked as if it might be better to level the whole thing and start over. A truck sat out front that had 'Coburn & Son' written on the side. A man stood in the front yard next to Amy and they were looking at Amy's sketchpad.

Tristan got out of his car and joined them. "This house has great potential," Owen was saying, "but most people can't see past all that needs to be done to it. You've got a good eye for design. If you wanted, you could go into flipping homes for a living."

"I only want to fix up one home." Amy's eyes were shining with anticipation. She turned to Tristan. "See what it could look like?" She showed him her sketch of the outside and he was impressed. It was definitely the same home with the same shape, but much more inviting.

"We'll need to replace the roof, the porch, the siding, and many of the windows," Owen said, "but the structure itself is pretty sound. Ready to go inside?" Connie had let Owen have the keys to get in so that they could get inside the property.

Amy nodded and Tristan followed, but he wondered if Amy knew what she was getting herself into. As they entered though, and she began showing them her floor plan, the design ideas she had, pointing out what things needed changed, and fixed, Tristan relaxed realizing that she was well aware of how much work this home would be to get into livable condition.

Owen made notes and nodded often. On occasion he would point out something that wasn't to code or that also needed replaced. After they had gone through the main floor of the house, Amy had a request.

"Could we go into the basement? The realtor didn't want to take me down, but I was thinking about making it into a guest suite so I want to see if that would work."

Owen opened the door and examined the staircase with a flashlight. Convinced that it was safe, they all went downstairs. The basement was unfinished, and smelled musty, but Owen didn't see any reason why they couldn't make it into a guest space. He pointed out that it would be good to widen the windows and add an outside entrance for safety purposes and together he and Amy figured out what the best configuration would be with the laundry and utilities down there as well.

Going back upstairs, Amy grabbed Tristan's hand. "I want to show you my favorite part." She pulled him out the back door and Tristan had to admit that the view was beautiful. "Isn't it great?"

"It is. I have to admit, you've put more thought into this than I expected."

Owen came up at that point and handed Amy a sheet of paper. "Here's my rough estimate on the project. Of course you have to consider that we may run into issues that we didn't expect that might drive that up. Over all though, I think this would be a good investment. The property is good. Lake front homes are automatically going to sell well because of the location. I think that when all the renovations are done, this house will be worth way more than you've put into it."

Amy had looked over the numbers on the sheet and now looked up at Owen with a big smile. "Thank you so much. I still need to consider a few other things, but I really want this house." Her gaze as she looked back on the house was so affectionate that Tristan almost thought she would pat the house lovingly before they left.

With the inspection done, Owen drove off leaving Tristan and Amy alone. "You think I'm crazy, don't you?"

Tristan shook his head. "I think you've got a great plan. What's keeping you from deciding?"

Amy's face fell. "My family mostly. And then there's Katie who works for me. They depend on me. I'm not sure I can just up and leave them."

"I think that with as long as this house has been on the market, it's not going to hurt you to make sure this is what you want to do." Tristan shrugged. "Like Owen said, though, when you're finished, you could always sell it and make a profit if you decide you don't want to live here."

Amy looked over at the house. "That's true. Although if I get it like the way I want it, I'm not sure I could bear to part with it." They walked towards Tristan's car. "Did your family make it safely?"

"Yep, they're all here. Which reminds me that I should be getting back." He turned to her. "Do you want to come meet them?"

"I do, but not right now. They just got here. You go enjoy them, and I can meet them later." She gave him a hug. "I'm praying for you." He watched her walk back down to the lake front and begin the hike back to Holliday Hotel.

It's time. Tristan sucked in his breath. Instinctively he knew what it meant. It was time for him and Amy to move to a different relationship. "My grandma only recently passed away. We're having her funeral in a few days. This is a horrible time," he muttered as he got into his car. *It's time.* Tristan felt his heart pound. It didn't seem like an ideal time to him, but how could he argue with God?

41

As soon as Tristan entered the house, Kylee and Liana were in his face.

"Where did you go?"

"What were you doing?"

"Why didn't you tell us you were leaving?"

"Are you okay?"

Tristan laughed. "You two could be twins."

Liana smiled mockingly and fingered her gray hair. "Not quite." Folding her arms across her chest, she returned to the business at hand. "Now, where were you?"

Behind the women the men had gathered. Kurt shrugged. Jordan wagged his finger in mock disapproval while Brendan drew his finger along his throat. Tristan tried to ignore the men and focus on his mom and sister.

"A friend of mine is thinking about buying a house here and asked me to go see it."

"They couldn't have picked another time?" Liana asked. "This isn't really the ideal week to do that sort of thing."

"She lives in San Francisco and has to leave Sunday."

"*She?*" Kylee emphasized. "Just who is *she*?"

"Ooooh!" Kurt, Jordan, and Brendan all chimed in together. They earned blistering looks from Liana and Kylee, but it didn't keep them from making goo-goo eyes and fanning their faces to mock the girls.

Tristan knew better than to laugh at that moment although he really wanted to. "She is Amy Juliette. She helped me design a logo for Holliday Hotel, and now she's found a house she likes here."

"You called her a friend," Kylee stated.

"She is a friend."

"A friend or a girlfriend?" She put her hands on her hips.

Tristan sighed. "Oh my goodness. For now, she is just a friend, but if I'm honest, I'd like her to be more than that."

Liana put her hands over her mouth, and her eyes filled up. "My baby boy is going to be married!" She threw her arms around his neck.

"I didn't say anything about marriage." By now the other men were bent over double laughing hysterically.

"How do we know she's good enough for Tristan?" Kylee asked.

"Because she drew this." Liana went over to the sketch and pointed to it. Everyone gathered around it, studied it for several moments and then turned slowly back to face Tristan.

"That's Grandma," Kylee said as if stunned.

"Yeah."

"She knew Grandma?" Brendan asked.

"Yeah."

"Is that her in the picture?" Kylee asked.

"Yeah."

"Is that all you can say?" Brendan asked with a teasing gleam in his eyes.

Tristan smiled. "Yeah."

"My brother's getting married!" Kylee shrieked as she jumped up and down.

Tristan made a helpless gesture at the men who just shrugged back.

Kylee dragged Tristan over to the couch and sat him down. "Tell me everything."

"I thought I just did."

The men shook their heads. "This won't work. He knows nothing about women," Jordan said.

"Hush!" Kylee told them. "Why is she here now? Does she know you like her? Is she moving here because of you? What's going on?"

"She came to visit Grandma before she died. Grandma asked her to come, and she came as quickly as she could. She sort of knows I like her. She's not sure she is moving here, and I don't know what's going on, because you're scaring me."

Brendan laughed loudly. "This is why I've been so thankful that God has called me to be single."

Kylee sighed. "You're no help." She turned and looked at her mom. After a moment they both nodded and turned their attention back to Tristan.

"I think you should invite her over for dinner," Liana said. "We should get to know her."

Tristan looked at the two women and shook his head. "I'm not inviting her over when you two look like that. You're going to pounce on her and tear her to pieces before she has a chance to get through the door."

"We wouldn't do that," Kylee said with great offense.

"Yeah, right," Jordan snorted. His wife glared at him.

"I'll invite her to lunch tomorrow if you promise that you can be normal human beings," Tristan compromised.

"What's that supposed to mean? We are normal human beings," Liana said huffily.

"No, right now, you're both sharks circling their prey. I don't know if you want to eat her or kidnap her and force her to marry me, but either way, I'm not exactly sure I want you around her."

Kylee huffed and stormed into the kitchen. Banging pots and pans around he supposed she was making dinner. Either that or she was wishing he was near enough to hit with a pan – preferably one of Grandma's old cast iron ones.

Jordan sighed and rolled his eyes. "I better go calm her down."

Liana stared at her son for several moments. "It's not terrible for us to be interested in a girl you're going to marry, you know."

"I never said anything about marriage. You did." Tristan sighed and ran his hand through his hair. "Just don't grill her when she comes over, okay?"

"Okay," Liana said shortly, and then went to join her daughter and son-in-law in the kitchen.

Kurt and Brendan took the seats next to Tristan on the couch. Kurt thumped his son on the back. “You’ve got a lot to learn about women.”

“They’re going to grill her, aren’t they?” Tristan asked.

“Oh yeah,” Brendan stated confidently. “Big time.”

42

The mirror reflected Amy's worried expression. She studied her outfit critically. Skinny jeans, lavender blouse with a floral scarf, and boots looked stylish yet simple and modest. A good outfit to meet your (What? Friend's? Boyfriend's?) parents in, right? She wiped her hands nervously on her jeans. Her hair shone and curled naturally under her chin. Her make-up was light. It was good. It was okay. Oh my goodness. Why was she so nervous?

She grabbed her jean jacket and went downstairs hoping to gain some confidence by a visit with Carol. She found her working at the front desk. "Don't you look nice today?" Carol greeted her.

Relief filled Amy. "I'm so glad you said that. I'm meeting Tristan's family today, and I'm so nervous."

Carol grinned at her. "Well you look lovely so that's one thing you don't have to be nervous about. Is there any special reason you're meeting the family today?"

Amy leaned on the front desk. "It's hard to say when I can't even describe our relationship. We're 'just friends who happen to not date anyone else'. What does that make us?"

"Confused," Carol answered quickly.

Amy laughed. "Yes. That's true." She sighed. "I've never really had much of a dating life. Is it always this confusing?"

"No." Carol's answer was short. She laughed at Amy's stricken expression. "But I suppose not everyone has your situation. You really haven't known each other that long. It's been what – three, four months? The majority of that time, you've been long distance friends. I'd be hesitant to jump both feet into a committed relationship with those criteria, too." She paused and studied Amy's face. "Do you want it to be different?"

Amy bit her lip and smiled girlishly. “I kind of do.” She sighed dreamily. “He’s so sweet, and I like being with him. I find myself comparing other men to him, and they don’t measure up.”

“Then say something.”

“Yeah, this probably isn’t the best time for that. I mean today I meet his family, and tomorrow is the funeral, and then I leave. So when do I say something?”

Carol frowned. “Good point. It’s probably not great timing.” She brightened. “Have you made any decision on the house?”

“No, but I got an estimate from Owen, and I think financially speaking it’s not only doable, but a good investment. I took Tristan to see it, and he likes my ideas. Tristan pointed out that there’s not much chance of it being bought out underneath me so I can take my time.” Amy shrugged. “And if someone else does buy it, then that’s God’s answer.”

“A very mature way to look at it,” Carol approved. “So what are you waiting for?”

“I need to talk to my family, and to my assistant. My moving here will affect them, too. I don’t want to make such a big decision without discussing it with them.”

“It sounds like you’re doing the right thing. I’ll keep praying for you.”

The front door opened, and Tristan came in. He stopped when he saw Amy. “Wow. You look great.”

Amy flushed. “Thanks. I wasn’t really sure what to wear.”

“I don’t think it really matters. You always look nice.” Tristan cleared his throat. “Are you ready to go?”

Amy nodded and said good-bye to Carol. She slipped on her jacket as they headed outside. “I’m so nervous.”

Tristan opened the car door for her and then came around on his side. “To be honest, I’m kind of nervous, too.”

“That doesn’t make me feel any better,” Amy said with a chuckle.

“I’m nervous that when you meet my family you’ll want to run out the door and not look back,” Tristan explained. “I know that they’ll love you.”

For the second time in just a few minutes, Amy felt herself blush. “Why would I want to run away from your family?”

“They’re going to want to know everything about you from cradle to the present. My sister and mom are especially going to be curious about you.” Tristan cleared his throat. “I’m finding it hard to explain our relationship to them. It’s like we’re more than friends, but not quite dating.” He pulled into his driveway and turned to face her. “So I was thinking that I’d like to make it clearer. What I mean is, would you like to be my girlfriend?” He smiled in embarrassment. “I don’t know how to do this very well.”

“I think you did just fine. And yes, I would love to be your girlfriend.”

The smile on his face made him beam. He took her hand and kissed it gently which tugged at her heart as she thought about how romantic an old-fashioned gesture can be. He got out of the car, and came around to get her. “Now remember to not hold my family against me.”

“Only if you promise to do the same when you meet mine,” she stated.

Before they even got to the door, it flung open and the whole family came out to greet them. Amy smiled nervously as they all watched her intently. “Amy, meet my family,” Tristan said with a self-conscious laugh. “My parents, Kurt and Liana, my brother Brendan, my sister, Kylee, and my brother-in-law, Jordan Dawson. Everyone, this is Amy Juliette.”

Immediately the whole family began exclaiming and talking. It was impossible to hear what they all said, but they all seemed happy to meet her. Suddenly she found herself being forced into the house and sitting on the couch between his mom and sister. The men all stood nearby staring at her and smiling as if anticipating something entertaining to happen.

“So are you Tristan’s friend or girlfriend? He didn’t seem to know,” Kylee said, looking at her brother with disgust.

Amy laughed. “We’ve sort of had an interesting experience. I officially became his girlfriend about two minutes ago.”

The men howled in laughter and slapped Tristan on the back.

Liana and Kylee squealed like teenagers and hugged Amy between the two of them. Amy looked helplessly at Tristan who just shrugged his shoulders in return.

"Do you think you'll be married here or in San Francisco?" Liana asked. "You'll probably want to wait a little bit so that Kylee and Jordan can plan to come with their kids."

"What? Married?" Amy's eyes widened. Had she missed something?

"Mom, she literally just agreed to be my girlfriend. Would you please not scare her off?" Tristan objected.

"Fine." Liana patted Amy's knee and whispered, "We can talk wedding plans later."

"It'll be so nice to have a sister," Kylee said happily. "Brothers are fine, but they don't get girl things."

"No we don't," Brendan agreed. "And we're very thankful for that."

Kylee stuck her tongue out at her brother.

"Why don't we go eat?" Tristan suggested. Amy jumped up off the couch, eager to escape the talk of marriage. As she headed into the dining room, she heard Tristan tell his mom and sister in a low voice, "Stop scaring her!"

After that, the men took over the conversation around the table. They asked Amy questions, told stories about Tristan, and reminisced about Carmen. Amy felt like they had discussed this strategy as a battle plan to keep the women from intimidating her. She noticed the look of gratitude on Tristan's face, too. As they were finishing up, Liana finally got a chance to speak. "Tristan said you came to visit Carmen and that you drew that lovely picture in the living room. How close were you with her?"

Amy shrugged. "It's hard to say. We shouldn't have been close at all, because I'd only known her a short time. In that time, though she became very special to me. When Tristan called to tell me that she wanted me to come before she went home," Amy's voice cracked and she cleared it before continuing. "Well, when he called, I knew I had to come. I got here as quickly as I could, and I spent a wonderful evening with her." Amy wiped a tear that had escaped. "The next morning I woke up before dawn and couldn't get back to sleep. I began praying for Carmen and Tristan. Finally, I felt a peace I couldn't explain. I went out on the balcony of my room, and drew the picture that I gave to Tristan. I felt at the time that Carmen was telling me good-bye. Soon after that I got the message that she had passed away."

The family sat in silence for a long moment. Kylee wiped the tears that were streaming down her cheeks. Liana sniffed loudly while Kurt held his wife's hand. "It's nice that you were able to come see Ma," Kurt said. "If she asked for you at the end, then we know that you were very dear to her."

Amy felt a glow fill her chest. It was nice to feel like the family accepted her as one of their own – even if they were pushing for more than she or Tristan were ready for at the moment.

They began clearing the table and then moved into the living room. This time it felt less like an inquisition and more like a friendly conversation. "What's your family like?" Brendan asked.

"My family is sort of interesting. My dad was not exactly a great husband or father. He was married three times after he divorced my mother, and I have three half-siblings from those marriages. My mom remarried several times, too, but I was her only child. She wasn't a great mother either so it's probably good that she didn't have any other kids. Recently I got saved and the very next day I found out my dad was in the hospital. One of my half-sisters had accepted Christ at a young age, and she was there, too. While we were there, my dad also came to Christ. Since then we've sort of been rebuilding broken relationships. We're still healing, but God is doing amazing things." Amy wondered what moving to Willow Creek would do to those budding relationships for the umpteenth time. She hoped that God would guide her clearly as she made her decision.

"That's amazing," Brendan said in a tone of awe. "God is clearly doing a work in your family's lives."

At his statement, Amy remembered that Tristan had told her that Brendan was a missionary. She asked him where he had been serving.

"I'm actually an itinerate missionary. I'm a dentist so I travel wherever I'm needed. Most recently I was in Haiti."

The conversation turned to the Romero family, and Amy learned more about each of them. Aside from the embarrassment of wedding talk, it was a nice afternoon.

Tristan took Amy back to the hotel and walked her up to her room. "Your family is nice," she told him.

"Yeah, when they aren't being obnoxious."

Amy laughed. "I suppose every family has their obnoxious moments. Mine certainly does."

He put his hands on her shoulders. "I'm glad you like them. I could tell that they genuinely liked you, too." He bent closer to her. "I kind of like you, too." His lips barely brushed against hers, but she felt a jolt so strong it made her heart race. Judging from the shocked look on his face, he felt it as well. He claimed her mouth again, this time lingering softly. He pulled back and took a deep breath. "I guess I'll see you tomorrow." His voice sounded as if he was having trouble catching his breath, and she was glad that she wasn't the only one affected by the kisses they'd shared.

"Tomorrow," she whispered. She leaned against the door and sighed. It seemed strange to start dating Tristan the week of his grandma's funeral, and yet, she knew that if Carmen could see from heaven she would be cheering loudly at the recent developments.

43

The day of Carmen's service was sunny and warm. There was a scent of flowers in the air, and everything seemed to be coming to life more that day than at any other time to date that spring. Holliday Hotel looked like a lady dressed in her Easter finest. The flowers in the window boxes and the flower beds made the old home seem even more welcoming than normal.

Amy stood on the large wraparound porch creating a somber note in a black dress with her arms wrapped around her waist. She looked up and down the street waiting for Tristan to come pick her up. The door opened and closed behind her. Turning she saw Carol come out with a sympathetic smile. "I thought I'd keep you company," she said. "Why don't we sit down while we wait?" She gestured to a couple of rocking chairs on the porch.

Gratefully, Amy sat down. She felt too many emotions to name – sadness, joy, nervousness, excitement - for a start. "These things make it feel final," she finally said softly.

Carol nodded and sighed. "Yeah, they do, but you have to remember that although it's Carmen's end here, it's only the beginning of her eternity with Jesus."

Both women rocked silently for long minutes. "Do you think it's inappropriate for Tristan and I to become a couple the same week his grandma passed away? People might think that we were hoping she'd die so that we could get together."

"Did his family seem upset?"

"No," Amy smiled. "They were overjoyed."

Carol clasped Amy's hand. "Then don't worry about what anyone else thinks. You know that Carmen wanted the two of you to get together so in a way, you're fulfilling her dying wish."

"That's true." Amy felt better after Carol's matter-of-fact answers.

"I know it's probably been a comfort for Tristan to have you here during this time."

Amy shrugged. "He has his family here now."

Carol looked at her face with a knowing smile. "As much as he enjoys them being here, I know that you've made a big difference in his life right now."

Amy blushed. "He's done the same for me."

A car pulled up and Tristan climbed out. He smiled as he saw the two women on the porch. "She's ready on time and everything. How lucky can a guy get?"

"Don't get used to it," Amy countered.

Carol waved. "I'll see you guys there."

During the drive to the church, Tristan noticed that Amy kept rubbing her hands together nervously. He placed his hand over hers. "What are you worried about?"

"I don't know," Amy admitted. "I've got so much going through my mind right now."

"That's okay. I feel the same way. I'm not sure I should be so happy during such a sad time."

Amy squeezed his hand, thankful that he understood her own mixed emotions. "Does your family think it's weird that we chose this week to get together?"

Tristan laughed. "You saw them last night. I think if I proposed at the funeral, they would cheer. I'm not going to do that by the way," he added quickly.

"I didn't think you would," Amy chuckled. "I'd probably have to say no if you did that."

The stone church brought back memories of Amy's one and only time in the church, and the message that had changed her life. "I remember seeing your grandma when I came to church with Carol."

"She was so excited that you had come. She knew God was drawing you to Him."

They climbed out and went inside where the family was

already gathered. Amy was thankful that Carmen had wanted a closed casket. She always had a creepy feeling with an open casket. The Romero family was gathered at the front where there were a few flower arrangements. Most people had donated to a charity to which Carmen had devoted much of her life volunteering.

Liana and Kylee were both quietly crying, and even the men seemed subdued. Liana gave her a hug. "I'm so glad you're here."

"Me, too. Even if I had gone back home, I would have come back for this." Amy was amazed at how quickly Tristan's family had made her feel like she belonged. She felt more a part of his family than she did her own. That thought made her frown as she went back to the question that had been plaguing her. Should she move to Willow Creek or stay in San Francisco? She sighed and tried to turn her mind to the present.

Pastor Westley came in and spoke his condolences to the family. He shook Amy's hand and looked at her as if he were trying to place where he'd seen her before. "I came here one Sunday with Carol Holliday. It was the Sunday before Valentine's Day, and you preached a sermon on John 3:16."

"Oh yes. You seemed like you were strongly affected by it. I knew God was working on you, and I was praying for you as I preached. You also made me pray that I would have the words God wanted me to say, nothing more and nothing less."

"God definitely used you. I came to Christ on Valentine's Day." Amy saw the joy that brightened up Aaron's face.

"Praise the Lord. He is so good."

Tristan placed his hands on Amy's shoulders. "God allowed me the privilege of being with her when it happened."

The pastor looked between the two knowingly. "It seems that God has allowed something else to happen as well."

Tristan smiled broadly. "My grandma had insisted that Amy was the right one for me. Turns out, she was right."

"What a blessing that God gave you joy in your sorrow." The church began to fill up and Aaron excused himself to go greet the others. The family spread out and began welcoming the guests, thanking them for coming. Tristan kept Amy at his side although she remained silent most of the time.

The service was lovely. The music was positive and uplifting. Many of the guests had lovely things to say about Carmen. The pastor gave a sermon where the gospel was clearly presented. Tristan kept his arm around Amy and would tighten whenever tears would begin to fall again. She noticed that his own eyes were watery at times, and his concern for her was even more touching.

Before they knew it, they were at the graveside watching the casket being lowered into the ground. The women cried openly now while the men stood silently stoic. Amy knew they suffered as strongly as the women, but held it inside. Turning away from the sight, Kylee said, "It seems so final now."

"She's better than she's ever been before," Kurt pointed out.

"I know, but I'll miss her," Kylee added tearfully.

"We all will," Tristan stated, his own voice cracking with emotion.

Back at the church they joined their guests for a luncheon. Amy noticed that a Christian funeral was a much more joyful occasion than any other funeral she had attended. Laughter mingled with tears. Smiles were seen more often than frowns. There was a hope that transcended life on this world.

When the last guest left, the family sat exhausted in the church's fellowship hall. A group of women were still in the kitchen cleaning up, and they could vaguely hear their chatter. Liana sighed. "It was a nice service. Carmen would have been pleased."

"Well, Ma did get to pick out every detail," Kurt said with a sad smile. "I guess that's the benefit to her lingering for so long."

"We should go," Brendan said. Of all of them, he had been the quietest. "They'll want to clean up the church."

"You okay, Brendan?" Tristan asked with a hand on his brother's shoulder.

Brendan nodded. "I was thinking that I should have made time to stop by between my mission trips and spent time with Grandma. I could have given you some breaks to go on vacation or something."

"Grandma and I got along great. You guys were busy," Tristan reassured him.

Kurt wrapped his arm around Tristan's shoulders. "I'm glad you got that time with Ma, but Brendan's right. We all should have helped more."

Kylee nodded. "I should have brought the kids more often."

"It doesn't do any good to have regrets now. Be sure that the next family funeral we have you don't have regrets," Tristan suggested.

Liana's eyes widened. "I hope that's not for a long time."

Tristan chuckled. "Me too, Ma."

Amy smiled as she watched the family climb into their cars and drive back to Carmen's home. She was sure they would make more time for each other in the future, and she knew that if Carmen knew that, she would be happy that something positive happened from her death. She looked over at Tristan. Well, maybe two positive things had happened.

44

The following day was overcast, matching Amy's mood as she thought about leaving Willow Creek again. She stood on the balcony soaking it in one last time. She had already attended church with Carol that morning, and Tristan had taken her out for dinner the night before on their first official date. It seemed oddly fitting to have their first date on the same day they remembered Carmen's life. She sighed heavily. If only she knew when she could come back again. Although she knew that she would keep in contact with Tristan every day, she would miss being face to face with him.

Going back inside, she finished packing making sure to carefully wrap the framed watercolor that Carol had given her. She looked through the suite one more time to make sure she didn't miss anything. Once assured that she was ready, she placed her suitcase by the front door. She felt an urge to pat the room affectionately before she left. It had become a special place for her.

A knock on the door interrupted her thoughts. Tristan pulled her into a hug as soon as he entered. He rested his chin on her head. "Are you sure you need to go home?"

Amy smiled and sighed contentedly as she hugged him tighter. "For now anyway."

He pulled back and looked at her. "You'll let me know as soon as you've made a decision on the house, right?"

"Of course. You'll be the first person I tell either way."

He grabbed her suitcase, and they headed down to the front desk. Carol was waiting at the foot of the stairs. "Somehow it's harder to say good-bye this time than it was last time."

"I'm sure I'll be back one way or another," Amy assured her

with a hug.

The door opened, and Owen and Willa Coburn came in. They greeted Carol warmly. "We didn't mean to interrupt your good-byes," Willa said.

"Carol invited us over for lunch since she thought she'd be lonely after you left," Owen explained.

"You aren't interrupting," Amy assured them. "I was just getting ready to leave. I'm glad Carol will have her friends with her."

"Have you decided anything about the house yet?" Owen asked.

"I need to talk to my family when I get home first. I'll let you know soon I'm sure."

"It's good to take your time on a decision like this," Willa encouraged her.

Amy stepped nearer to Willa, a look of concern crossing her face. "I've wanted to ask you how that little girl from your class is doing. Her name is Ava."

"Oh Ava. She's really blossomed lately, but that might be because she's in the process of being adopted now."

Amy smiled brightly. "She is? That's great!"

"Yeah, apparently Lupe convinced her uncle and aunt that they should adopt her so that they could be cousins." Willa's eyes twinkled as she told the story.

Carol explained further. "Lupe's grandmother is my best friend, Elena. She had two sons. Dave is Lupe's father. Ben and his wife, Veronika, have been trying to have children for several years now. Lupe convinced them that they needed Ava, and Ava needed them."

"Dave and Adriana are so proud of their tender-hearted daughter," Willa added.

"They should be. It would have been easy for her to ignore Ava. Not many children her age would have taken a step like that," Amy said.

"It's still a long process," Carol explained. "They have to make sure that Ava doesn't have anyone who's a closer relation who would want to take her. But they've gone through the course to be foster parents and are approved so even if things don't work out with Ava, I'm sure they'll be getting another child soon. There's such a desperate need for foster parents."

"I'll be praying that everything works out in the best way for Ava," Amy promised.

Willa thanked her, and then she and Owen moved off discreetly so that Carol could finish her farewell. "Let me know when you get home," Carol said in a true motherly fashion.

"I will. Thanks again for letting me stay with you."

"Anytime." Carol gave her another hug. "Come back soon."

"As soon as I can." Amy and Tristan gathered her things and headed out the door. Tristan loaded her things into the trunk of her car and then wrapped her in another hug.

"I wish you could stay longer," he said.

"Me, too." She laid her head on his chest. "I'm going to miss you." She felt his chest rise under her head in a deep sigh.

"Think we'll get through?"

She squeezed him tighter. "I know we will."

He lifted her chin and claimed her mouth with his own. His kiss was long and sweet. Amy sighed contentedly as he pulled away. He touched her cheek tenderly. "I love you, Amy."

Amy's heart raced. "I love you, too."

Reluctantly she climbed in her car and drove away. In her rear view she could see Tristan stand and watch her car out of sight. Her thoughts went back to their last moments. When Tristan said that he loved her, Amy didn't wonder if he meant it. She didn't wonder what he wanted. Deep down, was the knowledge that he had loved her for a long time. He had shown it to her in lots of little ways as he reflected God's love. Sure his love had changed through the months, but it had always been there. She had first seen true love through him. Then she had seen it in his treatment of Carmen, but now it was directed at her. He would be faithful, patient, kind, and thoughtful just as he had been with his grandma, of that she was certain.

She thought back to her relationships with Wright, Ivor and Rico. She had never told them that she loved them. She knew she hadn't. She didn't even trust them. Always having the feeling that they didn't know what love meant except when it came to loving themselves. Now that she understood what love was, she was even more certain that they hadn't truly loved her. And she knew for a fact that she hadn't loved them.

Her thoughts were so absorbed that the trip passed quickly, and before she knew it she was at her apartment. She unloaded her suitcase and went inside. What had seemed so homey before now seemed lonely and stark. An image of the abandoned home in Willow Creek flashed across her mind. She could do so much to make it seem like home.

She sent a text to Tristan and Carol to let them know she was home safely. Then she made a quick decision. One of the things preventing her from buying the home was her uncertainty of what her family would think. She had to find out what they would say and the sooner, the better. A text was quickly sent to her parents and her half-sisters to join her for dinner the next day. Rapidly they all accepted, and she thanked God that she could get things figured out quickly. She prayed that it would be clear after tomorrow what God wanted her to do.

Her phone rang, and she eagerly answered when she saw it was Tristan.

"I'm glad you made it home safely," he said.

"I thought about you the whole way," she admitted.

"I thought about you, too. In fact, I thought that I wouldn't have to wait for the next time you could come here. I can visit you, too." The sadness that had been prevalent in his voice returned for a moment. "I'm not needed here to take care of Grandma anymore."

"She would be glad that you're free to travel more." Amy sat in her favorite chair and curled her legs up underneath her.

"She would especially be glad if I was traveling to see you," he added laughingly.

"Your life is going to be so different now." Amy hadn't really thought about all the changes that Tristan could make now that he didn't have to care for Carmen. He could move, have a job outside his home, travel, get married – okay she may have thought about that last one, but distantly. "Do you want to stay in Willow Creek?" His answer may very well effect her decision as well.

"I've been here long enough that it feels like home. I suppose that I would rather stay here, but if you felt like God was telling you to stay where you are, I'd be willing to move to be near you." He paused and then added, "As long as it's God's will."

"You'd move here?" Amy had never considered the possibility that he could move to be near her if God closed the door for her to move to Willow Creek.

"Absolutely. I'd rather be with you anywhere than here alone." Amy smiled and snuggled deeper into the chair. She knew he wasn't really alone in Willow Creek. He had plenty of friends and a church family he was close to, but being with her was more important than that. "I'd want to be sure it was what I was supposed to do first though."

"There's no need to rush," she assured him. "Moving is a big deal, and our relationship is still new."

Tristan hesitated. "I know it's still new, and I don't want to scare you, but I'm sure that God planned for us to be together."

"And we are."

"No, I mean that He intends for us to be married - eventually."

Amy held her breath. "What did you say?"

"I know it sounds crazy, but I really felt like God was telling me that you were going to be my wife."

"When?" Amy's head spun with this new information. It felt too quick.

"Valentine's Day. As soon as you finished praying. It was as if He spoke to me."

"Are you sure it wasn't because Carmen wanted it?"

"She had mentioned something about it, but I hadn't believed her." Tristan took a deep breath. "Remember how you told me that you felt like a crazy person when you were arguing with God?"

"Yes," Amy said slowly.

"Well, I felt like a crazy person, too. It didn't make sense. Maybe it was the power of suggestion from my grandma, but look at where we are now. I'm not saying that we should get married tomorrow. We need to be sure this is what God wants for us, but I'm letting you know now that I'm not taking this lightly. I'm serious about our relationship, and I believe it will last."

"Whoa," she breathed. "That's a lot to take in."

"I know. I'm sorry. I shouldn't have said anything."

Amy smiled. "I'm glad you did. It's nice to know that you're all in, because it's not going to be easy with us living so far apart."

Tristan laughed. "For a moment I thought I'd scared you away."

"No way. I love you."

He sighed. "I love you, too."

Love never ends. Amy caught her breath. Suddenly she had a feeling that Tristan's confidence in their future wasn't so far-fetched.

45

When Amy walked into the office Monday morning, she was surprised to see that Katie was already there. Not only was she there, but she was pacing in agitation, muttering under her breath. "Katie? What's wrong?"

Katie jumped as Amy's voice startled her. She hurried over to Amy. "I'm so glad you're here. I need to talk to you."

"Is everything all right?" Amy led her to the couch they had for clients and sat her down. "Maybe I should get you some water."

"I'm fine." Katie waved her hands and then pulled Amy down on the couch next to her. "You know that I took your meeting with Wright."

"Yes." Amy's eyes widened. "He didn't do anything did he?"

"No, well yes, but not what you're thinking." Amy had never seen Katie so upset before.

"Why don't you start at the beginning?" Amy suggested.

Katie took a deep breath. "Wright came for the meeting and it went well." She smiled goofily. "It went really well. We got to talking, and then we went to lunch, and we talked some more. He's not as arrogant as you think he is. Anyway, I had to get back to the office, but he invited me out to dinner that night, and I accepted. And we sort of started dating."

"Wow. Congratulations!" Amy knew how badly Katie had wanted to be with Wright. "Why would you be upset to tell me that? You know I don't have any feelings for him, right?"

"I know that. I knew when you guys were dating that you didn't have any feelings for him." Katie's insight made Amy's eyes widen. Katie took another breath. "Okay, so here's the thing. Wright's asked me to work for him." She stared at Amy with a mix of fear and defiance on her face.

Amy's mind whirled with several thoughts at once. Wright could be using Katie to get back at her. He could also be taking advantage of Katie's crush to get her to work long hours for low pay. She wouldn't put it past him. But another interesting thought crossed her mind. One of her concerns for moving to Willow Creek was Katie. Her moving over to Wright's company would solve that problem and make it easy for her to move.

"Are you sure about this?" Amy had to ask the question. It seemed like God was helping her move to Willow Creek but she wanted to be sure it wasn't a decision they would both regret later.

"I've been thinking about it a lot, and as much as I've liked working for you, I think it's time I moved on." Katie's eyes pleaded with Amy to understand. "Sometimes I feel like you don't even need me. You make up tasks to keep me busy." She stood up and began pacing. "I know that Wright and I may not work out, but I think the job will. Besides I have nowhere to go here, but I can move up there."

"You've really given this some thought." Amy felt a peace settle over her. "If this is what you want to do, I think you should do it. I've actually been thinking about making some changes to the company, too. This seems like a good change for both of us." Amy stood up and gave Katie a hug. "I've enjoyed working with you, and I wish you the very best."

"I appreciate everything you've done for me." Katie teared up. "You've been a good employer and a friend."

"How long are you going to stay on?"

Katie brushed her fingers over her eyes and resumed her normal professional attitude. "I was planning on two weeks unless you need me longer."

Amy shook her head. "I think I can adjust things in two weeks." She smiled. "And if I can't, that's my problem and not yours."

"I don't want to leave you in a bind though," Katie worried.

"I'll be fine. I'm thinking of becoming all online and working from home instead of paying rent on this office space." Even if she didn't move to Willow Creek, the idea of not having the extra cost of having an office was appealing.

"That sounds like a great idea. Did that guy you were working with on the hotel logo suggest it?"

Amy looked at Katie in surprise. "No, but seeing how he ran his own company brought it to mind."

Katie smiled mischievously. "It seemed like you kind of liked that guy."

Amy smiled broadly. "I do like him. In fact, we started dating while I was gone this past week."

"I'm so happy for you. It's funny that we're both in this position at the same time."

"I think it's perfect timing." With that, they both turned their attention back to the business of the day.

By the time she got home, she was glad that dinner was ready in the crockpot. All she needed to do to prepare for dinner was toss a salad. Angela had said she'd bring dessert so everything was set.

Rhonda was the first to arrive. "What's this all about?" She seemed nervous.

"I need some advice from my family. That's all."

Rhonda looked at her skeptically. "You're sure this isn't about me and your dad?"

"Why would it be about you and Dad?"

Rhonda put her hands on her hips. "You don't want us to get back together. I could tell when we talked about it. Then your dad came and told me that he felt like we were too different now that he was religious, and he didn't think it would be good for us to get back together." She sneered. "I can only assume I have you to thank for his change of heart."

"Mom, I've wanted my family together since I was a child. Why would I convince him not to be with you?"

Rhonda sank into a chair at the dining room table in defeat. "I don't know. Why doesn't he want to be with me? Is it because I've aged poorly?"

"No, Mom." Amy sighed and sat down next to her mother. "I did talk to dad, but all I said was that I didn't want to see you guys torn apart again so I wanted him to be very sure before he pursued anything. You both have very different perspectives now. I don't want you to be hurt."

Rhonda raised her chin. "You don't think I'm good enough for your dad because I don't share your religion! How sanctimonious can you get? This is why people dislike Christians."

Amy heaved another sigh. "It's not that you're not good enough. For heaven sake, I lived with Dad. I know what he was like. He's not perfect. But what's going to happen when he wants to go to church and you don't? What happens when he's excited about something he's learned at church and you respond tepidly or worse, aggressively? If you don't think it'll be a problem, by all means, go for it. Personally, I don't see how it can work. You can't even talk to me without criticizing my faith. What would you do if Dad was talking about his every time you saw him?"

Rhonda slumped in her chair. "Why do I feel like I'm competing with God?"

"I think that feeling is fighting against God. I should know. I've been there before."

A knock interrupted their conversation. Answering the door she found Angela and April together. Angela handed her a homemade cheesecake. "I hope this is all right."

"I love cheesecake. It's perfect. Come on in." She led the girls to the dining room. Rhonda immediately stiffened at the sight of her ex-husband's other children. "Mom, you know Angela and April."

"Vaguely," her mom muttered.

"It's so nice to see you again," Angela said warmly as if she hadn't heard her.

Rhonda only smiled, but kept her mouth shut. Probably better that way, Amy thought. April hadn't said anything yet either. She looked terrified of Rhonda. Amy wondered what she had been told about her dad's ex-wife.

"April, why don't you come help me in the kitchen?" Amy suggested. April grabbed at the chance to escape the uncomfortable situation. Angela sat down at the table and began to talk to Rhonda.

She didn't seem to expect any response, which was probably a good thing.

"Your mom is kind of intense," April whispered.

Amy laughed. "Yeah, she can be. You can see why it didn't work out between my parents. They were both a little too much everything for each other."

"My mom said she was too much of a pushover," April confided with a shy smile.

"I guess Dad went from one extreme to the other." Amy handed the salad to April while she grabbed the crockpot. As soon as they put it on the table, there was a knock. Trying to save April a while longer, Amy sent her to get the door and went to get a pitcher of water to fill the glasses. Coming back into the room she entered an emotionally charged space. "Well, let's sit down to eat."

"Craig isn't coming?" Larry asked earning a frown from Rhonda.

"No, he's still not too excited about being part of the Juliette family." Amy sat down. "I think Coral tries to keep him away from us, too."

Conversation was stilted and awkward all through dinner. Rhonda tried to maintain an arrogant silence through most of it while April's silence was triggered by fear. Angela and Amy tried to keep things going. Larry seemed to be getting angrier as the meal wore on. Amy assumed it was because of her mom's treatment of his other daughters.

Over cheesecake and coffee, Amy decided to go ahead and tell her family her idea. The dinner couldn't get any more uncomfortable anyway. "I found a house I want to buy in Willow Creek."

Everyone focused their attention on her. "You're leaving me?" Rhonda asked. "They have each other." She gestured to the other three. "You're all I have."

"I haven't decided yet if I'm going to buy it. There are a lot of good reasons for me to make the move, but the biggest reason not to, is you guys."

"What do you think God is telling you to do?" Angela asked.

Rhonda huffed and rolled her eyes.

"So far everything is working in favor of me moving. It would be a great investment property. The house is right on Harper Lake. It needs a lot of work, but the price is really good because of that."

Larry leaned his elbows on the table as he critically examined his oldest daughter. "What about work?"

"My assistant left me only this morning for another job which was actually really good because I've been thinking about making the business solely online. Whether I move or not, I'm going to make that change so I can save some overhead cost."

Larry nodded. "Sounds like you've done your homework."

"I really have. Wait here." She jumped up and ran to her room. When she got back she laid out in front of them the estimates, the statistics on the house, photos she had taken, and her sketches of what she wanted it to be.

"You really have put a lot of thought into this, haven't you?" Her mom's tone was softening. Her eyes looked sad which made Amy wonder if she should stay.

"Why do you want to leave?" April asked. It was the first she had spoken at the table that night.

"I'm not sure it's about wanting to leave. It's more about wanting a home." She pulled the sketch of the house as she wanted to look when it was finished nearer to her.

"You can find a home here," April insisted.

Amy nodded. "I could, for a lot more money and a lot less space. And no lake view."

Angela put her hand on Amy's which brought her head up to look at her sister. "It seems like this is where your heart is. I want you here because I love being your sister, but I think if you stay you'll always be wishing you hadn't."

Larry swallowed hard and nodded. "I'm sorry I wasn't a better dad sooner, because I feel like I haven't had you long enough. But I think this is a really good investment for you, and it would be wise to go through with it."

Amy's heart fluttered. If all of them felt this way, she would go ahead with her plans. April's eyes filled with tears. "I don't want you to go. It's been cool to have another big sister." She sighed. "If you go, can I come visit you?"

"Yes, absolutely! I would love to have you come see me." Amy rummaged through the papers and pulled out the two sheets of floor plans. "On the top floor are three bedrooms. The master will be mine, the second my office, but the third will be a guest room. Then the entire basement will be a guest suite. I want all of you to come see me as often as you can."

April gave her a watery smile. "I guess it'd be kind of awesome to have a big sister with a lake house."

"Mom?" All eyes turned to Rhonda. She pulled the photo of the view of the lake to her. "This is your view?"

"Yeah, from the backyard."

"You always loved drawing water. It didn't matter if it was the ocean or a fountain." She smiled at the memory. Sighing deeply she said, "I guess you have to make your own decisions, and if that means that you choose to leave me, then I guess that's fine."

"Mom, I can stay if you want me to." Amy's heart sunk. Her mom was right. She didn't have anyone if she left.

Larry pushed over the drawing of the guest suite that Amy was planning. "I think you'd be pretty comfortable there."

Rhonda stared at the drawing for a long time. "It would be a nice place to visit, I guess." The words were spoken as if pulled out of her against her will. She took a deep breath and looked at Amy with tears in her eyes. "If you don't go, you'll just come to hate me for stopping you."

"I would never hate you, Mom."

"You should." Rhonda laid her head on her arms and began to cry. Larry came up behind her and rubbed her shoulders gently.

"We'll all miss her Ronnie. But it's within driving distance, and we can visit her whenever we want." Her mom's sobs lessened as she listened to his voice. "It'd be a great place to vacation at anyway. And think how happy she'll be there. We can't be selfish about this."

"But I want to be selfish," her mom whimpered like a toddler. Wiping her tears with her napkin, she sat back up. "Does this have anything to do with that guy?"

All eyes turned back to Amy. "Honestly, I don't think so. I fell in love with the house as soon as I saw it." She decided it was best to put all her cards on the table. "But to be completely open with you, I did start dating him this past week."

"What if it doesn't work out? Will you still want to stay there?" Larry's words carried weight with Amy since he knew about failed relationships. She took time to think it through.

"I think I would want to stay there even more. There was something so peaceful about the place. It would be a retreat for me." Amy knew that it was hard to say for sure how she would feel if her relationship with Tristan were to fail, especially with his confident words still ringing in her ears. "But even if I wanted to leave, I would make much more off the house if I sold it than I'll put into it. It would be a flip home then."

"Men always leave," Rhonda said bitterly.

Larry squeezed her shoulders. "Not always, and I'm sorry for my part in that feeling."

"Even if he does leave, this is my home – not our home. I can stay there if I want or I can sell it at a profit, move back and get a nicer home than I could afford now."

The confidence and common sense that she showed must have convinced her mom. "I think you should go," Rhonda said. "If you don't you'll always wonder what would have happened."

Amy's face lit up and she jumped out of her seat to hug her mom first and then the rest of her family. "I hope you'll all come see me often." Tears swam in her eyes as she added, "I'm really going to miss you all!"

Conversation was less stilted after that. They talked about helping her move, what colors she should pick, the pros and cons of various flooring styles, and what they would do when they came to visit.

Before she knew it, Angela was saying, "I have to get April home. It's a school night." She gave Amy a hug. "It's going to be great."

April also gave her a hug. "I can't wait to visit!"

Amy offered her parents another cup of coffee, but they both declined. "I'm a bit worn out. I think I'll head home," Rhonda said. Amy knew that the emotional roller coaster had taken a toll on her mom.

"I'll walk your mom to her car," Larry added. Amy knew that her mom would get the most comfort from Larry. He would make sure that she was fully on board with the idea, and talk her into it if she wasn't.

With the apartment all to herself again, she made the call she had been hoping to make. "Tristan, I'm moving to Willow Creek!"

46

It was August before Amy got to go back to Willow Creek. There had been plenty to do to get ready for the move. She had switched her business over to be online only. Most of her clients were happy to remain with her, and even appreciated the convenience, but she did lose a few over the change. What she lost though, God gave her back and more through new clients. The amount she saved by not having to pay for a pricey office and utilities was astounding, and she wondered why she hadn't made the switch long ago.

She had kept in touch with Katie, too. Her relationship with Wright had been short lived, but she loved her new job and had already earned a promotion. Amy was glad that Katie was doing so well. It even seemed like she may have a new romance brewing with one of the salesmen.

Her phone was kept buzzing with the constant contact between her and Owen. She would send him pictures of what she wanted, and he would update her often on what had been done. The hardware store had become a second home as she would run over and pick fixtures, flooring, paint colors, and appliances and let Owen know what she wanted. Owen wasn't the only one who kept her updated on the progress. Tristan and Carol both sent her their own impressions of the project along with pictures.

Rhonda had jumped on board with the move once she had come to terms with losing her daughter. She and Amy spent many Saturdays looking at furniture and décor for her new home. It was such a blessing to have this time with her mom before she moved that even when Amy thought she had plenty of items, she kept on going.

Angela and April enjoyed the updates on the construction. April had already claimed one of the guest bedrooms as hers. Amy was glad that her youngest sister was planning on visiting and prayed that she would do it often. Angela was a bit more subdued in her enthusiasm and Amy knew that it was harder on her to let her leave. By far Angela was the most loving and sensitive of all the Juliette children, so saying good-bye naturally was difficult for her.

Larry took his father role seriously for the first time in Amy's life. He was usually with her at the hardware store and telling her the benefits of one item over another. Always he left the decision up to her, but she generally chose the one he had thought best. She was so proud of how faithful he had become to God, his own personal growth, and his family. It was a new feeling, but she could tell that he was proud of her, too.

Tristan had come regularly to visit. Sometimes he came for the weekend and other times he took a full week. He helped Amy move all of her office furniture out of the office and into storage. He went shopping with her and Rhonda, and never complained which made Amy love him more. Her sisters absolutely loved him, and they would come over for a movie or game night when he was in town. Larry had given his approval as well, and even Rhonda determined that if any man could be faithful Tristan just might be the one.

Amy woke up on moving day with a tremendous excitement. She bounced out of bed with more energy than she could ever remember having first thing in the morning. She got out milk and donuts and brewed a pot of coffee. Angela and April had spent the night in preparation of the move. April had confided that Ruthie hadn't been terribly happy that they were helping their half-sister move and planning on staying in Willow Creek for a few days, but because she had now graduated from high school her mom let her go anyway. Soon Angela and April stumbled out of their room and joined Amy for breakfast.

Amy couldn't stop smiling. She'd been anticipating this day

for months. She finished cleaning the kitchen, put the coffee pot in a box that had been left open for that purpose, and hurried to get dressed. By the time Larry and Rhonda arrived, all three women were ready to go. Tristan had already taken a truck with all the items from her storage unit up so that was one less thing for them to worry about. Together loading up the truck took less time than Amy had thought it would, and before she knew it they were off. Larry drove the truck while Rhonda rode with Amy. Angela and April followed behind in the car that they would all ride home in. Amy was glad that Rhonda had softened towards her half-sisters so that the trip home wouldn't be entirely awkward. Rhonda had even invited 'the girls' as she called them on a few of their shopping expeditions.

In the car, Rhonda sighed. "I can't believe it's here. What will I do without you?"

"You're a strong woman, Mom. I know you'll survive. Besides, my door is always open when you need to visit, and I'm sure I'll come back to visit you guys as well." Amy's joy couldn't be dimmed that day. She knew this was where she was supposed to be – not because of Tristan or Carol – but because it was where God wanted her.

The drive went quickly, and Rhonda had even grown more excited as they got closer. When they pulled up in front of the house, Amy's heart swelled. The lawn was trimmed and the flower beds had flowers in them instead of weeds. The trees were full and provided welcome shade from the warm sun. But the house was what Amy couldn't take her eyes off. It was pristine and welcoming. The siding was a blue-gray with white trim. A porch swing swayed gently beside the front door. Amy felt tears well up in her eyes. "It's exactly how I pictured it," she whispered.

Rhonda nodded. "You did a good job." That one small phrase was enough. She knew her mom didn't want her to leave and would have found any reason to complain had she been able to find one. "And really, it wasn't that long of a drive," she added.

Amy smiled, thankful that her mom was making an effort to see the positives. Angela and April pulled up next, both exclaiming the minute they got out of the car about how beautiful the home looked. Finally her dad arrived with the truck. As he was backing the truck in, two more cars pulled up. Tristan got out of the first while Willa and Owen got out of the second.

"Carol sends her love," Willa said smiling. "She would have helped, but she had guests leaving today and had to stay at the inn. She is looking forward to seeing you all tonight and said that she would prepare dinner for everyone."

Introductions were made and soon everyone was unloading the truck with Amy directing where everything should go. She was glad she had worn shorts and a tank top as the heat steadily rose all day. Willa had brought a cooler full of water bottles for everyone, and it was a welcome relief. The electricity had only recently been turned on, so the refrigerator and air conditioning were still in the process of cooling down.

By the time everything had been unloaded, everyone was sweaty and tired. "I hope we have time for a shower before dinner," April complained. "I feel gross."

"Let's head over to the hotel now, and we should all have time to freshen up," Amy suggested.

Since they didn't have time to unpack the boxes or set any of the furniture up, the family had decided to stay one night at Holliday Hotel. The next day would be spent getting the house in order so that they could spend the night in Amy's new home that night.

Carol was waiting by the front door when they pulled up. She laughed at their obvious weariness. "I remember those days when I was getting this place set up. Go clean up and dinner will be ready when you're done." Willa, Owen and Tristan had all returned to their own homes, but planned on coming over for dinner after they cleaned up.

Carol gave them their room keys. "Amy, I put you and your mom in Sweetheart Suite. Angela and April you're in Resolution Room, and Larry, I have you in Daddy's Den." Amy led Rhonda up to the suite while Carol showed the others where their rooms were.

Rhonda gasped in delight as Amy opened the door. "This is

lovely," she said in awe.

"I've loved staying in this room. Why don't you go clean up first? There's either a tub if you'd like to soak or a shower."

"Oh, a nice soak in a hot bathtub sounds so nice for my aching muscles," Rhonda groaned.

Amy immediately moved to the balcony. The grass was thicker and darker than it had been in spring and the trees were full to provide homes for the wildlife and shade for humans. The lake sparkled sapphire blue under the hot summer sun. Amy got out her sketch pad again. Drawing the scene before her, she marveled at how it changed season to season. Under one of the large trees, she drew a lady sitting on a picnic blanket eating watermelon. A picnic basket was at her side and a bouquet of freshly picked wildflowers. Carol seemed to come to life under Amy's skilled fingers. It seemed like a perfect thank you gift for everything she had done for her. The idea had been in her mind for quite some time, so she carefully unpacked the frame that she had brought along for this picture and placed it inside.

It didn't take too long for everyone to clean up and come downstairs for dinner. Her family couldn't compliment Carol enough on her inn, and Carol beamed with pride one minute and flushed with embarrassment the next. She had pushed all the tables together to create one long family style table in the dining room. It had been set with her wedding china and crystal, proving what a special occasion this was for her. Lasagna, salad, and homemade breadsticks were placed on the table, and after the prayer, everyone hungrily dug in praising Carol for such a wonderful dinner. After a dessert of tiramisu, the group could barely move.

"I think I've eaten myself to death, but it was worth it," Rhonda exclaimed causing everyone to laugh.

Exhausted from the busy day, everyone soon separated to get some rest. Willa offered to help Carol clean up, but Carol wouldn't hear of it, and sent her off with a container of leftovers.

Tristan grabbed Amy's hand and took her to the back porch. He sat her in the very spot she had been in when she had become a Christian and they sat silently watching the moonbeams on the water for a while. "I'm glad you're here," he finally said, breaking the silence.

"Me, too. It feels perfect, like I'm where I'm supposed to be." Amy rested her head on Tristan's shoulders, weary from the long day.

"I was thinking that maybe we should merge our businesses," Tristan surprised her by saying.

Alert now, she sat up. "Really? Why?"

"We worked really well together before," he started with a smile. "I know you do good work, and I think our skills would compliment one another."

"Where would we work from?"

"We could work independently – for now. Maybe someday we can work together from our home." He intertwined his fingers with hers.

Amy suddenly felt the conviction that Tristan had felt all along. Someday this man would be her husband. The idea made her smile. "So what would we call our business?"

Tristan smiled with humor. "Romero & Juliette, of course."

Amy laughed heartily. "Why didn't I see that coming?" She tucked her head against his shoulder again. "I love you," she said with a yawn.

He kissed the top of her head. "I love you, too, but I think you should probably get some sleep it will be another busy day tomorrow."

Reluctantly she agreed. He walked her to her room, but before she opened the door, he stopped her. "You realize that you've been staying in the honeymoon suite every time you came, right?"

Amy nodded in confusion. Of course, she knew that.

"I haven't given it much thought until tonight. Now, I'm thinking that it would be the perfect place for us to spend our first night together as husband and wife." He kissed her tenderly, then caressed her cheek as he said, "Sleep well, my love."

47

Tristan's words kept repeating in Amy's mind the next day as she prepared to leave Holliday Hotel. Now that she lived in Willow Creek, the next time she would stay in Sweetheart Suite, she would be a married woman. It was hard to believe that so much could happen in less than a year. She'd met Tristan, Carmen and Carol, became a Christian, fell in love, altered her business, and moved to her dream home. God had been so good.

Clutching her suitcase in one hand and the picture for Carol in the other, she skipped down the stairs eager to begin setting up her new home. Amy could hear clatter in the kitchen and knew that Carol was cleaning up after breakfast. As she entered, Amy realized that she could visit Carol anytime she wanted to now, since they were practically neighbors.

"Ready to leave already?" Carol asked in surprise seeing Amy's suitcase.

"I'm ready to get my house in order." Amy's face radiated her excitement. "But first, I have something for you." She held out the framed picture.

Carol dried her hands on a dish towel and then took the gift. "It's me," she said in surprise. "How did you know I like to picnic under that particular tree?"

"I didn't. It simply seemed like something you would like to do on a summer day." Amy was pleased with Carol's reaction.

"Most Saturday afternoons in the summer, I'll spend some time under that tree. It's such a relaxing spot. It allows me time to rest and refocus. I don't get days off very often so those moments are precious." Carol pulled Amy into a warm embrace. "Thank you so much!"

"Thank you for everything you've done for me." Carol tried to brush Amy's statement off, but Amy wouldn't let her. "I mean it. You're a big part of the reason that I came to know Jesus, and I can't thank you enough for that."

"I'm honored that God would use me in such a way," Carol answered humbly. "I'm so glad you're going to be nearby now."

"I was just thinking that I'd be able to pop in whenever I want now." Amy smiled. "I'll probably gain weight from eating your cookies."

Carol laughed. "My door is always open to you. Come whenever you want."

Amy told her good-bye, but it wasn't as sad this time since she knew she'd be seeing her often now. Her family was waiting by the staircase for her, their bags in hand. Carol had told them to leave their keys on the desk when they were ready to leave, so they did.

Conversation and laughter rang through the house that had been vacant for so long as furniture was put together and placed in position, boxes were emptied, and items were hung on the walls. By the time the day was over, the house had been transformed into a home.

"It looks wonderful," Amy said with her hands clasped together in joy. It was exactly as she had pictured it, but somehow better now that it was a reality.

Her family stayed a couple more days, chatting, playing games and swimming in the lake. The day they were going to leave, they surprised her with a small motor boat as a housewarming gift. She stood on the porch waving as they drove off calling out promises of visiting soon. The quiet that enveloped her when she entered the house seemed heavy and oppressive. She wandered from room to room tidying up, but really remembering how happy her family had been together. That's when it hit her. God had healed her family. It didn't look the way she had pictured it, but He had melded them together in a strange, but wonderful way.

Her parents had already made plans to come back to her place for Thanksgiving, and she was going to San Francisco for Christmas. April had asked to spend part of her Christmas break from college with her, and she had happily agreed. Angela had told her that she'd better have the guest room ready at all times, because she planned to use it often.

When the year had started, she had been such a lonely isolated person. In her desire for independence she had shut herself off from the world, but hadn't realized that her solitude had become oppressive. Now she had friends, family and more love than she could have imagined. The best part was that she had a relationship with Jesus that nothing could destroy.

Hearing a car pull up, Amy moved to the front porch to find Tristan coming up the steps. "I thought you might need some company," he said as he pulled her tightly against him.

"You came at just the right time," she assured him, and he had.

Epilogue

The week before Thanksgiving, Carol hosted a large dinner for anyone in the community to join in. She prepared the turkey, stuffing and mashed potatoes, while the guests brought the sides and desserts. It was a crowded, noisy, cheerful affair. In the living room, she had baskets of construction paper leaves which the guests were supposed to write what they were thankful for on and then pin them around the room.

Amy was in shock at the amount of people that attended her dinner. "I can barely breathe there are so many people here," she told Tristan.

"Fill out your thanksgiving leaf, and then we'll step outside and get some fresh air," he suggested. "I'll go get our jackets."

While he was gone, she grabbed a leaf and a marker. Without hesitation she wrote 'love' on her leaf. She hadn't even known the beginning of the word earlier this year, and now she was blessed to know what true love was and experience it in so many different ways. God's love had brought her to Him. Her family had healed because of love. She had new friends because of love. And Tristan daily showed her his love for her. She pinned the leaf up just as Tristan rejoined her.

He smiled at her. "Somehow I knew that's what you would put." They stepped out on the back porch and put their jackets on. With arms wrapped around each other, they walked through the multi-colored carpet of dried leaves enjoying the crunch of their steps as they headed towards the lake. A few golden and crimson leaves clung tenaciously to the trees, and Harper Lake's waters glistened dull gray in the cool autumn air.

When they got to the edge of the lake, Tristan pulled out his leaf. "Want to see what I'm thankful for?"

Amy nodded, then smiled tearily as he showed her his leaf. All he wrote was the word 'you'. She swallowed hard as he placed the leaf in her hand. It felt different, heavier, than hers had. Curiously, she flipped the leaf over to find a diamond ring taped to the back with the words, 'Will you marry me?' written next to it. She looked back at Tristan who was now on one knee. "Will you?" he asked.

She nodded vigorously as she pulled him up from his knee and threw herself into his arms. "Yes! Of course I will."

He took the ring off of the leaf and carefully placed it on her finger. Taking her face in his hands, he kissed her long and sweetly. Putting his head against hers, he said, "I'm so thankful that God picked you for my wife."

Amy clung to him tightly. She had no words to express the amount of love she felt for this man, and it was only a fraction of the love that she experienced from God. One thing she knew without a doubt. To know true love, she had to know God first.

Dear Reader,

This was a story that I was anxious to write. The story of God's love is one that never gets old. It is truly remarkable. It is through Him that we can experience what love truly is. Christians should be a reflection of that in our interactions with everyone. Love should be our defining characteristic – so much so that it draws others to God.

I know it's not surprising that a romance author would be excited about writing about Valentine's Day, but more than the romance between Tristan and Amy, I was eager to share about the unconditional love of God. I hope that it was a good reminder to those who have already experienced His love, but my biggest prayer is that someone might come to know Him personally through this book.

Come check out my other books, my blog, and more at courtneylyman.com. You can also find me on Facebook. I love hearing from my readers!

Happy Valentine's Day!

In His Service,
Courtney Lyman

Made in the USA
Middletown, DE
09 September 2024

60661588R00161